PLOWING UP A SNAKE

Merle Drown

PLOWING UP A SNAKE

The Dial Press
New York

Published by
The Dial Press
1 Dag Hammarskjold Plaza
New York, New York 10017

Although the situation portrayed in this novel is based on an actual event, the characters and the plot are fictitious.

Copyright © 1982 by Merle Drown
Manufactured in the United States of America
First printing
Design by Francesca Belanger

Library of Congress Cataloging in Publication Data

Drown, Merle.
  Plowing up a snake.

  I. Title.
PS3554.R64P59   813'.54   81-19460
ISBN 0-385-27433-5   AACR2

For my mother and father

"Thou was not bold; thou was not true."

The Scarlet Letter

ONE
Spilled Milk

1 / *Red* L

In the early morning hours of the first day of January 1956, three men waited in the cold dark of Forrest Langley's barn in Enoch, New Hampshire. Amidst the quiet oaths that they muttered there was no mention of what they would do with Langley. The hiss of their breathing mixed strangely with the lowing of the cows waiting to be milked. Later than usual, though still early, Forrest Langley elbowed open the door from the milk room, his hands full of tools. In the same moment he saw the three men moving toward him his tongue worked a curse.

"We want to talk to you," one of them said.

"To teach you a lesson," another added.

The tools clattered to the floor. Before Langley could reach the green army blanket, folded on the bench, the third had hit him in the face. Under the blanket lay a simple, single-barrel sixteen-gauge shotgun. Finding that, the three men kicked and hit Langley. When they were done, they rehid the shotgun, dragged Langley's body across his back pasture, and dropped it off the bridge into the river.

Saturday, December 24, 1955

A week earlier, when Billy Harmes punched in at Land's Dairy at six, he saw two jugs full of bad milk, each jug painted with Langley's large red *L*. Jelly Enman, the fat man who stood all day by the scales weighing and judging the raw milk that came in from the farmers, was returning these two jugs that had come in the day before.

"Christmas or not," he told Billy, "I'm not going to credit him for the weight either. One drop of that stuff got into the system, it'd taint the whole batch." The fat man blotted the sweat from his brow with a white handkerchief, then slipped it into his back pocket.

Billy said nothing because it was not his job to judge or return the milk, and he was thinking of the party they would have at noontime when all the work was done. Still, he waited, because by the way Jelly hitched at his yellow apron, Billy knew the fat man had more to say.

"If Langley didn't try to squeeze and drain everything dry," said Jelly, "then he wouldn't have this trouble. I've let it go a couple of times, like last summer I figured maybe it'd got too warm on the way in." Jelly grinned out of one side of his mouth, the other side holding back the name of the kid who picked up the milk and the story of why it had arrived warm. Both kid and story Billy knew well, and it wasn't more than half funny to him either.

"It was only Langley's that went bad," he said. "I don't feature it was the kid's fault."

Jelly knocked the lid from one of the forty-quart cans on the rollers in front of him. Shielding his face, he smelled the raw milk before dumping it into the scales. "Now," he said, "that's fresh product. When Langley opens those two jugs of his, you'll be able to smell them clean back here."

"A man's grasp shouldn't always exceed his reach," Billy said. From the pocket of his wool jacket he pulled a fifth of white rum that he held gently at the shoulder of the bottle. "I'll just keep a good grip on this until the party."

"Even Langley couldn't spoil that," said the fat man as he knocked the lid off the next can.

Following the milk lines, Billy walked out to the larger room with the pasteurizers and bottling machines. Next to the short-time pasteurizer was a wooden case the foreman called his ammunition box. In his middle twenties, Jack Niles, the fore-man, was a few years older than Billy and looked enough like him to be his older brother. They weren't related. They were friends, and Billy did what he could to look out for Jack. As he laid the bottle of rum into the box, he winked at the foreman and told him it was a cold morning.

Looking up from his figures, Jack flipped back the thick black hair that hung in his face. "And it'll be a cold day in hell before I talk to Langley again," he said.

"Jelly told me about returning the milk," Billy said, taking off his wool jacket.

"I told Langley we'd warned him about it before," said Jack, "and he told me he didn't need any drones warning him about anything."

"Maybe you shouldn't have called him," Billy said. He knew that neither he nor Jack nor even Jelly would have to face Langley, and the kid who would return the milk was smiles enough and six and a half feet enough to withstand all of Lang-ley's guff.

"I had to." Jack returned to his figures with a look that said he didn't run Land's Dairy. He was only the foreman. Billy didn't see any benefits to that conversation, particularly when it would hold him back from setting Jack's machine.

Every morning Billy checked the switch on the bottle washer to make sure that Jack had turned on the rinse. Other-wise the bottles would come out filmed with poisonous alkali detergent. The bottle washer that Jack ran had an adjustment to determine how hard the bottles would drop onto the conveyor belt. Whenever Jack fiddled with the adjustment, he set it so that either half of the bottles smashed right at eye level or all of them went through to the glass filler, where the weak ones ex-ploded after they were filled with milk. Saying nothing to Jack or the others, Billy would return the setting to its proper posi-tion, where only the bottles with defects would break from the drop.

On his own machine, the paper filler, was an adjustment

for fill capacity. By law and regulation a quart had to be a quart or more, never less. Billy reduced the margin by which the machine exceeded a quart until the line over the legal minimum nearly disappeared. At twenty-two Billy already had a face aged with a grainy texture of skin caused, Jack joked, by too much attention to detail and not enough to women. A constant growth of beard met the darkness that seemed to spread from his thick hair and his dark pupils. Stripped to T-shirt and chinos, he worked quickly with hands made horny with hide by the detergent. He was marked with seriousness and pleased with the art of his work. His adjustments saved Land's Dairy and Mr. Land thousands of dollars, and he feared neither law nor Mr. Land, however little good that was about to do him with Forrest Langley.

At eight o'clock Mr. Land himself came out, wished everybody a Merry Christmas, and distributed their bonus money. In each brown envelope was an extra week's pay. Then he left. Billy knew that the owner had told them he was leaving so that they could drink at their party. Mr. Land knew they drank, but he didn't want to catch them.

Billy didn't worry about being caught. He knew that Sonny Rutherford, the nineteen-year-old who picked up milk for the dairy, worried about being caught, even though he wore a smile like a constant advertisement for good nature. Jelly cautioned him, and Jack threatened him, for they both agreed that the long-legged gink had reason to worry. Sonny, always late, goofed off on the job when he finally did arrive. Billy knew the protection of Sonny's father, who was plant manager, could not extend outside the dairy, could not extend to the fathers of the girls he fooled with (even on his routes) as if they were a dangerous and exciting hobby he had taken up. All of that energy fouls Sonny up. Here it is after eight, and he hasn't even begun his day's work.

When Sonny did stride in, it was closer to nine. Billy was glad the kid had arrived because Jack was still riled from his conversation with Langley, and he could yell at Sonny. Besides that, the foreman wanted to get the pickup runs started because they couldn't begin their party until everything was done. Billy was waiting to break the seal on his bottle of rum.

"You work hard most all day," Jack told Sonny. He took the toothpick from his mouth and replaced it with a cigarette. "But come Saturday morning you're not worth getting up for. What kind of girl you got wears you out like that?"

Sonny grinned. His hand rested on the pint of whiskey in his pocket. "Local girl," he said.

"Good thing we're off tomorrow," Jack told him, "or you probably wouldn't even get here." Jack reached for the bottle of whiskey, but his hand was locked before it touched Sonny's coat. Billy stepped away from his machine and watched the kid, still grinning, release Jack's hand. "I'm not going to take it away from you," the foreman said. "But don't you so much as sniff the cap while you're in the truck."

"I didn't think you was," Sonny said. He looked down at Jack and winked, then went to load up the empty cans to return to the farmers on the first pickup run.

The past summer Sonny had spoiled half a load of milk when he took the tarp for himself and a girl to lay on under the trees while the truck sat square in the sun. If that had been Cloudman's daughter and had Jonas Cloudman found them there, there would have been six and a half feet of Sonny Rutherford sprayed up against the very trees he lay under. Though it hadn't been Linda Cloudman then, she was letting him come into the kitchen now, as if he weren't six and a half feet of gink. Billy tried not to let mysteries annoy him, though from what he knew of Jonas Cloudman, he thought it foolhardy for Sonny to dally too long with that man's daughter.

Billy was thinking of the rum and grilled cheese sandwiches that would await him when Sonny got back from the third run. He was thinking of rum mixed with cranberry juice when he saw Dubber Handley scratch his balding head and push the button to stop his machine, the bottle filler. That meant that the line of bottles from Jack's glass washer would lock tight on the conveyor belt. If Jack wasn't quick enough, the next cycle of his machine would smash half a dozen quart bottles. The sound of exploding glass told Billy the foreman hadn't been fast enough.

Jack snared Dubber between the cases he was loading onto a dolly. "Why the hell do you do that?" Jack asked him.

"The number of bottles are written plain on the piece of paper I clip to your machine every morning," Dubber said. His chin uncurled from his skinny neck. "If you can't count from the time I start to when you should stop, it's not my fault."

Jack, keeping Dubber hemmed in, pointed a finger at him. "A man would need a microscope to tell just when you stopped stopping and started starting."

Billy knew that once Dubber began filling the bottles from the washer, he would work along at a rate designed to bring him just ahead at nine o'clock. Then he would amble like a man walking his last mile down past the time clock to the brown veneer door marked EMPLOYEES ONLY—MEN. Today at ten he had done the same thing. But now Jack stood blocking his way.

"Sonny's not back from the second run," Jack said.

"He's fooling with Cloudman's girl," said Dubber. "You going to do something about that?" Dubber began to move forward, not so much with his feet but by swelling his bony chest and extending his arms.

Jack, hesitating a moment, moved his stocky body back. "I thought since you're so rapid in your work and all on schedule in working and shitting, maybe you'd have time to pick up that third run." He leaned back against the cases, and the sarcasm left his voice. "If we get that third run in, we can start the party."

Dubber squeezed by the foreman. "I'm not doing Sonny's job or your job," he said. "And I'm not the one who's going to return Langley's milk," he added before sauntering off to the toilet. Jack asked Billy if he wanted to pick up the short run so they could start the party. Billy knew Jelly would be needed to dump Sonny's load when he got back in with it. Out from Jack's mouth came the toothpick, to be replaced by a cigarette. As Billy agreed to go he felt sorry for Jack. The foreman hadn't wanted to ask him.

Out back Jelly helped Billy roll the empties onto the black truck. In all the times Billy had picked up milk he had never returned any full jugs.

"Do you know why Jack's not taking this run himself?" Jelly asked. He ran a pudgy hand behind his yellow apron to pluck a cigarette from his pocket. "He's not going," Jelly said as he sat on the rollers for the cans, "because he called Langley to tell him we're returning the product with no credit for the weight. Langley wasn't partial to that at all."

Though Jelly's story lost him, Billy could feel in it the edge against Jack. "So?"

"So Jack told me if he went out there himself, he'd break Langley's face."

Jack brought a glass of cranberry juice and rum for Billy. "Must be something in those red L's Langley's painted on his cans." Billy saw the half smile the foreman tried on Jelly. "Must be those L's turn the milk bad."

"He insisted on it," Jelly said. "Everybody else's got numbers."

Billy finished his drink. He put his wool jacket on. "Milk won't get warm today," he said.

It was noon when Sonny got back from the second run. Jack said nothing to him, just let the kid unload the truck. When Jelly started to dump the milk, Sonny went to move the truck.

Jack took the toothpick out of his mouth. "Let it sit," he said. "I guess you can wash cans for a while."

After the load was finished, Jelly told Sonny to take the lunch orders into the kitchen. It was a narrow, hot-smelling place, decorated with red and green crepe paper. Flora Handley, Dubber's wife, was in charge.

"I suppose they'll let you drink, too," she said to Sonny. She stood stern and strong as he bent down to her.

"I brought my own," he said. "You come out with the lunches, I'll give you some."

She ripped open a loaf of bread and began brushing butter on the slices. "That's more than Dubber will give me," she said.

On upturned milk cases the men sat with glasses of rum or whiskey mixed with things from Land's cooler: cranberry juice, orange juice, grape drink, or eggnog. Dubber poured more rum into his eggnog.

"This is the only way I ever liked Mr. Land's eggnog," he said.

Jelly bit into his sandwich. "The only way you like anything is if it's free." He took another bite, and crumbs fell down his yellow bib.

"That's why I got married," Dubber said.

When Flora came back with some ice cream, Jack told her what her husband had said. "Next time he gets it up," she told them, "he'd better spend some time in the freezer so he can keep it ready."

"With the rum and all you'd think Billy'd want to hurry back," Sonny said. "There ain't a woman on that route you'd want to linger with."

Jack told him to shut up.

At the bottom of Langley's drive Billy touched the brake. Stretched across the back of the truck, the chain clinked as it was struck by the sliding empty cans. The second time he touched the brake there was no noise except the crunching of snow. At the back of the truck the milk cans lined against the chain like decapitated dwarfs. In the truck cold air entering from the hole near the shift lever had stiffened Billy's pant cuff so that it creased when he touched the brake the third and final time. Swinging the wheel to the right, he watched the loading platform grow in the mirror. There were no cans on it.

In the back he moved the full cans from the other farms out of the way and unhooked the chain. Two at a time Billy began carrying the cans with the red *L*'s into the milk room. Forrest Langley, standing erect by the new bulk tank, watched silently as the cluster of red *L*'s grew. Taking the last two cans from the truck, Billy grunted. He grunted when he lifted and again when he lowered each can. Billy saw Langley's lips draw together as if there were something bad in his mouth and he were holding it in.

Billy hoisted the first can over the doorstep and rolled it on edge to the group of empties. The second sloshed a little when he started to roll it. From the floor came the smell of bad milk, peculiar in the cold air. As Billy pulled a jug out of the cooler and tilted it, Langley held up his hand. From the shelf over the cooler he got a yellow cloth and wiped up the spill. Billy smiled at him, but Langley just stood there in his cotton drill pants and green jacket, as though, Billy thought, he were in uniform. Without any more spills Billy loaded the truck.

"Open it," Langley said.

Cautiously Billy walked to the last can he had unloaded and, hitting first one side then the other with the flat of his hand, removed the top. The same odor that had come from the spill now permeated the room, an odor not sour with growth like buttermilk or cheese, but rancid and ugly. Shaking his head, Langley turned to the remaining full jug and pointed at it. Billy removed its cap, releasing more of the foul smell.

"You ruined it," Langley said. "Sending it back here isn't going to allow Jelly Enman to cheat me of my weight."

Billy stopped himself from saying that he was only bringing it back, that he had had no part in denying Langley any credit. Instead, holding the top on both hands like an offertory plate, he backed off a step. "You can smell it's been gone bad a long time, Mr. Langley," Billy said.

The concentric inner circle of the top Billy held was white with the bad milk. As he moved it the milk coursed around the ring. Against his fingers the metal felt cold. Langley was looking at Billy as if he were the source of the smell. Billy handed him the top.

Langley pushed the top in his face. On the floor Billy felt the cold milk around his eyes where his glasses had been. From his cheek spread a stinging pain, a pain surrounded by numbness. Langley was above him, pouring the rancid milk over him. Some of it got into his mouth. Scuttling away, he watched Langley raise the can over his head. Billy's arm rose and crashed back to his body. Pain carved a path from his forearm to his shoulder.

He was being kicked to the doorway, hard, methodically; kicked in the side, in the ribs and stomach, and finally in the head. It was a relief to be lifted and thrown outside. The snow caressed his face. The slamming door and Langley's curse blended into a single sound.

The woman helped Billy get into the truck. She said nothing, just kept looking at the milk room as if, Billy thought, she expected her husband to fling himself out of there. In the truck he turned the key and pressed the gas pedal to the floor to engage the starter. After the motor started, he automatically pushed on the choke, but it hadn't been left out. His left arm, alive with pain, lay in his lap. He spoke to the woman.

"The chain," he said.

Through the side mirror he saw her pull herself up to the bed. She pushed the final jugs screeching along the metal bed to the front. Stretching the chain across the necks of the jugs, she attached it to a stake on the other side of the truck. Her hat blew off. Billy watched her leg descend from her skirt as if she were undressing.

She was by his door now, and he looked down at her and smiled. She started to say something, and all the parts of her face seemed to be moving toward the center. He waited a moment for her to speak before he drove back to the dairy.

None of them were drunk when he arrived. What effect the holiday liquor had had quickly disappeared. Dubber and Sonny working double unloaded the truck while Jelly dumped the milk, writing the weights in a hasty scrawl. Normally a neat man, Jelly shook his head at his illegibility. Jack took Billy to the hospital in Newfound. While Sonny and the fat man were finishing with the load, Dubber played live steam over Billy's machine. The hose hissed and roared. Every Saturday, standing there like some mad river god, Billy cleaned his machine with live steam. Dubber did not look like a god; he looked like all of the other men, grim and angry.

When Jack got back and saw that everything had been done, he said to Dubber, "Turn that damn thing off."

In the quiet, Jelly handed him a drink. None of them interrupted while Jack was telling his story. When he was finished, each picked some part of the story to make his own.

They talked about disfigurement and blindness and the aging effects of Billy's injuries. They wondered how he had been able to drive the truck back from Langley's. They were in the middle of those practicalities when Jack spit out his toothpick and replaced it with a cigarette.

"Somebody," he said, "just ought to kill that son of a bitch."

2 / *Down the Hatch*

Sunday, December 25, 1955
On Sunday, Clay Freeman wanted to know what had happened between his cousin and the Harmes kid. Clay had been gone all day Saturday, getting home at midnight to discover his wife, angry beyond tears, sitting in the middle of the packages he had expected to wrap. He had told her he had got tied up, and she had gone to bed without speaking to him. As he placed the presents on the boughs of the tree, he had muttered to himself that it was true, that he had been tied up. It happened often enough, he thought. She ought to believe him. The next morn-

ing after church Clay first heard the anger that the event at Langley's barn had generated, though he didn't learn the details. Gladys, annoyed and exasperated, wouldn't let him linger to talk about things she considered none of his business. Since he had crossed her the night before and was going to cross her again this night by going to the weekly meeting with his three friends (Christmas or not), he went along home with his curiosity under his hat. This curiosity had been whetted on the mystery of why an ordinary fight, what sounded like an ordinary fight, had become significant. Why did the town of Enoch consider it vital to talk with such hatefulness about his cousin, a hatefulness that seemed to be turning purposeful, even on Christmas?

"Well, what about the Harmes boy?" Clay asked his friends Sunday night in the Down the Hatch Lounge. "What exactly is all the fuss about?" He had refrained all day, and now he wanted the story, all at once, drink it down with one slug and leave the subtleties for chaser.

"Langley kicked hell out of him," Zack said. The big man strained, sucking his highball up through the straw. Clay thought his concentration on the straw was odd, though he had seen Zack concentrate the same way on a rusted U-bolt at his Mobil station. The muscles of his chest would force the red horse on his shirt to move his wings. Then just as the bolt snapped, the concentration would rush out of Zack in a quiet breath that said, Got the bastard. "He just kicked hell out of the boy. There are no two ways about it."

"There are always two sides," Clay said. "Sometimes half a dozen." He rolled his back against the leather of the booth to give himself some movement. He wished they would sit at one of the tables in the middle of the floor where he wouldn't be hemmed in by Zack's huge frame, but Duncan Hatch, whose place it was after all, insisted on the booth.

"We didn't know if you would make it tonight," said Davis Scales. The undertaker looked at Clay with a half smile that

Clay identified as the beginning of a rib about Gladys. Clay knew that the undertaker got a hard time from his own wife, especially about his drinking with the others, which she felt lowered him. Neither Zack nor Duncan joked about wives. "We thought you'd have to stand up and tell us all about why Gladys kept you home."

Every Sunday for years they had met there with no purpose or laws except the rule that every missed session must be explained. Because his maple sugar business frequently took him out of town, Clay had had to deliver a good many explanations.

Each of his friends knew that Clay's only alibi would be the truth, and around the table they grinned at the thought of him telling them about staying home. "I may be late—" he started.

"You usually are," Zack said.

"But I wanted to know what's the fuss over Langley. There's got to be more to it than that he beat the kid up."

Duncan Hatch shook out a Lucky from his pack. "Of course there's an explanation," he said. "If that's what you're looking for." He passed the cigarettes around. As usual Davis took one, Clay refused, and Zack pulled out a cigar that he would unwrap later. At the end of this ritual Clay noticed the Lucky Strike package left in the middle of the table, its red circle like a target.

"What got him riled is that the dairy returned some of his milk," Davis Scales said. "It wasn't the Harmes kid himself. It was the idea the dairy could refuse something of his."

Duncan's cigarette moved through his fingers in intricate ways. "Billy'd had a drink before he went over there," he said.

"Oh Jesus," Clay said, "Forrest's death on drinking." Then he asked, "It was just the milk?"

"What he did to that boy wasn't even human," Duncan said.

Duncan Hatch had on the V-neck sweater they teased him about and the matching slacks he'd had made in Boston. There was a softness about his clothes that gave his restaurant, where he wore tie and jacket to greet his customers, a kind of elegance. That was why, Clay thought, he has some sense of Forrest's dreams. The difference is it all comes out in loneliness, where Duncan, a lonely man, has to open his doors to the town.

"Langley prides himself on having the best of everything," Duncan said. "The best farm, the best cows—he wouldn't believe that his milk was bad."

Now Zack lighted his cigar, sending a wreath of smoke over the table. "Jelly Enman told me that when he knocked the lid off that jug, it was all he could do to keep from puking. Now, as the man who dumps the milk, he ought to know." He spoke louder, as if he sensed an argument. "What pissed Langley off was he knew the milk was no good when he sent it, and they caught him at it."

"And by way of denial," Davis said, "he beat up a twenty-year-old boy that no one in this town has ever spoken a bad word of."

Langley had to answer every insult as if he had not proved himself with all the dollars he had earned, with every improvement he had made to his property. The recognition he wanted marched farther away with every step he took toward the people of Enoch. The more he succeeded the more they hated him, until finally he had turned all chances of acceptance into dust. As he himself, Clay thought, had not. But then he had not succeeded like either his cousin or Duncan Hatch.

"Holidays busy for you, Clay?" Duncan asked.

"Oh, I guess it is," Clay said. "It's a good two months before the sap will run again, which makes it over two months before I can buy syrup and boil it into sugar. Everybody wants it right now, for the holidays."

Zack leaned against him. "Well, if you don't have it, you can't sell it to them. Right?"

"I wish I'd been selling during the war," said Clay, backing away from Zack. "Then everybody wanted sugar, all the time. Now I got to run around trying to find any of last year's syrup while I'm making arrangements for next year's run."

"And eating holes in your stomach," Davis Scales told him. The cigarette in his thin fingers pointed to Clay's drink. "No wonder you drown that Scotch in soda."

"Gladys said if I lived a normal life, I wouldn't have to pour soda into everything I drank." He paused, allowing the silence to ask politely what it was he had replied. "I told her I like soda."

"My wife says I come home every Sunday night with my tavern smell," said Davis Scales. He waved the Lucky he had bummed over his glass of beer, as if to conjure up the very odors his wife objected to. "But I told her if she could put up with the smell of acid that's always on my fingertips, she could put up with the smell of a man's night out."

"I've heard there was talk about doing something about Forrest," Clay said. Atop his swizzle stick perched an angel, which he tapped quietly on the table.

"We know he's your cousin," Davis Scales said, "but Pistol Pete was Zack's cousin, and it never made a bit of difference to him when we did what we had to to fire Pete."

"One thing's sure," said Zack. "Right's right." The smoke from his cigar had formed a cloud around the crepe-paper Christmas bell that hung over his head.

Clay thought Pistol Pete Zakrzewski should have been fired long before he was.

"You took care of that little matter with Pete pretty well right here," Clay said. "Hardly broke a glass."

"That still bothers you, doesn't it, Clay?" Duncan asked.

It had been the pretense Clay had hated, the deception. Despite the soda in his drink, his stomach began to churn. They had set Pete up, waiting until he was drunk in the Down the Hatch, then calling in the doctor from Newfound to commit Pete to the state hospital. They had put him there long enough to make Henry Dodge chief. And Dodge, then Pete's one officer, a kid who wore his uniform even off duty, did what they told him because he wanted to go on wearing the uniform. They had even called the doctor early because no one wanted to hold on to two hundred and fifty pounds of rampaging Pete Za-krzewski while the doctor drove up from Newfound.

"Over in Vermont," Clay told Duncan, "they hold the bartender responsible for anyone he gets drunk."

"Nobody ever had to get Pistol Pete drunk," Duncan said. "Do you know the law on lounges and Sundays? We're all breaking the law right now."

"This is different," Clay said. "We're just friends having a drink. The place is dark, there's no entertainment, and no money is passing hands."

"Maybe you'd like to explain all those fine points to Henry Dodge," Duncan said. "Or maybe it'd be a lot easier just to keep it to ourselves. You know I had to build all those motel units because the law says I can't have a lounge license unless I have so many rooms under the same roof. Enoch's not exactly a convention center, so I figure the license came pretty dear. Now I'm getting another round if the legal discussion is over." There was a crèche on the bar next to where he fixed the drinks, and he nearly knocked it over when he picked up the tray. "You know," he said when he brought the drinks back, "Nancy was a friend of Marjorie Langley's." He lowered his head as he always did when he spoke of his wife. "At least as much of a friend as she ever had in this town, and Nancy said she never talked about Langley, not even so much as mentioned his name, except to say, 'I've got to go home to put on Forrest's supper.' You know women, always gabbing about their husbands, but she'd only talk about plants or the boy."

"Billy'll be out of the hospital in another day or two," Davis said. "I understand Langley's paying the medical bills."

"And well he ought," said Clay, "if what you've told me squares with the facts."

"When it was me and mine, Clay," said Davis, "you told me it ought to be more than medical bills."

"And you followed the advice," Clay said.

"You're damned right I did. Like Zack said, What's right's

right." He stubbed out his cigarette. "And that case between my son and the Reed girl was a hell of a lot different from this one."

"We all know what it's like to have problems at home," Clay said. He knew it wasn't much of an argument, but he was beginning to feel excluded.

"His problems at home are no excuse," Zack said. "And I'll tell you another thing." His fingers gripped the cigar he pointed at Clay. "His troubles are his own making. His own, you understand?"

"Like any man's," Clay said.

"More than most men's," Zack said. "This wasn't something his son did or something happened to his wife or his cousin. What comes to him, he brought it on himself."

Duncan sat back. "There's no arguing what he is."

"But who would have guessed he would have done something like this?" Clay asked. But he knew. After growing up knowing Langley's father, he didn't wonder that Langley had struck the Harmes boy. The wonder was that he hadn't gone down to the dairy and cleaned house.

"Anyone can fly off the handle," said Duncan. "Jonas Cloudman like to tear this place apart once, but it's the arrogance of a son of a bitch like Langley who in the cold of the morning just does it and goes back to his chores like nothing happened."

"Or will happen," Zack added.

Clay stared at the thick, blackened thumbs of the mechanic. The liquid in the highball glass magnified them, showing off the lines of grease that had worked their way into the skin. Davis had his acid smell, from embalming, and Zack smelled of the garage; Clay carried the sweet aroma of maple syrup, but Duncan smelled of neither liquor nor food. Duncan smelled not at all.

"We've heard people talk," Duncan said. "They're not talking money."

Davis put out his cigarette. "People are angry, Clay. You

understand that." He rubbed the butt around the ashtray, cleaning the ashes from the sides until it glistened. "This was not an accident."

"In that case," Clay said, "Henry Dodge should pay Langley a visit." Though he wouldn't call him Forrest in front of them, he didn't think it was a sign of agreement.

"You use Henry to chase kids who break windows," Duncan said.

"And he's none too good at that," Zack said.

"He's our policeman, our law," Clay said. He leaned back so that he could speak to all three of them. "He was good enough when you got rid of Pistol Pete."

Duncan laughed to himself. "When Jonas Cloudman was in here, drunk as a lord, I watched Henry go by in the cruiser, then I went and called Zack to handle him. After Jonas's wife died, you remember he turned so ugly there weren't many men in Enoch would walk crosswise of him unless they were armed. As it was, Zack broke the glass out of the front door taking Jonas out of here."

"And Cloudman hardly stands five five," Zack said.

Clay sipped his Scotch. He and Cloudman were about the same height, though he outweighed the farmer by thirty pounds. "So what's the point, Duncan?"

"The point is that Jonas walked in here a couple of days later and personally thanked me for not siccing Henry Dodge on him. 'I'm real runty when I get to drinking,' he told me. 'I'm afraid I might have killed that kid cop.' "

Clay had always figured Duncan was close to Jonas because as widowers they were both in the same lonely boat. Cloudman, though, had two daughters, which had to make some difference. Clay wondered what they would be thinking of doing if Pistol Pete were still cop. "I don't suppose anybody's talked to Billy Harmes about this."

"Don't have to talk to him," said Zack. He relighted his cigar with great gulping puffs. "You just have to hear what he looks like."

"You might think of this as a case much like Pistol Pete's," said Davis, "where the town has to take some responsibility."

Clay told him that Forrest Langley was neither crazy nor drunk.

"What do you call it?" Davis asked.

"Mean," Clay said.

"Jonas Cloudman's mean," Duncan said. "He doesn't go around riling people up."

Clay finished his drink. "People shouldn't be so quick to go around getting riled up."

"Well, somebody's going to fix that son of a bitch," Duncan Hatch said.

In the parking lot of Hatch's Diner, Clay stared out where street became highway. The restaurant marked the verge of town, just beyond which Pistol Pete used to hide with the Bonneville to exact justice as policeman, judge, and revenue collector. Pete hadn't thought of himself as guardian of Enoch as much as Clay's three friends had. The arm of motel units Duncan Hatch had built seemed to Clay to stretch jealously toward town. Perhaps Forrest Langley's case, Davis Scales to the contrary, was not at all like that of Pistol Pete Zakrzewski.

They hadn't needed to lure Pete to the lounge because he was there and there drunk regularly. Clay thought Pete's rage must have erupted when he found his own patrolman, Henry Dodge, trying to put handcuffs on him and a doctor from Newfound standing behind Dodge saying something about the state hospital. So they had got what they had wanted, even if it had taken both Duncan Hatch and Henry Dodge to get Pete into the cruiser.

It was all pretty funny, Davis Scales had said. The town had pretty much agreed, Clay thought, because all he had heard were snickers and jokes about Pete giving out tickets to speeding loonies at the state hospital. Duncan Hatch, however, hadn't laughed, not only because his lounge was a wreck, but also because on the way to Concord, Pete had called his wife a whoring bitch. Duncan had raised an egg on Pete's head with

Henry Dodge's flashlight. But it had all come out clean in the exploratory hearing when the judge said that Pete had been legally committed for evaluation and (having been found as sane as the rest of them) was free to go.

Of course, they had dropped the assault and drunk-and-disorderly charges, and he had dropped his suit for damages. Very clean, Clay thought, and no one had to admit it had been a mistake to hire Pete in the first place. They had just given his wife his severance pay while he was in the hospital and raised up Henry Dodge to be chief. If there was any resemblance to his cousin's fracas with Billy Harmes, Clay thought, it was when Duncan had wielded the flashlight.

None of his friends had come out. Clay got into his beach wagon and pulled back through town. With snow covering the common in front of the church, Enoch looked like a picture-postcard New England village. Clay thought of all the times he had been on the road he had never sent Gladys a postcard. Never cheated on her either, though, he thought. Along the iron rail that bordered the common, scoops of snow had been stolen by kids from the youth group. Before getting into the Reverend Treadwell's car, they pelted each other. Tall and lanky Sonny Rutherford from the dairy had Jonas Cloudman's daughter on his shoulders. As Sonny pranced about dodging snowballs, Clay wondered if Billy Harmes still attended the meetings or if he was too old. He wouldn't be here tonight anyway.

At the turnoff to go over the river, Clay hesitated. He could stop at Forrest's and tell him about the Reed girl, because that was really what his situation resembled, even if Davis Scales didn't want to admit it. The undertaker wouldn't want to admit it, Clay figured, because it was his son who had sat in the boat fooling with matches. Blond and fair and not yet thirteen, the Reed girl had been pretty and still was except for her scarred legs. Davis Scale's son was too young to be out in the motorboat with a girl anyway. Clay turned down the hill and drove across the flats to the bridge. He could call Forrest from home.

Gladys said nothing to him until he went to the telephone.

The desk the telephone sat on was a red-oak piece that Gladys kept polished. He was proud of the desk and the way she kept it, in fact of the whole house, a two-bedroom Cape he had had built five years before. It wasn't anything like Forrest's spread, but then, he thought, I'm not anything like Forrest.

"It's nearly ten o'clock," Gladys said. She sat her book beside her on the couch and looked at him with her wide blue eyes. Her short hair had begun to gray a little lately.

"I know," he said, his hand holding down the telephone as if he were hiding something.

"Whom do you expect to talk to at this hour of night?" She pulled her yellow cardigan around her shoulders. At night she never put on her gown or pajamas until she got into bed. For some reason, though he had never told her, he liked that. She tugged at the sweater again.

"Forrest," he said. "I've got something to tell him."

"About what?" she asked. "I thought I told you this morning to stay out of that business."

"I know what you told me. I think I can do some good. He is my cousin." Clay's hand left the telephone and flashed, open-palmed, at his wife. He told her he wanted to suggest Forrest consider paying some money, as with the Reed case. Clay had told Davis Scales to pay the Reeds money over and above the doctor's bills.

"That was an accident," Gladys reminded him.

"The Scales boy was the cause of the accident," said Clay. "I told Davis what good is money if you can't use it to smooth over problems."

"Davis Scales must have wondered if his son had sat there deliberately tossing matches into the gasoline spreading under the Reed girl, so what you wanted to do was convince Davis that his son hadn't done what he thought he had done."

Clay shook his head. "If I had thought the boy did that, I wouldn't have interfered."

Gladys smiled at him, revealing the large white teeth he had always admired. "You're more transparent than you think."

"I think Davis judged me bold."

"You always dress things up in the best clothes."

"Sometimes in their most ordinary," Clay said. "But I have a real respect for the lack of certainty."

"Just don't get me mixed up in it," Gladys told him. She nestled back into her yellow cardigan and returned to her book.

As Clay gave Forrest's number to the operator, he could feel his guts gurgle as if someone had pulled a plug.

3 / *A Short Dark Man*

Monday, December 26, 1955

Jonas Cloudman, a short dark man, walked through the ell, slipped his coat onto the peg, and went on into the kitchen. His forearms, stiff from the milking, were rigid with swollen veins as he made his coffee on the fat iron stove. He made just two cups, for he was a frugal man, a poor man, but not a cheat. He couldn't abide a cheat, a man who'd claim good for bad or a kid who'd sneak around while you were gone. Jonas thought his daughters managed meals well enough, but he didn't trust them to be making the coffee. At seventeen Linda was already of an age to sit after supper with her own cup. Jonas hoped he wouldn't have to worry about Jane, too. Not yet, he guessed, not at thirteen. If he hadn't already started this job for Langley, he might not go today. While he was over there, Sonny Rutherford would be picking up milk at his place.

After what he had heard about last Saturday at Langley's, Jonas thought he might find reason to turn down any more jobs over there. It was too bad because working for Langley suited him. Langley told him what he wanted done, and Jonas did it. A week or so before the job Langley would call, and he wouldn't expect a man to linger through milking time or to come when he had his own place to keep. And Langley paid right, according to what the job was worth, not how long it took a man to do it. Still, this business Saturday smelled rank, and Jonas had never found any reason to like Langley at all. And that damn Sonny Rutherford would be right in the kitchen, sitting at this very table with the smooth, cold oilcloth under his arms as he reached across the table for Linda's hands.

The girls were awake now. Jonas could hear them talking in the other part of the house, talking softly as their mother always had. He knew people thought the girls had been a burden on him, but not even counting the cooking and cleaning they'd done, for ten years they'd kept laughter in the dark rooms.

Linda kissed him when she came in the room. She laughed, as her mother had, without giggling or wrinkling up her nose.

"We need some syrup opened, Jonas," she said without turning to him.

From the closet he got a gallon of maple syrup, heavy, dark, grade B syrup that Jonas liked more than the better grades. This can was from a batch Clay Freeman had been taken on, and when the dispute was over, he had given the can to Jonas. Every spring Jonas earned six gallons for working at jobs on Clay Freeman's candy kitchen, but that was honest stuff. Jonas accepted this syrup because it was a gift without value to the giver. Clay Freeman, who wouldn't hold him to a gift anyway, hadn't even told Jonas the name of the man who had sold him the syrup. Milk could go bad too, he thought, but sending it to the dairy that way was no better than overgrading syrup.

With his jackknife he prized the metal seal in the can's spout and poured off syrup into a mayonnaise jar. As he returned the syrup to the cold closet, he heard the swish-slap of Jane's feet, loose in her sister's slippers. Her hands were full of forks and knives, and she kissed her father and moved quickly around the table. Though at thirteen she was nearly as tall as Jonas, she was his toy, his stuffed animal, always rising later than her sister, always rubbing the wrinkles from her eyes. At night when he sat by the stove, he imagined her married, living in one of those new long, low houses surrounded by grass, a woman with the face of a thirteen-year-old.

"You don't need to be feeding Sonny Rutherford when he comes by to pick up the milk," Jonas told both of them. He went back to his coffee and waited for Linda to answer.

"It's just a cup of coffee, Jonas. You won't let me make you any." She shook her ponytail as she looked at her younger sister. He wondered if she and Jane shared some secret.

"His father manages that dairy. I'd guess he can afford to keep his boy in coffee." He couldn't find it in himself to be hard with Linda. "It ain't mooching food I'm talking about."

Linda's ponytail nervously brushed her shoulders while she flipped pancakes onto the platter beside her. She covered them with a large white dinner plate, inverted to hold the warmth. "It's not anything bad, you know, Jonas."

He smiled at her when she brought the pancakes, a golden brown, the color of her hair. "How's a man like me supposed to know about a thing like that?" Sometimes he didn't know how to take his words any better than she did. "I don't want it to become my business to find out."

"Oh, Daddy," Jane said, "quit talking."

Jonas was glad of the girl's interruption. He mistrusted his luck, and Linda took after him like a thief in the night. So wasn't it only natural to expect her to come to grief and natural, too, to worry about what he feared he couldn't prevent?

Out in the yard he greased the universal joint on the tractor. He crawled under the pickup and drained the oil into a galvanized tub. From underneath he could look up at the pedals. He went into the ell looking for sheet metal to patch the holes in the floorboards.

"Aren't you going to Mr. Langley's?" Linda asked. She was dressed now in dungarees and a sweater. "It's nearly eight o'clock."

To dilute the exhaust that came up through the floorboards, Jonas rolled down the windows as he pulled out of his yard. He thought Sonny Rutherford was probably just down the road, waiting. Usually the kid would pull in, chattering like a radio announcer, or singing some rock and roll song. By the time Jonas would get to the cooler, Sonny would be snatching out cans and swinging them up onto the truck bed. In the ease of his motion was a kind of insolence that went along with saying "Jonas" every third or fourth breath while Jonas stood stolidly by the cooler and yanked the cans. Few people in Enoch called him "Jonas." He was damned if he knew why one of them had to be Sonny Rutherford.

Langley had him working on laying lines to tie the milking system into the bulk tank. According to Langley, it was the wave of the future. It would do away with coolers and cans. Everyone would come around to it, he said, or go out of dairying. Of course, it would close up people who couldn't afford it. Jonas nodded. He was one of the ones who'd be closed up. Langley talked right along. The truck from the dairy would just pull up, hook on to your outlet, and suck out the milk. And it'd be weighed and graded in the process, clean, neat, and efficient.

Jonas lay down the adjustable wrench he was using to tighten connectors. "They won't pay you any more per hundredweight," he said. "You can bet on that."

"Yes," Langley said, "but it will eliminate that goddamn Jelly Enman. I'm for something that will do that." He picked up the wrench. "Been a bulk tank all hooked up here Saturday, it wouldn't have happened."

When Jonas saw that Langley had walked off with the adjustable wrench, he started measuring the hole to be cut through to the milk room. If Langley didn't come back before he ran out of work, Jonas would just pick up and go home. He hoped Sonny Rutherford wouldn't be there. Before he had finished scribing the circle on the wall, in came Langley with a Thermos. He offered Jonas some coffee.

"In a minute." Jonas completed the circle. Langley never brought him anything, gave him no coffee breaks. After all, this was his time. He punched no clock. Still, there didn't seem to be any more strings to this coffee than there were to the gallon of maple syrup Clay Freeman had given him. Jonas didn't see he had any reason to refuse.

With no question of cream or sugar or how Jonas might like it, Langley awkwardly poured the coffee. "Cloudman, you a drinking man?"

"I've had a drink," Jonas said. "Times I've had too many drinks."

Langley looked up from the sawhorse he sat on. "How many when you've had too many?"

"A ways down the road from the first one. Sometimes a long ways down the road, but then it's worse." Clay Freeman talked to Langley because they were cousins, and Clay liked to talk as well as he liked to eat. The Reverend Treadwell talked to him because he was paid to talk and anyway he would talk to anybody. Right now Jonas figured he must be the only fool available to listen, though he wished he were being paid for it. "You meaning to get tight New Year's?"

"When Billy Harmes came here Saturday, I smelled liquor on him." Langley spat on the floor, something Jonas had never seen him do in the barn. "I suppose you know about Saturday."

"They have a little celebration at the dairy before Christmas." Jonas wished it were Billy Harmes who picked up milk at his place instead of that sneaking Sonny Rutherford.

"You know about Saturday?"

"I heard some," Jonas said. "I heard they wouldn't credit you the weight."

"Celebrating too much. Someday Jelly Enman's going to fatten himself up just about enough to fry."

Jonas was quiet. He figured there were other steps in what was going on, but he was far from sure they went along any road he wished to travel.

"They paid," Langley said. His face lowered so that he stared only at the silver cup from the Thermos. "Billy paid."

"So?"

"So what I'm saying, Cloudman, is that I was wrong."

As Langley talked Jonas scarcely listened. He was not used to revelations from anyone. His daughters were no good at deception. They had all they could do to hide the gifts they bought for him three times a year. Few other men talked to him of intimate things except Duncan Hatch, who traded loneliness with him. He didn't share anything with Langley other than the air. When the man handed him the wad of money, he was amazed enough to wonder if Langley was frightened.

Jonas had been to Billy Harmes's house before. Over a year ago he had come to plow the garden plot, though despite their coaxing he hadn't entered the house for a cup of coffee. After that, Billy had asked him if he wouldn't assist on some repair work around the house. It seemed that Billy's father increased each chore as he attempted it, so that at the end of the day only the setting sun ransomed him from his work. If he went to nail down the tar paper on the shed roof, he would discover the hammer handle was split and the roof boards had rotted with rain. Repairing the plaster on the hallway wall, he would sever the wires for the light switch. And when he was done and had washed his hands, the faucet would taunt him with the slow drip of a worn washer. Billy had hired Jonas to put an end to the broken trail of tasks that grew with every step the old man took.

It had gone well for a while because Billy's father was amazed at the success of anything connected even vaguely with himself. Though Billy was far more competent than his father, when he paid Jonas, he, too, seemed to express that same humble fatalism his father lived by. Finally, Billy told Jonas that they would hire him only for the major jobs. Billy said that the more things that Jonas did, the longer his father's list grew, and it was driving his mother crazy.

Without so much as a sign of work about him, Jonas got out of his truck and knocked on the Harmes's door. The wad of money in his pocket pressed against his side like an unnatural tool. A rapping on the front window drew his attention to a crooked finger that invited him into the house. He stomped the snow from his rubber boots onto the hair mat and spoke to Billy's father, who met him in the kitchen.

"Your boy home today?"

Billy's father nodded toward the living room. "I got him from the hospital. Do you want a drink with us?"

"Hospital?" Jonas said. "Yes, a drink." It wasn't yet noon, but a drink might help him conduct his business. He didn't ask what kind of drink. As he crossed the linoleum he left wet bootmarks ridged with waves.

Jonas put his hand on the cloth bag with the wad of fifties and hundreds that Langley had counted out. He had handed it to Jonas there in the barn without asking for a receipt. After years of receiving cash in hand with neither bills nor receipts, Jonas didn't wonder about the lack of forms but only the amount of money. When he saw Billy, he understood all at once why Langley had sent him and what he was up to and why the amount was so large. Billy's face, the part that wasn't covered by the bandage for his left eye, looked like the bloody sawdust on a butcher's floor.

Billy's father gave Jonas a glass of rum and cranberry juice. "I didn't know," Jonas said. Lowering himself just to the edge of the couch, he put his hands on his knees. He watched Billy pick up a huge book in one hand and set it aside. The other arm was in a sling. "I should never have told him yes."

"Peculiar warm weather we're having," Billy's father said. "For this time of year."

"I'm on a false mission here," Jonas declared. "I was deceived about the job. A man should never cheat you about the nature of a job, and now that I commence to understand it, I'm inclined to be shut of it." He explained to them that he didn't know how badly Billy had been beaten.

Billy settled back in his chair. "I trust you to do what you should, Mr. Cloudman."

"How much is it?" Billy's father asked.

From the cloth sack Jonas drew out the money like a dangerous snake. "Five thousand dollars."

"It'd buy you a lot of stamps," Billy's father told him.

Billy pointed to the stamp album he had set aside. "I started that in 4-H," he said. "But there just hasn't come any natural end to them. The rabbits I sold at the Newfound fair, and the suit I made doesn't fit anymore. But my sister didn't want the stamps, so I just kept them."

"I wouldn't be such a fool as to sit here," Jonas said, "except that I took the money, so I guess I took the responsibility of it."

"What are you going to do?" Billy's father asked him.

"I'm going to take it."

In a single swallow Jonas finished off his drink. After dropping the burdensome bag onto the stamp album, he rubbed his hands on the back of his pants, then let them fall. He remained standing. He wanted to go, though not without a release from Billy. Stepping back, he looked for a place to rest his hands, but clutter covered the tops of everything.

"What are the conditions?" Billy's father asked. He ran his fingers up and down his suspenders as if he were tuning them.

"Ought to be conditions on him," Jonas said. He leaned toward Billy. "I wouldn't accept another chore of him if it was shoveling sand into his grave at a dollar a minute."

"He didn't say anything?" Billy asked.

" 'Give it to Billy' was all he said."

Then Billy asked Jonas to do a favor, and having already done one for Langley, he didn't see how he could shunt this one aside, though he'd hoped to get home before Sonny Rutherford stopped there.

At the dairy he found the men, including Sonny, all working. He wasn't sure if the kid had returned from the run or hadn't gone out yet.

Jonas stood on the cement floor waiting for them to stop.

In the midst of the steamy noise the men worked their machines, Jack Niles taking Billy's place on the paper filler. Sonny Rutherford, long arms smacking into the cases of empties, fed the bottle washer, and Jonas figured that if the kid had already stopped at the house, he hadn't had time for so much as a penny's worth of coffee. One by one, as they noticed Jonas, the men shut down their machines. Into that silence Jonas spoke.

"If Billy hadn't asked me to come down here, I wouldn't be telling you this because it ain't something I call myself proud of." He told them about giving the money to Billy, then he added an explanation. "And while I'm telling things, you ought to know I hadn't seen Billy when I took that money. I ain't any closer to Forrest Langley than milk to shit, and the next time he asks me for something I'm liable to take job, money, and everything and fling them right into his teeth."

He waited a minute, his hands going in and out of his pockets like dogs worrying a hole in the ground. Sonny Rutherford laid a big hand over a case on the rollers as he slouched against his machine. After his apology Jonas couldn't dig out words to speak to Sonny, so he let the men's silence give him leave to go home.

The men at the dairy were sitting on upturned cases eating their lunch. Jelly had finished one grilled cheese sandwich and was starting on the other. "You shouldn't've sent Billy on that run Saturday," he said.

"Of course I shouldn't," Jack said. "Ain't I already been in to explain that to Paris Rutherford?"

Jelly's plate was empty. "I mean you should have known not to send Billy on that run," he said.

Jack shook a cigarette from his pack and spit out his toothpick. He put the pack back in his T-shirt pocket. "And just how do you figure that?"

"You should have known how Langley was going to be when that milk came back." Jelly dropped his voice. "Meaner than a mink, right?"

"You sent the milk back." Jack thrust his cigarette at Jelly. "You decided not to credit the weight."

"But you sent Billy with it, you dumb son of a bitch."

The plate cracked neatly in half across the top of Jelly's forehead. A line of blood creased the skin. Kneeling on the overturned fat man, Jack pressed against him. It looked as though they had had an accident.

"Don't ever call me dumb," Jack said, his mouth open, loud breaths rubbing against his teeth. "I mean what I do."

Sonny Rutherford held a grin that didn't quite dare become a laugh. Against his glass filler stood Dubber Handley. The safety of his body had been his first concern. Mr. Land was his second. He looked into the passageway and saw that it was empty. Then he picked up the two halves of the broken plate.

"Flora'll want some money for this," he said, nodding toward his wife's place in the dairy-bar kitchen. "She's already over her breakage allowance for this month."

"Maybe she'll let them take it out in trade," Sonny told him.

"What do you do in bed?" Jack asked. "Worry about the telephone bill?" He stood up.

"Sure," Jelly said, "it keeps his mind on something interesting."

Jack replaced the cigarette that had fallen from his mouth, then handed the pack to Jelly. With their coffee the men were silent. From the long room that connected the plant to the dairy bar came the sound of Mr. Land making ice cream. Usually he made it at night, but he would need extra for the holiday. Nodding his head toward the sounds, Jelly raised his eyes and blew a breath of narrow escape. Not that he thought he would be fired, but God knew he didn't want Dubber Handley for a foreman. And that would be the only choice if Jack went, because Sonny being what he was, even his own father wouldn't promote him. Paris Rutherford agreed with Mr. Land about the seriousness of the dairy business, and neither of them would tolerate fighting. At least, Jelly thought, they didn't want to see it, any more than they wanted to see the drinking that went on Christmas, New Year's, and the Fourth of July picnic, or the loafing that went on practically every time Sonny Rutherford left the plant in a truck.

"Cloudman might have skimmed some of that money off the top," said Dubber. He was glad to sit and talk on dairy time. "It might have been ten thousand."

"Maybe Billy could get more out of Langley," Sonny said.

Jelly stood up, his empty cup in his hand. "Jonas Cloudman wouldn't take money, you numbnuts. He's as safe as mold on a cheese." His forehead pained him.

Sonny said, "Billy's a rich man."

Sonny's father being plant manager and Sonny's great height protected him from being either bullied or fired, and even goofing off, he could get his work done. But the men at the plant merely tolerated him. If it were him beaten up, there would be no talk of taking it out of Langley's hide. They would probably just laugh about it. That was all right because he wasn't going to get beaten up. It was the girls who scared him. It was for them that he goofed off, and neither father nor height was the slightest advantage when it came to their warm mouths and the nooks and crannies he discovered in their bodies. With them he was foolish, and looking at Jonas Cloudman had reminded him he was also in a cold kind of danger.

"You know, that money makes me worse than mad," Jack said. "He thinks he can buy a man like he pays for a cow." He got up to signal them back to work.

Dubber hesitated. "If Billy gets a lawyer, Langley will be paying more than five thousand."

"Hell, if we had a real law in this town, he'd be in jail," Jelly said.

"It ain't the law," Jack said. "It's the son of a bitch himself."

After he cleaned the short-time pasteurizer, he would have to clean Billy's machine. Deep down in the guts of the pump where the spinning blades forced the milk into tubes, butter formed, a greasy butter, brighter and richer than ordinary butter. Whenever he got to it, Jack put some in his mouth, letting the cold lump slide tasteless from side to side. The wire cone from the homogenizer needed replacing, so he took a new one from the cardboard box in his drawer. Thousands of gallons of milk passed through this small cone every day, the mesh of wires breaking down the fat globules so that the milk was one white consistency that wouldn't separate. Mr. Land claimed that it wouldn't be long before all milk would be homogenized, an extra penny a quart so that you wouldn't have to shake the bottle to mix in the cream. No butter formed on the tight wire cone.

4 / *Snakes*

Tuesday, December 27, 1955
She was a short woman, dressed in a suit and a purple hat, as if it were Easter. After her car had rolled down the driveway, she tumbled out onto the lawn. Only it was from the passenger side, as though she hadn't been driving and whoever had had just disappeared. About fifty, smelling of lilac, she didn't move at first, just lay there waiting for something to pass. When she turned, we could see it coming out of her sleeve.

It looked like corduroy, colorful bits of cloth strung on a wire. She wasn't hurt from the accident, only quiet and embarrassed because of the thing that moved past her hand. I've had a serpentile infestation, she said. We thought of worms. Though no one here has worms, and it was coming from her sleeve, still it was worms that we thought of.

Helping her back into the car was a chore. Not only was

she heavy, but the thing kept waving its head. Somebody said, they carry their eggs on their bodies. It brushed against us, neither slimy nor wet, but warm, smooth, and hard. In the car her jacket opened, revealing the body of the thing from the arm-hole, across her chest, and in between the buttons of her blouse, where it pulsed like a vein. It's in my heart, she confessed.

We fell back. Someone shut the car door, with her still on the passenger side. We went inside, hoping to wash it away. In her heart, we said, but no one watched her, and soon the car was gone.

Though she sometimes took a nap while Peter lay upstairs in his bed, Marjorie Langley was afraid the dream would return, so she tried to read a magazine. The phone rang. Forrest was in Newfound seeing about something for the bulk tank. As the phone rang again she put down her magazine. Since Saturday she had not been able to concentrate on a book, and now she was interrupted in a magazine. She allowed the third ring to finish, then picked up the receiver.

"Langley?" The man's voice didn't give her a chance to say "hello."

"He's not here now," she said. "May I ask who's calling, please?"

People seldom called Forrest. There wasn't much they wanted to talk to him about. Most of the phone calls were for her. She didn't recognize the voice.

"You can't shield him," the man said.

"Please, who is this?" Forrest would be angry about this as it was. He would be angrier if she had no name to give him. "I'll have him call you back."

The man laughed. "We'll get back to him. Tell him that. That's his message." The line clicked.

When the operator came on, Marjorie realized that she was still holding the receiver above the cradle. She mumbled an apology and set the phone down. No noise came from Peter's room. The dry south wind blew from across the road, raising silent swirls of snow. On the radio would only be the chitchat from the Newfound station, a noise that worsened her loneliness. They said that televisions in Enoch could pull in more stations now. There were new ones in Manchester and on Mount Washington. With a high antenna you could get Boston at night, but at night all the radio stations came in. She could listen to music from New York or Chicago or Montreal. Other children in town enjoyed watching television, so maybe Peter would like the shows. Forrest called it an expensive toy, though he would buy one if she were to ask him. His disapproval, she knew, was not at the cost, but because he considered it frivolous. He was too serious about so many things, and now it had gotten him into trouble.

Under the radio the record player gently swung out on elaborate hinges, offering itself to Marjorie. She stacked up the five heavy records for *Madame Butterfly* and pushed the switch. Its thick metal made more of a thud than a click. The console, which stood solid and short like a servant, was a wedding gift. Marjorie wondered if her mother had known how much she would need it.

When Marjorie had moved into the house, there had been no telephone. Forrest had grown up without one. On the road he had used the telephones in the stores he serviced, the hotels where he stayed. Marjorie had had to explain to him that her mother would want to call her. Once he understood, he made arrangements with the telephone company. When her mother died, she told him there were other people that called, people from church, and she still wanted the phone. She didn't say that he used it now, too, because he knew that. Nor would she say that she "needed" it, because that would have been false, and there was never a time to be false with Forrest. Today she wished she had never asked him to have it installed.

She did not think Forrest was a cruel man. Like most men he had trouble seeing beyond himself, and because he was so strong he could close off a lot of life from his own view. It seemed to her a wastefulness, a carelessness that was unlike any other part of him. She had had to teach him how to hold Peter because she wanted to be sure that he loved Peter. At first she was uncertain if it was just Forrest's awkwardness or some horror at Peter's affliction that made him so strange with his own son. Even though the doctor had said it was in the nature of an accident, with no likelihood that it would happen again, still Forrest would not have another child. Marjorie believed that he thought of Peter as the only failure of his life, a failure few men, even his father, ever had to face. And though his father had failed at practically everything, he had never taught Forrest anything about it, except to avoid it at all costs. Marjorie was glad she never had to talk to her father-in-law because she was afraid she might hate him.

Before Forrest had learned to hold the boy, he had learned to hold Marjorie. He had lain in bed apparently expecting something like spontaneous combustion to occur. His innocence seemed to her another wall between him and life. Only gradually had she got used to his question. After supper, when he had finished the paper or done his production records, he would say, Are you ready tonight? And if she could, she always said yes, unsure whether he asked because he wanted to or because he thought it was time for her.

Now she knew he was afraid. He told her he had taken care of the Harmes boy, but he lacked the confidence to tell her how. That betrayed his fear. Maybe she shouldn't tell him about the telephone call. When she had found she was pregnant and had sat down to talk to him, she first thought he was trying hard to imagine her as a woman and not one of the cows about to freshen. Then the confusion revealed that his feeling was fear, something neither his strength nor his confidence could conquer. Pregnant, she was outside his bounds, and he had marveled at her.

The phonograph arm reached the center post, touched it briefly, and the twin supports, like empty hands, opened. The final record began to replay. Rather than turn the records over,

Marjorie shut the machine off and slid the player back into the console.

She decided to call the minister. The people in Enoch had never been mean to her; it was her husband they thought was a monster. Just being married to Forrest Langley made her, in their eyes, stranger than Jonas Cloudman or Ned Grimsley. At church the people spoke to her, though no one invited her home or asked her to join a club. She hadn't had a friend since Nancy Hatch died. She baked for the sales and suppers, receiving thanks without praise or teasing. She had kept her membership in the Newfound church until she tired of asking Forrest to drive her every Sunday and wearied of making excuses as to why he didn't attend. (He had told her he wasn't church people.) At the Enoch church the Reverend Treadwell was warm to her, but he had been in Enoch only three years, far fewer than she had. In Enoch she answered to no one except her husband. She was Forrest Langley's wife, and that alone defined her.

Soon after he arrived, she told the minister about her dream. She thought there was something feminine about the Reverend Treadwell as he sat across the table from her, his hair a bit long, his face too smooth, his hands white like paper. He was young, barely thirty, and Enoch was only his second church. She felt as though she were confiding in a friend, the way she and Nancy Hatch used to talk.

"The terrible thing about the dream," Marjorie concluded, "is I can't tell who I am. I seem to keep switching around from watching it to being the woman in the car. And when I watch it, I keep thinking 'we.' It makes me nervous."

The Reverend Treadwell sipped his coffee. "Mostly people accept themselves only on the surface," he said, "as one, so they can deny the confusion that comes from the many they are inside." He set the cup in the saucer as if he had said something important and expected Marjorie to think about it. "I would not try to interpret your dream because my counseling isn't of that sort, but I would tell you not to trouble yourself about playing two roles in the dream. It's far more common than most people realize, even in real life."

As he talked on Marjorie noticed that his sentences were long, as long as the ones in his sermons. They were not like the sentences of anyone else's conversation except those of Clay Freeman, who went on stretching things out and along and along until you couldn't figure out where he stood. It was hard to know what to think about it. In Clay she thought it was a nervous need to cover every possibility, to let no stone go unturned, and he didn't always speak in ungainly sentences. The Reverend Treadwell's speech, almost like the French she had learned in high school, seemed to trip out without clues to its identity. Lengthy, and once again almost womanlike, his speech was as confusing as her dream. One of her childhood storybooks had a picture of a huge ball with no seams or openings. From it came a muffled voice that cried for help. She couldn't remember anything else about the story except feeling frightened of being trapped in the ball.

On the floor Peter rolled a truck toward the minister. Making engine noises, Treadwell backed it up to the boy. Peter handed him the toy, a metal stake truck, painted red. As Treadwell turned it upside down, exposing the dull silver of its empty engine cavity, Marjorie felt strangely excluded. When the minister returned the truck, Peter smiled and rolled it over to the stove, where he had his pile of blocks.

If she told the Reverend Treadwell about the phone calls, she would feel obligated to tell Forrest, though Forrest himself might already have gotten one. Still, knowing that she knew about them might force him to do something, something like with the Harmes boy. If he knew who it was. He must not know, she decided, or he would have had a mean word for them. Forrest could never keep his temper hidden. She hoped he would never again do anything like the thing with the Harmes boy. If he thought she was aware of what he was up to, of what was going on, Forrest wouldn't do anything, but she didn't know what was going on.

"I got a terrible phone call today," she told Treadwell. She felt a little foolish because now the dream would seem merely an excuse, a long and awkward introduction to her real horror. Yet the dream had horror enough, and her horror had grown daily since Saturday, when she had helped the Harmes boy back into the truck. She wished Peter wouldn't play with that truck. Threatening a man on the telephone, she told Treadwell, seemed so brutal.

"Some of the men are very angry," the Reverend Treadwell said.

Though their coffee cups were empty, she didn't offer more. "Who?"

"A number of them." Treadwell looked over at Peter cautiously. "A lot of rumors and people saying unpleasant things about other people."

What could be just the minister's careful honesty, his meticulous balance of truth, could also be the oily words of one who was already in violent alliance against her. She worried that she might have betrayed Forrest. "What rumors?" she asked.

Looking directly at her, the minister's face seemed to show heaviness, as though he had put on weight in his few years in Enoch. No longer was the jawline cleanly visible. "I don't take them all that seriously," he said.

"It's the most serious thing since I've lived in Enoch." Her voice made Peter start so that he dropped the blocks out of his truck. He dropped the truck, too, and began to cry. "Except—" she said, but instead of finishing she went to Peter and held him.

The Reverend Treadwell stood up. "Of course they're frightening," he said. "I don't mean to say that they're not; what I do mean is that I don't think anything will come of it, though I would, of course, notify the police."

"Henry Dodge?"

He said, "And I will talk to whomever I can to discourage this harassment. This season of good will and peace places a special duty on me which is in my province of promoting the spirit of Christ and forgiveness, and that duty is not something that I take lightly.''

"Do you know which ones?'' She wondered at her directness.

"I don't know who called you," he said. "I don't know who called, but terrible as it is, I think it must be someone in town, one of your neighbors.''

"Of course," she said. "Who else would it be?''

She let him leave without telling him that there had been two phone calls, and she couldn't tell if it had been the same man both times. She wondered about men who could see anger as superficial, and she believed it was not only the minister's folly but the error of most men. She fixed Peter some hot cereal so that when Forrest arrived home she could eat supper alone with him.

Wednesday, December 28, 1955

The large pores on Ned Grimsley's face made him seem open to the world, which was fine with him as long as the world demanded no explanations for what it saw. Now Clay Freeman wanted to talk about Langley because Ned was attached to Langley in a fashion everybody knew about and no one mentioned.

Ned didn't want to talk about it. He lived next door to Langley and didn't say five words to the man day or night. Ned just wanted Clay Freeman to come and get the goat's milk he trucked off to Newfound three times a week. He didn't want his wife or his mother and father to have to listen to talk about Forrest Langley or his sister.

Ned dipped his brush into the basin of hot water, then swirled it in the soap. He liked to be clean-shaven for Louise, even if his father did call him "half-modern," as if he were a bastard for using a brush but not a straight razor. Ned thought the old man was fortunate he had a son to take over the house and keep it from falling down over his ears and fortunate that he had a wife and a daughter-in-law to listen to the jeremiads he delivered after meals like some antigrace. That was the other reason (and the only one that Ned told his wife) that Ned kept his second-shift job. It was a man's business to live in the world and explore it, but whether he chose to publish his discoveries was his own affair. Not the world or his father or Clay Freeman had any claims on his purposes.

Ned smiled at himself as he wiped the remains of the soap from his face. It was a smile few save Louise ever saw, but Ned was smiling at his own vanity, at the pleasure he took in his taut skin and clear eyes, the bit of gray that mixed with blond just above his ears, At forty, though he neither looked it nor felt it, he kept his joys to himself and his mistress. He liked the word "mistress," preferred it to the one Enoch used about Langley's sister. To them Louise was just his woman.

Ned carefully washed his hands before going out to the goats. Even the perfume from the shaving soap could taint the milk with an off-flavor. In the barn he put some grain in the goats' buckets and washed their teats. Squeezing their bags in the familiar opening and closing of his fingers, Ned imagined himself back in Europe listening to the music of some rural church. With the milk from Anita's teats he played a warm and frothy counterpoint, zoup, zoup, into the pail.

Clay Freeman, in his usual way of never being on time but always showing up, came at twelve. When Ned finished cleaning out under the rabbit hutches, he found Clay in the kitchen. The old man, sitting by the stove as if to bring one last summer to his bones, was talking about Langley. Ned wondered if Clay had brought up the name.

"Not that I got anything against a man that works," the old man said. From the pocket of his sweater he took a handkerchief. "Works hard, Langley does, always has. Can't take that away from him. Same's you," he told Clay. "Must run in the family. But every man's got a position in life, and he's got to live up to it whether he likes it or not."

"Your position's by the stove," Ned's mother said. She refilled Clay's coffee and brought Ned a cup.

Why the old man persisted in this position business, Ned couldn't understand. He knew perfectly well that Langley, the poor boy who had made money, was just as much out of place as Ned himself, the college graduate who milked goats and worked second shift in the Newfound mill. Langley's beating up the kid was just as much violation of the scheme of things (though not the same kind of violation) as Ned's keeping a mistress. Of course, Ned didn't hurt anyone in Enoch except his own, if they knew. He was sure that none of them knew, unless you counted Langley, but he didn't think anyone counted Langley.

Dinner was on the stove. All three of them, mother, father, and wife, waited to see if he would invite Clay Freeman to eat. Ned asked him to sit down with them because he didn't want to go out to the barn with Clay and talk about either Langley or Langley's sister. As soon as he sat down at the table, Clay went right ahead and talked about Langley.

"Ugly talk around town," he said. He heaped his plate. Ned noticed Clay always had a good appetite despite whatever it was he couldn't stomach. Ned's mother looked around for a place to pass the bowl of mashed potatoes.

"Give that here," the old man said. "Think anything will come of it?"

"Not so long as people behave as befits them," Clay said. He drank some water to help flush down his mouthful. "Still, you were talking about position a while back, and I think the town has a position to maintain. I'm not saying Langley was right—far from it—but the man has paid money and the law has been notified. I would think the rest of us could try to hold ourselves a little better than what's been talked about."

"In fact," Ned said, "more money than Billy would make in the course of a year working at the dairy." What little Ned ate, he ate rapidly. He was nearly finished.

"Still, there's the insult involved," the old man said. He had his red handkerchief out again.

"It's the men who're insulted," Clay said.

"As if it were a prizefight," Ned said, "and Billy didn't represent them well enough." They thought everybody in town had to represent them. He wondered what they thought of Clay Freeman.

Clay's plate was empty now, and he looked to be offered more. "I'd hate to see anything happen." Without a word Ned's mother began passing dishes to him. "It's not only Forrest I'm thinking about, cousin or not."

Family, relative, it wouldn't make any difference to Clay Freeman. Ned was sure he would find a way to get himself buried into this right up to his haunches. Interfering was supposed to come hard to New Englanders, but Ned knew that that never stopped them from talking. On the contrary, gossip had never gone out of style. Ned knew he gave them something to talk about. And not just talk, for they must draw lessons from their gabbing, identifying homilies from the spin of their neighbors' lives, as though they were unknowns precipitated from a chemist's centrifuge. Then at some point you test the substances you gathered, touch a match to the assembled compounds, and see what blows. Was Clay Freeman a pure scientist? A mind full of mischief could pour the vitriol of town secrets into available ears and await the results. Perhaps even simple gossip without malice could become dangerous. The catalyst to turn words to deeds could be words themselves, even the words of the innocent.

Out in the barn Clay Freeman tallied the quarts of milk. "I'll bring you more empties next time," he told Ned.

Ned nodded. If Clay forgot too many times, there just wouldn't be any bottles for the milk, and he could buy it by the bucketful. "What are you getting for it now?" Ned asked, just to rile Clay a little.

"Stores are asking seventy-five a quart," Clay said, "and

getting it." Ned took some of the bottles, and Clay lugged the remainder out to Clay's beach wagon. "Somebody might go over there to try to rough him up and teach him a lesson."

"Over ten years he's been neighbors to us," said Ned, looking across the snow to Langley's house. "He hasn't done me harm enough, nor favor either, to make me want to teach him anything."

Clay followed his gaze to the house. "I wasn't thinking of you. The boys at the dairy are awful ugly about this, and I've heard talk from other men who ought to know better."

"Wasn't me who kept Langley's fence in good mend," Ned said. He slammed down the tailgate on Clay's beach wagon. "I'm not going to be one of the neighbors who helps tear it down, but I don't believe Langley's got a fence strong enough to keep all the people out who'd like to get in."

"You aren't just a neighbor. Neither am I."

Sometimes Clay knew how to take the sting out of what would be offensive in another man. "You want to know something, Clay? She doesn't talk about him half so much as you do, and I don't even say a word." People said that Clay Freeman didn't ever know when to let up, so it gave Ned considerable satisfaction to watch him get into his car and pull out of the yard without either of them once mentioning Louise's name.

At eleven o'clock, his shift done, Ned went to Louise's apartment. The talk about him and Louise was no more than the tree falling in the forest when no one was there, because no one close to him heard it. As long as they just let the tree fall and didn't interfere, then it was the tree's own business. Ned was confident that no one, not even Forrest Langley, would interfere with him. They had no call to, though he wondered if Clay Freeman was suggesting some subtle similarity between him and Langley, a similarity he himself had already noticed.

Over a business block on Newfound's Main Street was Louise's apartment. Ned liked the neat, closed quality of the place. The door opened into a kitchen tight with stove and refrigerator, table and chairs, and a polished glass serving table that held a toaster and coffeepot. In contrast the living room stretched out to the windows overlooking the street; her portholes to the world, Louise called them. On a coffee table rested a television set that was never on when Ned was there. Around its perimeter glowed a green light, as soft as a bored angel, Ned remarked. He laughed about boredom and angels. He lay on the bed and looked into the walk-in closet where most of Louise's possessions were stored. All of his were scattered in the barn, the attic, and the cellar, and still, he thought, the place belongs to the old man.

He held the drink she brought him and watched her while she got into bed. Under her shorty nightgown her skin flowed as smooth and warm as any fabric. She wore no panties. She looked at him holding the drink and asked her question almost automatically.

"What's the matter?"

"This time of year things are slow for Clay Freeman," he said, "so he turns into an original fool."

She slid her arm around his back. "No one ever bothers you, do they, Ned?"

He looked down where the nightgown parted at her breast. The sight of her body still excited him. "It's not about us," he said. "It's that business with your brother."

"Did Forrest hire Clay to do something for him?" She moved out of the bed and, holding her glass in one hand, indicated his empty one with her open hand. There was no liquor in his house. The old man wouldn't allow it.

"No, he got Jonas Cloudman for that. Clay's doing this free lance." He swiveled his legs to the floor and followed Louise to the kitchen. "To hear Clay you'd think this was just one big family squabble."

"I always liked Clay," she said as she mixed the drinks. "Out of the relatives, he was the only one who never had a bad word for us."

"He's going around taking testimony."

She gave him his drink. "Sides?"

He put his arm around her. "There's only one side. Lining up against your brother." It was bright under the fluorescent ring, much brighter than in his own kitchen. "Working themselves up like fools at a hanging."

"It won't come to that?" She tasted her drink.

"No," he said quickly. "Clay Freeman's going to stop it. He's just got to be careful not to heat it up. People got nothing better to do than to get into someone else's life." He snorted. "I don't mean Clay. I mean all of those dung beetles stirring up shit about your brother."

"It's all talk," said Louise.

"Talk that got him scared enough he'd pay five thousand dollars to get it quieted down." In Ned's voice was a satisfaction at Langley's fear, a gratification he didn't want Louise to hear.

"Money won't work with those people," Louise said, a frown furrowing her forehead. "They hate him for the money he has already."

That was one thing Ned didn't hold against him. "It was a slap in the face because it denied recognition of them. They won't stand being treated as if they were no more important than stock." He didn't want to frighten Louise, just to let her know there were men who hated her brother far more than he did.

"All the men talking about this"—she searched his face for a moment, her eyes small with suspicion—"have they been to the Harmes boy?"

Ned laughed. "They wouldn't go to him because he'd have no part of it, even before the money. If Forrest thought he was buying off peace, he paid the wrong party."

"Who should he have paid?"

"There isn't anybody special," Ned said. "I heard somebody from the dairy was making telephone calls."

"Then it's just talk," she said.

He led her back to the bedroom, and they finished their drinks naked. She didn't know the danger of talk. She'd been away from Enoch long enough to have forgotten. Ned didn't know there was that much time in the world. Clay was right about talk, Ned thought, because if they do too much talking, some mule will have to do something. In Enoch there were bound to be a considerable number of mules. If Clay wanted to save Langley, it would be different. That he could do. But he wanted to save Enoch, and Ned didn't think that was possible even with God and the devil both on your side. With Clay trying, he just might talk them into doing the very thing he feared most.

When Ned came back from where he had lost himself in Louise's body, he began to talk. "There must have been a mistake in my birth," he said. "The only men I ever felt I was like were the Italians I met when I was stationed there. The New Englanders who work hard and go home to their drafty houses and their drafty skinny wives aren't like me. Their only sense of glory is celebrating somebody's death."

"Esther's not skinny," Louise told him.

He was surprised to hear his wife's name. Louise spoke it no more than he said "Forrest." "Well, there's an awful fatalism to both Latins and New Englanders, so I suppose I'll live right on here until I die."

He kept wife and mistress as separate as his Latin and New England selves. He appreciated his mistress and worked for his wife. He was faithful to two ideals simultaneously. Of course, Forrest Langley was out of place, too, though Ned thought that the only ideal that man served was *more*. Perhaps the merger of conflict between Enoch and Langley would be that each would deserve what they got. Ned felt no loyalty to either.

"My brother's going to be there until he dies," said Louise. "I thought with the trouble either he or Marjorie might call me."

Ned knew Langley would call no one for help, and if he wouldn't call himself, he certainly wouldn't let his wife call. Ned was sure of that because it was no different from what he would do. He put an arm around Louise's bare shoulders.

"I'll do what I can," he said. He knew that between Clay

Freeman's talking and Forrest Langley's paying there was little he could do. About the most he expected of himself was to stay out of it. When the phone on the passageway rang, he thought instantly of Forrest. No one knew he was here, and who else, he wondered, would call Louise at this hour. Louise stood next to the chair whose sole purpose was to hold the telephone. Naked, he took the phone from her.

"Better come home now," said his father. Ned wondered why the old man was up at this hour. Then he wondered how he knew where to call. "Mother's dead." Before Ned could answer, the old man had hung up.

Louise worked her empty hands in front of her as if she were making something. She said nothing.

"Goddamn it all to hell," he told her.

She grabbed him, digging her fingernails into his forearm. "What? What is it?"

It wouldn't have dared to come in anger, friendship, or as a joke. Only when there was a moment terrible enough to pierce his privacy with had someone let the old man know; and he had used the swift, convenient dart of the telephone. What delight people took in picking until they had turned everyone into an open sore.

"I'll find out," he told Louise. "I don't care who it is; I'll find out."

There was one man who knew where Ned was and hated his being there enough to pass on Louise's telephone number. All men, he thought as he clumped heelheavy down the stairs, have some part in what happens to them, but that bastard's going to have more than most.

5 / A Proud and Stiff-necked People

Friday, December 30, 1955

Before Forrest Langley began thinking about the day, he first did the chores. All of the problems the day might offer could wait until he had fed and milked, just as a man must wake before he can act. When Forrest awoke, he was up. Lying abed daydreaming was the waste of a man. He thought a woman might do it because her day started later or because she was given to mind spinning, but a man had to be about his business. After chores, of course, he'd be a fool not to plan out the day, but a man didn't have to plan to do the chores. He just got up early every morning and did them.

The first thing he had to do this day was to call on Jonas Cloudman. From hoisting the cans into the cooler a tired ache spread up from his lower back until it reached his shoulders. The bulk tank would be a real time-saver, freeing him from this step of production and allowing him to expand the herd. He was sure he could get Grimsley's pasture on lease. Ned, whoremaster that he was, would still do business with him, even when money wasn't pressing the Grimsleys. Some of these folks would rather starve than deal with him. He would have to call on Grimsley, too.

Clay Freeman wanted to buy sap from him. His cousin would provide a steady market for his sap, sap he hadn't even bothered to collect, less boil down. Forrest thought it would be fine as long as he didn't have to hire anybody on. It was hard enough in the good times, and now he wasn't even sure of Cloudman. At least machines didn't talk back or lie to you. They certainly didn't use the telephone. Maybe those bastards just wanted to hold him up for more money because they weren't getting any. Unless Cloudman disbursed it. Anyway, it amounted to robbery and blackmail, no more than what you might expect from a town whose men had the ambition of a dead dog. With Marjorie home he couldn't even use the telephone. She nearly fainted every time he went near it.

In the house Peter sat at the table behind a cereal box. Forrest's father had given him nothing from the nothing he had, and now Forrest with so much could give little to Peter. What he had already given to Billy Harmes seemed to be more a problem than a solution. Maybe Clay had been wrong about how money could help, but at least Forrest could keep Peter from going to Laconia State School. There would be no charity for any of his, charity that provided cheap goods at high prices and gouged it out of your taxes. That institution, a holding tank for lunatics, soaked the state by overcharging, getting surplus food, and hiring help that, no matter how little you paid them, would underwork. And what did anyone learn at that school? None of the lunatics ever came home. His son could sit at his own table and eat food Forrest had paid for. Charity and depending on others just weakened you. Like those time-payment plans, it took a down payment of your soul, and month by month by month ate your heart away.

Making a motor sound, Peter slowly revolved the cereal box. Forrest knew that wasn't right because the back of the box offered not cars but service rings, circles of brass or tin with the insignias of Army, Navy, Air Force, or Marines. Fifty cents and two boxtops to turn his boy's finger green. Wouldn't they like that. People in town hated Peter the same way they hated him. They're not as good as either of us, he thought.

"Rings, Peter," he said. "Look." He pointed to the rings on the box. The boy should learn what he could. They should always watch to see if there was a chance for him to learn something. Slowly, as if he were a machine handling a heavy object, the boy turned the box back. "Rff," he said. The sound lowered as he stopped the box.

"Can't he even understand a picture?" Forrest asked his wife.

"He's just playing." Marjorie laid her hand on Forrest's shoulder. It was a gesture she had taken up since the weekend, as though she would keep him from rising. To what, he did not know; nor, he thought, did she. She just comforted him and worried, and she would worry even more if she knew what he kept in the barn.

Her hand pressed against him. "It's the box he likes," she said. "The picture doesn't mean anything to him. You don't wear rings."

"I can't," he said, "working with the machinery." But he knew what she was getting at.

Across the table Peter smiled at Forrest. "Rff," he said. The box began to turn again.

"It's hard," she said, then stopped.

There was no more to be said about Peter, hadn't been for years. And there was absolutely nothing to be said about this other business either. "I'll be out for a while," he told her. "Should Clay stop, tell him to wait." When he stood, her hand didn't leave his shoulder. "I'm going to Cloudman's."

He hadn't seen her cry since they'd learned about Peter. Even now she wouldn't let him see her cry, but he knew that if he turned back and went into the house, she would be hunched over the sink, scrubbing dishes while the tears ran down her face. Their telephone calls had done this. There wasn't a one of the bastards worth Peter, not one. He'd heard them talking about sterilizing idiots as if they were bull calves to have wires twisted around their ballocks. They'd meant for him to hear them. As far as he was concerned the whole town of Enoch ought to be put out of its misery; then they wouldn't feel so envious and worry themselves over what other people had or did.

Back near the hills where Forrest had grown up was Cloudman's place. Three dogs of no related variety lay about the yard like scrap wood saved for some useless project. Cloudman worked hard, but Forrest couldn't see anything he did ever came to anything. Maybe he figured that money Forrest had given him would be a shortcut to wherever he might be going. When Forrest got out of his truck, the dogs just lay on the frozen ground, their eyes peering up at him. In the warm kitchen sat Cloudman and his two daughters.

"I didn't hear you knock," Cloudman said. Hunched at the table, he looked like a boy.

"I'm in a hurry," Forrest said. "It's about the money." He looked at the girls, waiting for them to leave. The older one went to the stove and asked him if he wanted some coffee.

"He's in a hurry," Cloudman said. "He don't want no coffee."

The girls remained in the room, watching him. Forrest felt like a freak. He felt too big for the room. If he owned it, there wasn't a thing in it he would save.

"What about the money?" Cloudman asked.

Forrest looked at the girls. "It's business." He wanted to sit, which struck him as strange because he never did business sitting. He didn't want to be brought to something that would go wrong again, not in front of a man's children. The edge of the counter stuck in his back. He gripped it.

Cloudman finished his coffee and pushed the cup aside. "They're family," he said.

"Where's my money?"

"Where you sent it." Cloudman leaned back in his chair.

Forrest released his grip on the counter and walked to the table. "Then how come I still get phone calls?" He grabbed the table. "I want what I paid for."

He watched the three of them. He had been threatened enough this week to see the menace in Cloudman's hands, the deceit in the eyes of the girls. In anger he had beaten a boy, and he had tried to pay for it. Now all he found was hate, not fear. This was not something simple between him and Cloudman, and it didn't even seem to concern Billy Harmes anymore.

"I thought you prided yourself on being an honest man," he told Cloudman.

Cloudman looked up at him, his narrow face busy like a rat. "I took the money."

"Yes, you and how many others?"

"Get out of my house."

Forrest stood back. "I keep a loaded twelve-gauge."

"Good," Cloudman said. "Good for you."

As he drove back, Forrest decided that he must be careful whose house he went to. Before pulling into his own driveway, he stopped at Grimsley's. Their Christmas wreath, usually not removed until Easter, was off the door. Mary Grimsley, he remembered, was dead. Still, he could probably talk to Ned; he would be the one to make the decision about the pasture anyway. From the barn came a rough yell. Forrest closed the door of his truck and went toward the side porch.

"Here," Ned said, as if he were calling a dog to heel. A hay fork dangling from his hand, he came out and stood on the cement step.

Forrest didn't see the old man anywhere. "Sorry to hear about your mother." He stopped. His hearing lately wasn't good and he didn't always read people right, but something here was wrong. Maybe he just didn't realize how much his mother's death would bother Ned. "Maybe this isn't a good time."

"What have you got to tell me?" Ned said. "You seem real skillful at telling lately."

Forrest explained how with the bulk tank he could expand his herd, which meant he would need more pasture. He also told Ned about Clay Freeman's plan to develop a sugaring operation. His cousin would do most of the work, and Forrest and Ned would benefit without much effort at all.

"What do you care if I spend nights with your sister?" Ned stepped down. "At least I don't beat her."

"You know how I feel about that," Forrest said. One more man with his brains between his legs was what he had called Ned, but now he had done passing judgment on Ned and Louise. "I don't think about it."

"Well you should have thought about it before you went flashing your tongue around."

"I don't talk about it," Forrest said. "I haven't got a hint in hell as to what you're talking about."

"Tell me, Langley," Ned said, "could you lie as fast with one of these tines stuck in your goddamn throat?"

Stabbing forward, the fork rushed at his face. Forrest jolted back, then ran to his truck. He didn't look at Ned, but he could hear his awful laughter. Worse yet, it was not the laughter on the telephone.

In his own driveway Forrest found his cousin grinning like a jack-in-the-box. "Happy New Year, Forrest." Clay Freeman was practically the only one in town who called him by his first name.

"Maybe it'll be a better year," Forrest said. "Better for business anyway." This was more like the way he liked to conduct business, standing outside, unless it was bitter cold. Then he went inside the barn. Today was warm, getting unnaturally warm.

"Hope it's better for my beach wagon," Freeman said, looking over his shoulder at the car, "because every time we run into a wet weather, she just quits on me. This has been the only winter I've ever prayed for cold, too many nights of it growing up."

Forrest nodded. He didn't have to talk about those years with Clay because they had grown up close enough to know them and now they were different enough not to share them. Clay, of course, would remember the cold. Forrest remembered his father.

"Twenty years ago," Clay said, his eyes brightening as he stepped toward Forrest, "we were sitting in a hotel in North Woodstock, and you were standing me to a hot bowl of oyster stew."

They had done that, too, traveled through New Hampshire and Vermont and even part of Maine as manufacturers' representatives, he for Sunshine Biscuits, Freeman for a spice company. Rich with cash and cars, they had enjoyed themselves. "The best feeds," said Forrest, "were the venison steak spreads we used to have at the Coolidge Inn." All the boys on the road, even the ones with competing lines, would meet there during deer season and again in the White Mountains during the New Hampshire deer season.

Clay Freeman threw back his shoulders as he looked up at Forrest. "Back then a dollar would buy the best spread in the place."

"And today five thousand won't buy off a mistake," Forrest said. He jerked his face away, ashamed to look at his cousin.

"Do you remember that little crossroads store of Snow's?" Clay asked.

Forrest kept his gaze across the street to the barn, where melt from the sun-drenched roof sheeted from the eaves. "Where that display of pickling spices burned?"

"I had chipped beef for lunch." Clay was laughing. "Because Gladys had a devil of a time getting the cream sauce off my lapel afterward. She said they must have used white paste instead of flour, and all the time I was trying to tell her about the fire."

"Those bottles of white vinegar Snow put in the window worked like so many Boy Scout lenses." Forrest scratched his chin and smiled. "He gave you a hell of a dressing down, as I remember."

"We nearly lost the account," Clay said. "Of course, it's a wonder the whole store didn't burn down. Snow said I was responsible for the display of goods and should have warned him."

Forrest said, "He wasn't talking responsibility. He was talking blame."

All of us were ambitious, Forrest thought. None of us stayed with those jobs. I got the farm, Pelletier built up a couple of supermarkets in Manchester. We got free of companies, supervisors, road schedules, and put our names on our own work. Even Clay's got something.

"People pass out blame a lot easier than they give out credit," Forrest said. "Let's hear your scheme."

"Work at it," Freeman said. "It's all you can do." He wanted to tap all his sugar maples this spring. He could do it all with plastic pipes, run it right into the shed and boil it down. A paper with a list of equipment unfolded in Freeman's hand. March was pretty much slack time anyway, Forrest thought. After setting up the bulk tank, he could see how he could tie into all the trees and drain down to a collector.

Freeman refolded the paper. "The amount of syrup you could produce would really cut my travel."

"Always thought you liked to travel," Forrest said.

Freeman was serious. "It cuts into the business at both ends, production and sales. After the funeral tomorrow, I have to go to Vermont to make arrangements with one more supplier."

Forrest laughed, the first laugh of the day. "No telephones in Vermont?"

"Those guys don't deal on the telephone," Freeman said. His head never went down, his feet stayed rooted, but his hands were in constant motion, like a man trying to warm himself up.

"Good sense in that. Telephone's just a black worry," Forrest said. He looked over to the empty yard at Grimsley's. "Oh, her funeral, isn't it?"

"Terrible, a death like that at Christmas," Freeman said. "Shocked the hell out of the old man, though better to go like that than to linger on. Ned's just furious, you know, which doesn't seem right. I never expected a man of his caliber, educated and all, to go under so, talking right off his head."

"I didn't know he was that close to her."

Freeman stared up at him. "His father had to call him in Newfound with the news." Even Clay wouldn't speak Louise's name. Forrest thought it was a strange sort of respect after the encounters he had had this morning.

"How come you want to use my trees?"

The little man in front of him stopped his hands and pointed to the grove behind the house. "Sandy soil," he said. "Usually grows pine, but yours has got maple. It makes a syrup with more body. Like Vermont syrup, the kind I use in the sugar. Makes a superior sugar."

Forrest laughed again. "You must be the only man in Enoch who figures I got something sweeter. Maybe that's because we're related."

6 / *Many Mansions*

Saturday, December 31, 1955

Louise Langley did not attend the funeral of her lover's mother. Even before she could ask, Ned had told her that if he were to see a wrong look on someone's face, he would kill him. Louise was worried that he had not found out who had told his father where he was Wednesday night when the old man made that terrible telephone call. She was worried because he suspected her brother, despite the fact that she was sure Forrest would not interfere in her business. Although Ned said nothing about Esther (Louise never thought of her as "his wife"), Louise knew that he didn't want them to meet. Of course, she knew Esther, a short-legged woman, absolutely plain, always in a yellow something, usually a pretty something. Keeping them from being face to face helped Ned keep them apart in his mind. His feelings now were probably too confused to be tested in a way that might end up by destroying all that Louise had with him. Comforting was what he needed, a comforting she had never given him. Because he wasn't dependent on her, they had lasted for years, far longer, she knew, than most people did, even married ones. She didn't give Ned anything that he couldn't get elsewhere, which kept pure the reasons he came to her. The afternoon of the funeral she spent cleaning the apartment and thinking of two men in Enoch: one who threatened to kill; the other, threatened.

Forrest didn't go to the church. Like his sister, Louise, he wasn't expected. In fact his appearance there would have been not just the shock hers would have been, but an insult, too. It would have angered them, and once they had heard the sermon, there were some who would have put their feelings to action, for they were contrary people. Forrest himself, of course, never considered going. Even before Ned had thrust that fork in his face, it had occurred to him at the subtle level where instinctive decisions are made that he didn't belong in a closed space with any of these people. If he ever had, they had since excluded him. Without Jonas Cloudman to help him he needed extra time to connect his bulk tank. As it was, he wouldn't get it done before the first. So he worked, wondering as he connected tubing and tightened fittings whether his sister was also frightened of Ned Grimsley.

Marjorie Langley was afraid. A fear not undefined, yet far from specific, inhabited her. She worried about having called Timothy Treadwell at all. The anonymous phone calls during the week had frightened her so that the fright had taken on a presence of its own beyond the temporary and horrible voice in her, extending to the shadows and the wind and the sounds Peter made in his bed. If she had not called the minister, she might have dared go to the funeral. In her absence people would assume she was home taking care of the boy. And she was, though he slept most of the afternoon and needed no more care than a house or a barn. She had nothing to tend; even her plants didn't need watering.

First, even before the Reverend Treadwell arrived, Davis Scales opened the church. Before Davis had left his house, Ned Grimsley had called him one more time because his father wanted to be reassured that a closed casket was not a sign of disrespect. The old man said he had only seen the casket closed in an accident case where the man had burned to death. Since Davis had left it open at the funeral parlor, wouldn't it seem odd to have it closed at church? Davis knew that Ned wanted it closed and would have had it shut from the beginning with neither cosmetics nor Formalin. He said to tell the old man there was no disrespect; in fact, some people considered it more formal, more dignified, than an open casket. Correct, Ned said. I'll tell him it'll look "correct."

After the call it occurred to Davis that the Reverend Treadwell ought to know about the old man's concern in case he wanted to make a last-minute fuss at the service. It would have been simple enough to bring along tools to open the casket, but Davis knew the old man was avoiding an acceptance of the final act, as though his wife weren't yet dead. Not until the spring would she be placed into her grave. The closing of the casket, then, was the seal of her death. The Reverend Treadwell said he had been over the same ground with the old man. He said something else, also; just a hint, but it was sufficient. Davis Scales had dealt with trouble for too long not to recognize it.

Zack closed his gas station at eleven and set the hands of the cardboard clock on the "be-back" sign at three. After changing his clothes he went to the church to help Davis Scales arrange the flowers. He liked working with Davis, and he had done so often enough so that he no longer bothered to tell the priest about each Protestant service he attended. All the priest would say, Zack knew, was not to take part. And Zack knew he would participate in any damn thing he wanted.

Arranging the baskets (mostly gladiolas) for best effect, setting the bouquets on the wooden stands to create a frame, were things he did better than Davis, undertaker or not. Even the women's group, who knew his ability, left him alone. They spent their time downstairs in the kitchen. As far as he was concerned, they didn't sing well either. The sermon usually bored Zack. He couldn't understand how that was supposed to provide consolation for the living or ease the passage of the dead. No temptation to participate ever threatened him, but his neighbors appreciated his presence and told him so. They praised his work with the flowers, and he sat, quietly bored, through the service. This time, however, the sermon moved him to feelings that would be called sinful, Catholic or not.

Duncan Hatch stood at the doorway by the table stacked with folded paper programs. On the other side of the doorway was Jonas Cloudman in a tight-fitting blue suit. Duncan couldn't think of a more unlikely looking pair than he and Jonas Cloudman made. Duncan had gone to work dressed for the funeral, so that all he had had to do was to close the restaurant and tape to the door the sign his waitress had lettered: IN RESPECT TO THE MEMORY OF MARY GRIMSLEY WE WILL BE CLOSED UNTIL FIVE O'CLOCK. Ever since his wife's death, Duncan had been head usher. Every Sunday morning, despite having to close up at one the night before, he seated people in the church just as proudly as he greeted them at his restaurant. He also passed the collection plate and even stood silently during the sermon and counted the congregation. In the afternoon he would cash up from Saturday night, and by evening he would be ready to meet with his friends in the closed lounge. At the funeral service there would be no collection, no counting of the house, so he wouldn't have any reason to stand during the sermon. But when he heard the sermon, he felt he should rush down the aisle and pluck the Reverend Treadwell out of the very pulpit.

To Jonas it looked like a wedding, except there was no music and no waiting for the shift to the joyous recessional. One day he would be here with Linda, not walking her down with her sister to their pew, but escorting her to a man at the end of the aisle. On a simple stand off to one side rested the coffin. Jonas thought you'd have to look for it if you didn't know it was there. Since about twelve thirty he and Hatch had been busy passing out programs and seating people. When the old man Grimsley arrived, he went to his usual pew at the back. Jonas told him that Ned and the others were sitting up front. He wondered why they had left the old man to come in alone. To please the old man, Jonas snapped the velvet rope across the Grimsley pew so that no one would sit in it. As the old man walked down the aisle he told Jonas that the empty pew would show respect for her. It would look correct, he said.

Most everyone from the dairy was there. Dubber Handley sat on the right with his wife, Flora, who had closed up the dairy bar at twelve, changed into her long black dress, and driven Dubber to the church. Every few moments he raised the sleeve of his suit jacket to look at his watch. On the other side were Paris Rutherford and Sonny, heads above anyone else. Mrs. Rutherford, who was home with the flu, usually sat between them, and even now a space not quite large enough for an adult separated the two tall men. Jonas had seated his daughters considerably behind Sonny Rutherford. In fact he had told Duncan Hatch that he would seat that kid on the end of his foot if he could kick that high. Jack Niles and Jelly Enman, smelling of the dairy soap, sat in the same pew, each with his wife. Both of them fidgeted as though the quiet of the church made them uncomfortable. Still bandaged, Billy Harmes came with his father and mother, who limped along on a leg bad with arthritis. In his suit Billy looked almost dignified, the contrast with the white bandages giving him an air of seriousness. Clay Freeman, late as usual, the last one in as usual—so that the Reverend Treadwell knew to begin after Clay arrived because there would be no other mourner—sat with Zack in the last pew. His wife didn't even turn around to see if he was there. He had just time to tell Zack the flowers were beautiful when the service began.

"Let us pray," said the minister. The congregation bowed their heads, indicating an agreement with Treadwell none of them felt, one they would soon outright reject. Timothy Treadwell was known for his prayers that went far and wide and included enough people to cause his parishioners to listen to the words. But they didn't expect him to exercise his social conscience at a funeral, therefore they were shocked, though not surprised, when his prayer went beyond Mrs. Grimsley and the surviving Grimsleys and included the Negroes of the South, the starving millions of India, and other peoples whose material wants (if not their spiritual needs) were lacking. The hymn chosen by the old man came as a relief from the prayer. Though they knew the words by heart, the congregation pointed their faces at their hymnals.

"In my father's house," began the sermon. However familiar was that text, it sounded like a veering from the subject. Those in the pews feared they would hear more about the poor and suffering in faraway places and little of their dead neighbor and her grieving family. Soon, however, Timothy Treadwell was more personal than they would want, personal enough to change their apprehension to anger. "There are many mansions." Suspicious as they were of the minister, they listened to him, and indeed he spoke of "Mary Grimsley, that good and gentle woman, most deserving of our prayers and thoughts, whose place in God's mansion is surely prepared."

An older minister, a man who knew Enoch (the congregation was sure), would have been able to mention a thing or two about Mary Grimsley's life and from them draw some gentle homily, a message reassuring to the Grimsleys, pleasing to the congregation. Though Timothy Treadwell had been in Enoch but three years, he took his homily from the town itself. He pointed to the police chief's wife, who was pregnant. The people were reminded of the renewal of life that children were. As the old died, the young were born. "What will that child be told?" the minister asked. He spoke not of the mystery of death and eternal life that would be explained to the child, but of the horror of sin that would need no explanation because it would be all too evident even to an innocent child. "A child," he reminded them, "whose very father is the symbol of obedience to law, as the Father of us all demands obedience in His law."

There were no smiles. When the minister said that the Grimsleys had their secrets and Mary had to live with those secrets, it was Ned whom the congregation looked at, seeing between his thick hair and his stiff white collar the redness of shame and anger. The old man never moved or shifted position, and people in the congregation believed he must not have heard the minister's words.

"Mary Grimsley was burdened with secrets," the Reverend Treadwell said. "Knowing sins she could not prevent troubled her. She felt the pain in her heart as though every guilt grew there. Jesus said, 'Let not thy hearts be troubled; but believe in me.' Let us have a moment of silent prayer." They thought it was over. It was terrible for the Grimsleys, at least for Ned and his wife, but the people in the pews were glad it was done with. "How can we pray for Mary Grimsley's soul in the spirit of Jesus who said, 'I am the way, and the truth, and the light,' when we have not that spirit?" Timothy Treadwell was not done; he was finally including the congregation in his net. "Secrets and hatred are harbored, and plans laid, plans not only of sin, but of crime. Thoughts of violation of both holy and civil law infest this town with an illness surely more deadly than any Mary Grimsley suffered. Little will it comfort Mary or her family if this town disgraces itself before God and man."

Old man Grimsley liked the music. He could almost make himself believe that Mary, too, could hear it, not in the closed box in front of him, but in the mansion in the sky where Christ most assuredly had taken her. He felt annoyed when he noticed that Ned wasn't singing until he thought that grief had taken away his son's words. But it wasn't grief at all, and soon the words would return.

Downstairs the women prepared the tables. Despite their long dark dresses they moved with the same ease as in their own kitchens. Across the hall was the punch bowl, which Flora Handley filled. Expertly she began ladling into the paper cups on the table. The groups of men who stood by the tables said little while the women brought out the food. Clay Freeman and Zack Zakrzewski set up an extra table for trays of cookies against the back wall. Ned Grimsley waited, and when the Reverend Treadwell entered, the other men turned to listen.

"Exactly what secrets were you talking about, Reverend?" Ned said.

"The things your mother told me had little to do with you," the minister said. He smiled at the women behind the food table. "They had to do with the community in which she lived."

"I never knew my mother to be much on Catholics. When did she take to confessing to you?"

Treadwell stopped smiling. "It wasn't personal," he said.

Ned watched him for a moment. "Town meeting isn't until the first Tuesday in March." Treadwell started to smile again. "I don't like my mother's funeral being the occasion for your speeches. And I'll tell you another thing, the man who interferes in my business will find himself a sorrowful man."

The Reverend Treadwell excused himself and moved to the food table. He walked with a step that mixed a bounce and a waltz. As he walked along filling up his plate, his smile returned.

Davis Scales said that he could not remember when a minister had so bollixed a funeral. He said Marjorie Langley must have talked to Treadwell. "There's not another soul in Enoch that could raise any sympathy for Langley," the funeral director said.

Among the people there was little doubt that Davis Scales was right. Esther Grimsley stood next to the minister while old man Grimsley thanked him. The others, assuming without saying that they were the subjects of the sermon, stayed away from Treadwell. With little verbal acknowledgment they agreed among themselves that it had been wrong of the minister to mix business of that sort in with Mary Grimsley's funeral. Preaching, after all, was supposed to be preaching. The Grimsleys had never had much to do with Langley. There was a silence while they thought of Langley's sister, but they did not mention her name. They were neighbors, they said, but in Enoch we're all neighbors. By his sermon Timothy Treadwell had succeeded where he hadn't wanted. He had brought them together.

Throughout the murmured criticism of the minister, Zack felt uncertain as to what to say. The proprieties were not automatic for him, the Catholic. Still, he said, "If Treadwell wanted to talk about sin, why didn't he talk about the deed that was done? And Billy sitting there in his bandages."

Duncan Hatch grabbed Zack's big hand, as red as the gasoline that he pumped. "Because the woman got to him," Duncan said. "God knows what stories she filled him with."

Clay Freeman, leaving early, said that he was late for his appointment with a Vermont farmer who had some of last spring's syrup. The farmer had held it over, hoping to sell it at Christmas, but now he was stuck with it. Clay asked Davis Scales to go with him.

"Last time I had to bring the syrup back in the hearse," Davis said. "If the Board of Health knew that, you couldn't get an approval seal for water out of the tap."

"Well, it saved me a trip," Clay said. "How about you, Duncan?"

"Restaurant will be busy tonight," Duncan said.

"I went on one of those trips," Zack said. He poked his finger into Clay's ribs. "It's an hour of talk before you even mention syrup, and by the time you get to the farmer's daughter's dolls' names, it sounds like Clay ain't going to buy or the farmer ain't going to sell."

"This farmer's going to sell," Clay said.

"Then there's the mud," Zack said. "It's all mud and us wrestling five-hundred-pound drums of syrup."

Davis laughed. "And in Vermont they never heard of chain falls."

"That's not the real fun," Duncan Hatch added. "The real fun's driving back with Clay doing seventy and the rear end of the beach wagon trying to break away on every curve."

Clay joined in their laughter. "There'll be no mud this time," he said, "but I won't be home until morning."

"Maybe they'll make some mud for you," said Duncan. "It's warm enough to rain."

When Henry Dodge in his uniform came into the room, they were all reminded of Treadwell's sermon, though no one mentioned it. They had even stopped talking about the Grimsleys. Only the strange warm weather kept the conversation going.

"Too bad for Clay to miss New Year's," Duncan Hatch said. "I hope he doesn't end up stuck in the mud somewhere."

"All of us do," said Davis Scales. "Sooner or later."

7 / *Sunday*

Sunday, January 1, 1956

It had started to rain New Year's Eve. Now early New Year's Day, it was raining steadily. Through the towns of snow and Christmas lights Clay heard the horns blaring the violent greetings. His answering blast, though moving, seemed more settled, ordinary, as he drove along with the two five-hundred-pound drums of syrup in the back of his beach wagon. From his radio came the music of the ballroom bands, tempo varied from station to station. The windshield wipers swept back and forth, constant, out of time with the music.

He was late, of course, and if Gladys complained when he got home, she could just remember that it was she who had held him up. He hadn't minded taking her home after the funeral, though he had assured her one of the boys would be glad to drive her back. After all, the kid was being watched. She should enjoy a chance to get out. But no, she'd ridden home silently, waiting until they were home and the girl paid and gone before she'd said a word.

"Did you tell him to preach that sermon?" she asked. Her shoeless feet were perched on the hassock.

"Maybe I'm partially responsible," Clay told her. "He asked me which men to see, and I told him he would have to see all of them." He had been pacing, stuck, wishing to be on the road. "I can no more sort out sheeps and goats than he could. It's all feelings, even Forrest, not plans or schemes or acts."

Gladys reached up to rub her knee. He felt awkward looking at her leg. "Of course you had no desire to pick goats because these are all your friends, Clay Freeman. You think they're all your friends. They'd rather deal with feelings than go to the law or even the church. They, just as much as you, forced Timothy into that foolish speech. He the more fool for listening to you."

Times like these he wished she smoked or drank so that he could do something other than stand before her defending himself and all of Enoch. "The law here is Henry Dodge and the church is Timothy Treadwell, two men, with just as much feeling as any other flesh and blood in town. When people think of the law or morality, they think of those two."

"Two good men."

"I didn't say they weren't good," Clay told her. He heard his voice rise and quieted it. "But incompetent in Dodge's case and ineffectual in the other."

"Like most of the men in this town," she answered.

It was a sneer he chose to ignore. He didn't imagine the men in Minnesota, where she had moved from after high school, were any better than his friends, than men anywhere. Sometimes people were thrust fiercely out of their depth. Not just sometimes, he thought; sooner or later it was inevitable.

"I have to leave," he said, putting the burden of his staying on her.

"Be careful, Clay," she told him. "The weather's turning funny."

She had gotten out of her chair to kiss him. Even in her stocking feet she was nearly as tall as he, but she had bent her head back to receive his lips. He had gripped her broad back for an extra moment before he had left, whistling the start of a tune he couldn't remember.

•　　•　　•

Enoch was dark, the radio practically silent, as Clay spun the knob from station to station. The rain, hard and dark, hid what few parties might still be going on. The sign on Hatch's Diner was out. The lower windows of the lounge all were black. No cars were left in the parking area. The directional signal clicked an insistent rhythm. Before turning, Clay braked the car, but it only slowed, its weight gently coming to rest like something lighting on the earth.

Clay moved the shift lever to *L*. Ahead the road disappeared. From Langley's barn came not a bit of light. As Clay turned down the hill he saw a gleam of reflection, a large square of light in the road. He rubbed his eyes and pumped the brakes. The square of light grew larger and encompassed the road. At the bottom he hit a huge puddle of water, bright like a reflecting pool. Water splashed up into the motor, and it died.

Clay coasted nearly to the bridge, so that when he stopped, he was equidistant from the two hills. There was something of a shoulder to pull onto, muddy as it was. Clear across the field and all the way down to the riverbank was all snow. Clay pushed the shift lever up to *P* and tried the ignition key. The motor turned uselessly. He hammered the dash with the heel of his hand. From the floor in front of the passenger side he took a gray frock coat, balled it up, and pillowed it against his window. Soon he was asleep.

It could have been a dream. A dim glow of light seemingly coming from the snow itself rather than from above was interrupted by two figures. Or three figures. It was colder now. From in back Clay pulled a wool shirt. He put it over his chest like a blanket. Between the figures was a shadow moving slowly away from him. Clay sat in the middle of the seat as if awaiting a passenger and a driver. No one came.

January 1, 1956

There was never enough, Forrest Langley thought as he pivoted his legs from under the covers. Not in Enoch, New Hampshire, not in the entire world, free or otherwise, was there enough to satisfy them. They would always want more and never be satisfied to a pennyweight with anything he ever accomplished. At forty-two Forrest Langley had accomplished a great deal. Yet, he thought, no one save Clay Freeman, who's my own cousin, will so much as say it. He looked back at his wife, curled on the bed like a sleeping question mark.

Stealing down the dark stairs, Forrest thought of all the mornings he had come down out of the loft to read by the fading heat of the kitchen stove in the old place. He had decided that his father must have hated him to raise him in such a place as the worst section of Enoch, and he had also decided that there was neither percentage nor advantage in depending on or following his father. No good to be gotten from a man who'll raise his family in a shack in the Birches, he had said. No good in most men, he told himself now, thinking of the telephone calls he had gotten all week.

He drew a glass of cold water from the sink and stood with his face in the window. From the stove clock shone the only light in the room. As a boy he would get up early mornings and study his school books. At night his father wouldn't let him go to bed until his chores had all been done and a man-sized pile of wood stacked beside the stove. He got to inventing chores for Forrest to keep him from going to bed. Forrest glared at the black window. That alone, he thought, was enough to make me hate him.

There was time yet. There was always time enough because Forrest rose early to get the jump on everybody. Even God, he thought. Even the sons of bitches who try to snare me with that telephone. Five drops of vinegar fell into his glass of water, counted out of the brown gallon jug just as his mother had counted for him every day in the old place. Best natural tonic there is, she would say. Adam's ale and cider vinegar. Once he had had Marjorie give some to the boy, little good that it did. Puckered him up, and he didn't even have words to complain. You'd think that would be calamity enough for them—

his boy lying up there like a baby, a baby all of his life. And when Forrest's mother had died, his father had told him, She ain't no wife of mine. I never paid clerk nor preacher nor woman either for the only pleasure God ever gave straight to man.

Forrest let the water sit in his mouth until he puckered. He knew he was delaying the walk across the road to the barn. A wish, a weakness he thought it, came to him. He wanted to talk to someone. Mornings walking to school with Clay Freeman, he used to talk about getting out of the Birches and going to college. But after school his cousin was always playing ball with the town kids, leaving Forrest to go home to the Sisyphean tasks his father assigned. Unlike Sisyphus, Forrest was confident he would escape, sure that even his lack of money when he graduated from high school in 1932 would not keep him from college. It didn't. His father told him he would have to stay on the old place and work until he was twenty-one. Wasted all them mornings getting up, didn't you? His father laughed at him. Valedictorian—fool.

People were always calling him names, he thought. All week on the telephone—even so his wife could hear. They'd probably tell Peter, too, if they thought the boy could make any sense out of what they were saying. In the closet hung the Pendleton shirt Marjorie had bought him for Christmas. Even if she had had Clay take her to Newfound for it, he knew that shirt had cost her thirteen dollars. Thirteen Dollars when five dollars would buy you the best dress shirt in the store. It was pride that made Forrest close with a dollar. All of those years on the road, wholesaling to the little store in the North Country and over into Vermont, he had stashed money away. Early one morning he had gotten up and driven his coupe to the assessor's office to pay the taxes on the Henderson farm. Wedged into his trunk was his gladstone full of samples, which he didn't take out even when he traded the coupe for a truck. He had gone to Newfound to borrow money to fix the place up and stock it with Holsteins and had gone back to Newfound for a wife. Now the sons of bitches in Enoch resented his living with them. They resented everything he had, and they wanted to take it all away from him.

He drank the last of the water. Though he didn't often think about his looks, Forrest Langley, standing just six feet tall, was a handsome man. With his wide forehead, long ears, dark eyes, and a nose as straight as a wedge, he thought he looked hard. All except for his lips, which were soft, puffy—because, he told himself, I've had to swallow far more than my peck of dirt. Inside his stomach the tight-curled snake was neither dirt nor water but fear, a fear Forrest would not name, even to himself. Across the road he walked, his head down against the unseasonable rain. Be cold later, he thought as he went into his barn.

January 1, 1956

Jonas Cloudman, looking for his daughter and Sonny Rutherford, was also abroad that night. In the dark rain he closed the door to his house and looked up at the bedrooms to see that there were no lights on. The two dogs by the truck raised their heads and lowered their hind ends at his approach. No sound passed from the dogs as they stood in the rain and watched him enter the truck. He pulled the choke out full, turned the key, and stepped on the starter. At the road he paused before turning right.

Through town there were no other vehicles. Around behind Zack's filling station the only car he found was a thirty-two Ford coupe with its hood up and its motor torn out. Jonas got out of his truck and urinated onto the snow beside the Ford. Out on the street the town cruiser passed by, a single red light on top of the roof like an unnatural nipple. His trousers unzipped, Jonas crouched by the fender of the Ford until the cruiser moved by. Back in the truck he drove in the direction from which the cruiser had come until he cut onto a road that led toward the hills on that side of the river. At the gravel pit he slowed down and killed his lights. After rolling down his window, he still could hear no noise; only the rain came in, warm, without wind.

Patches of snow showed in his sudden lights, patches of snow and the slow curtain of rain.

Over other roads he went, never encountering another car, not even so much as a light. Nor did he see the cruiser again until he passed Henry Dodge's house, where it was parked. There was no sign of life in the policeman's house. At the south end of town he saw a light on in Langley's barn. Stopping by the top of the drive, he looked down into a yard of shadows, only shadows.

He left the truck on the road and walked down the drive, carefully testing his footing as he went. Inside, the milk room was warm. Folding his arms around himself, he stood there a moment and looked at the black windows. The cows made no noise when he entered the barn. He walked past the stalls until at the last one he found a pitchfork. He picked it up and continued to the bales of hay double-piled on the floor.

Gripping the middle of the fork's shaft, he climbed the ladder to the loft of loose hay. His feet made slow and silent contact with each rung. At the top the air was warm, almost thick, with dry hay. It was quiet. Jonas could see nothing. When he reached the floor again, he set the fork against the stall and walked back to the milking machine. There tubing led to a hole cut through to the milk room, and by the hole was a slender three-cell flashlight. Without turning it on, he slid it into the wide pocket of his jacket. Once more in the loft, the fork again in his hand, he played the flashlight over the hills of hay.

He left the flashlight and fork where he had found them. Across the road at Grimsley's a car pulled into the garage. Jonas stood by his truck and watched, but no one got out of the car. Depressing the clutch, Jonas coasted the truck down the hill toward the river. Halfway across the flats was Clay Freeman's beach wagon. Jonas could see no one in it as he passed the car.

During his search of the east side of the river, it began to snow. By the time he returned to his place, it was coming down hard. There were no marks on the fresh snow in his yard. The dogs had gone under the tractor. In the kitchen a bit of warmth found its way from the stove, which Jonas stoked until there was a blaze. As he lay his head on the table his arms encircled the empty space in front of him. Through the door came the girl, so quietly that he looked up twice before he rose from the table. She kissed his cheek and went back upstairs. First Jonas opened the door from the ell to let the dogs in, then he, too, went to bed.

January 1, 1956

At the house next to Langley's, Ned Grimsley sat in his car parked in the garage. He had sat there for some time as the car lost the heat of its journey from Newfound and turned cold. After Cloudman's truck came darkly up the drive from Langley's barn and turned to go over the river, Ned wiped his eyes. There were no tears there from his mother's death. Out of the car Ned moved slowly, steadily, paying no attention to the warm puddles he stepped in, but suffering (despite all of the whiskey in him) some inner cold. Avoiding the snow-filled ditch, Ned walked down the middle of the black road. Past his house he stopped to peer down the drive to Langley's barn. A small light, dimly yellow, shown from the milk room. With a shake of his head he turned and walked back to his garage. A wooden stake set into the ground to mark a corner for an extension of his rabbit hutches tripped him, and he fell headlong into the snow.

In his garage Ned opened the trunk of his car, took out a quart whiskey bottle, and stuck it into his coat pocket. He slammed the trunk lid down. At the sudden noise in the closed, cold space he looked up at the second floor of his house. He shook his head at the darkness and went into the ell, where he had left the light on. When he clicked the switch off, it was too dark, so he pressed it down again hard enough to leave a square indentation on his finger. Goats, their bags growing full, moved about in their pens. Sitting on a wooden milkcase, he went from goat to goat. As he squeezed the milk from their teats his body sagged and slumped, as though it were falling slowly a great distance. The whiskey bottle, nearly empty, sat on the bench beside the refrigerator.

When he was done, he strained the milk into thick glass quart containers and lined the bottles up in the refrigerator on a single shelf, where they sat white like maids. Sweat beaded along his temples.

The whiskey bottle in his hand, he went outside and watched Clay Freeman come up from Langley's barn and turn onto the road. Clay was holding something yellow in his hand, keeping it away from his body as though it might be contaminated. With one hand on the door jamb and the other gripping the whiskey bottle, Ned watched Clay take the road down to the flats. He watched him until Clay disappeared below the hill. Langley's house was dark, but the small yellow light in the barn was still on. Ned held the bottle upside down, forming a small circle of pink in the snow beside the pool of his vomit.

In the kitchen of his house he set his boots on some newspaper, dried and yellowed, that was laid near the stove. He shook the wet from his jacket and, reaching around the corner into the hallway, hung it on a wooden peg. His black hair glistened. Trickles of water itched his neck. At the sink was a tall glass, which he drank from, spitting out the first two mouthfuls before he swallowed any of the water. He refilled the glass and took it to the table. Pushed against the wall with its leaves down, the table looked like a bird with its wings broken.

Kerosene from the barrel in the entryway foamed into the glass jug. The smell of it was thick and slippery. In the kitchen Ned flipped the jug upside down in a single motion and set it on the white stand beside the stove, then jiggled the bottle to make sure that the spring top was depressed in its fitting. As the burner began to warm, he slid the coffeepot over the flame. The pot made a gasping, sighing sound, and its glass eye slowly went black.

Ned found the aspirin bottle in the cupboard. He spilled the pills out onto the table so that he could form triangles of them. Lined up on the edge of the wooden surface were sixteen white groups of three. With his glass of water he toasted the empty bottle, then swept the nearest triangle into his hand and swallowed the pills all at once. At the hall he caught a glimpse of white not the dawn.

Ned's stockinged feet were nearly silent as he walked over to the stairway that rose from the hall. The door at the bottom was partially open. He listened, but from the second floor the only sounds were an old man's snores. Ned shook his head. Back at the table he dropped the aspirins one by one back into the bottle, like pebbles off a bridge. After replacing the bottle in the cupboard, he finished his water and left the glass by the sink. The cup of coffee that he fixed himself kept him company for a very long time before he went up to bed.

January 1, 1956

It was still raining. From across the snow-burdened field to the steel bridge everything was white. In the false dawn even the breath of the river was white. Like an old woman the river had been preparing for bed, but now, on the first day of January, it swelled against its banks and rose as if there were a man in the house, as indeed there was. On the other side of the bridge was a steep hill where the road wound slowly up to the ridge. A warm mist floated through the leafless trees.

Clay Freeman stirred, as if pierced by the light or made suddenly aware of the decline in temperature. Turning his wrist toward the window, he looked at his watch. A wind from the opposite direction began now, hurrying the mist but not dispelling it. Hunched over the wheel, race-fashion, Clay twisted the ignition key through its clicks to the start position. The motor, responding sluggishly, turned over several times without catching. He let the key fall back to its original position, pulled the shift lever toward him, and dropped it down so that the red line went from *P* to *N*. After trying twice more, the motor shrieked a high-pitched whine. Clay released the key and slammed the heel of his hand against the steering wheel. Sitting back a moment, he stared at the bridge as at some distant enemy. He kicked the dashboard.

Outside the rain was turning. Clay pulled his coat collar around his neck. He wore no hat. The hood of the car came up with a groan, water running off it to splash into the sensitive insides. After twisting the distributor cap free, he dug in his pocket for a paper tissue. The one he pulled out in a lump was a wadded ball; hard, dry, useless. His hand closed around it, but instead of throwing it away, he thrust it back into his pocket. He set the distributor cap back over the rotor and ignition points as if he were covering a sleeping child. Just past the car he turned, went back, and put the stiff white tissue on top of the distributor cap. It could neither dry the points nor prevent more moisture from getting to them, but he left it there anyway. He lowered the hood, which did not pause as he expected but crashed shut with a sharp, short noise.

It was getting colder. Pellets of hail mixed with rain and crunched under his feet. By the time he reached the hill at the head of the field, the road had become slippery, and the pellets stung his face.

The light from under Langley's barn shown hard into the turning weather. Across the road the house was dark, as were the two places farther along. Clay slid down the incline to the barn, his hands held out like an impromptu skier's. At the side door of the barn he neither knocked nor spoke but simply peered into the window of the milk room. The trim on the window was clean, its paint dry but not cracked. Inside the door was a large stainless-steel bulk tank waiting to be attached to the milking system. A conventional cooler for the old forty-quart cans stood by the wall. Clay was alone in the barn. The cows shuffled about in their stanchions, some lowing, and Clay wondered if they were disturbed by him or only waiting to be milked. On a shelf over the cooler he found a soft yellow cloth, started to stuff it into his pocket, then just held it in his hand as he left the barn. He carried it like a sign of peace, a demonstration that he was not a common thief.

Back on the road he turned to the barn, then to Langley's house, obscured now by the snow. The darkness of swirling snow balanced the increasing light so that even though it was near dawn when he reached the car, he could see little more than when he had left. Switching the yellow cloth to his other hand, he turned the key in the ignition. As the motor began to turn without firing, he flicked the key off, got out, and lifted the hood. There on the disconnected distributor cap sat the wadded tissue, as if to taunt him. Brushing it onto the ground, he secured the cap, got back into the car, and once more turned the key. The motor spun easily and caught. Clay pitched the unused yellow cloth to the floor. It had finally gotten cold enough for the car to start.

The falling snow would cover the ground again, cover the few bare spots created by the rain. As the motor idled it grew warm in the car. He had seen the three men before he heard them, had seen them, the two separated by something, and the third following. Slowly they had moved across the wet field toward the river. When they had come even with the car, he had seen that the two were lugging something, dragging it and hoisting it over the uneven ground. At the bank they had turned to the road and had gone onto the bridge. There they had swung their burden over the rail. It must have been a calf born dead, he thought. A hell of a way to start the new year. He hadn't seen them come back. Maybe he had fallen asleep. He couldn't remember if it had been before he had gone to Langley's barn.

Racing the motor, Clay brought the red line of the shift indicator down to *D* and pulled away from the ditch onto the road. On the bridge he stopped. It was perfectly white, unmarked, undisturbed. Perhaps he hadn't seen anyone. The river would freeze now. He drove on toward home.

January 1, 1956

Marjorie Langley sat alone in the cold house. Upstairs Peter lay awake in his bed. He would not need any attention until noon.

Marjorie wondered why he still took a nap (for he didn't often sleep), as if having the brain of a child he kept a child's habits. Unless there was something wrong, he napped after lunch. When he was sick, he slept like a man, lying through the morning curled slightly to hold in some essence he wouldn't reveal as either child or adult. As she had since he was first born, Marjorie listened for him, though he said little enough when he was wide awake and standing right beside her. As the years had passed she had allowed herself to stay in the kitchen, where, she had learned, she could be attentive enough.

She shivered in the kitchen and shivered again as she skirted the grate. Turning the round dial of the thermostat on the wall, she felt she was violating a rule or presence. Since Forrest had had the oil burner installed, it had always been he who twisted the burnished gold disk and listened for the click and whoosh from the cellar. From the dark hole in the floor she heard before she felt the rush of warm air. Even now, after two years, Peter would not walk across the grate. Forrest had said it was because the boy was afraid he'd fall in, so he walked his two hundred thirty pounds over the crisscrossed bars. See, he had said, it will surely hold up a hundred pounds of boy. But Marjorie knew it wasn't fear of falling that kept Peter off the grate. Because she felt it herself, Marjorie knew it was a fear of being snatched by something that would grab her ankles, slide up her legs, under her skirts, and pull her down. Forrest was never afraid of things getting him. He didn't even listen for Peter's breathing.

The heat of the burner warmed Forrest's coffee into bitterness. Marjorie had let it grow cold and oily, had reheated it, and now made herself a cup and poured the rest into the sink. It amounted to exactly the two cups Forrest always drank. The eggs in the dish in the oven had grown together, losing their fresh yellow color. The coffee tasted worse than bitter; then she realized that she was drinking it without sugar, the way Forrest did. She neither added sugar nor poured out the coffee, but left it there on the table unattended while she put on her coat and overshoes. At the top of the stairs she listened for Peter before she went out into the sheen of the outdoors.

Through the thick and treacherous snow she walked, hearing the cows bawling before she was even halfway down the hill to the barn. He's dead, she thought. When she didn't find him slain in the milk room, she thought he might have burst with rage among the cows. She was afraid she would find him among the pipes and hoses of the milking machine, his arteries and veins stretched and torn, rent by the terrible pressure of his proud heart. But the only pressure in the barn was in the full udders and pained teats of the unmilked cows.

Back across the road she walked and called their neighbor, Ned Grimsley. Hearing her request, he laughed as though she had told him a joke. "I'm sick," he said. "I could barely milk my goats." She wondered how many laughed behind her back. And Forrest's back. Men did that, especially the sort of men who had made those telephone calls. Forrest did not laugh at people; he seldom laughed at all. And the telephone calls that had come for him had not asked for help in milking cows. But surely, she thought, Ned would help. If not because he lived next door, then at least because of Louise. His voice, thick though it was, did not sound heavy with a cold or some illness. It just sounded tired, as if he hadn't wanted to be bothered.

Next she tried Jonas Cloudman, planning to pay him whatever Forrest would have given him for such a job, but his daughter said he was sleeping. She told Marjorie that he was in a black mood and wouldn't do a favor for God himself. Marjorie couldn't imagine Jonas Cloudman sleeping in on any morning, regardless of whether it was a Sunday and a holiday, because he wouldn't have been invited anywhere the night before, nor gone if he had been. And now Forrest's absence required that she do no less than cross the road again and do her best at milking, though once more, before she left, she went to the top of the stairs and listened for Peter. With the machinery she felt helpless, a mood that passed as she fitted the cups to each udder. She did not know that the bulk tank was not attached to the system, so it wasn't until she went to the milk room that she saw the morning's milk white and warm covering the floor. She did nothing. She said nothing as she walked through the inch-deep milk. Only in returning to the house, when she saw that the truck and the car were still in the garage, did she say aloud that they must have killed him.

She may have thought it when she rolled out of bed and tiptoed down the hall to check on the boy. So many mornings of waking to an empty bed had not numbed her to that final absence. She had certainly thought about it as his breakfast sat wasting on the stove. The cry of the cows had confirmed what she suspected sometime earlier, the culmination of those horrid telephone calls: the morning-empty bed and the full garage.

When Marjorie called the police, Henry Dodge's wife answered the telephone, but she soon had her husband on the line. He asked Marjorie if it were police business, and when she told him Forrest was gone, he did not react at all. He said it was New Year's Day. So she told him that Forrest had been murdered. By nine o'clock this morning she knew that, even if she couldn't find him. She was not able to say "his body." Henry Dodge asked her if she and Forrest had had a fight the night before.

They never fought, she said. Besides, what did that have to do with it? Did he think she had murdered her husband? He laughed, not the same laugh as Ned Grimsley, but rather a shallow laugh of the sort he may have used in school when he answered incorrectly. Last night was New Year's Eve, he explained, and many people got into difficulty with drinking, one thing leading to another. Forrest didn't drink, she said, never drank. Had they been to a party? he asked, and Forrest just not home yet? Many people slept it off right at the party itself; that way they didn't have to worry about driving home.

She had thought that what she knew about Forrest and about the town of Enoch led to a conclusion in a logical way men seemed to think was solely their province. Now logic wasn't in it. Now everything, including the position of Henry Dodge, was secretive and dangerous. Only in pregnancy had she learned the burden of carrying a secret, the knowledge to ascertain danger. She asked Dodge if he knew what was going on.

"Do I know what's going on?" he repeated, stalling. "Look, maybe your husband was only kidnapped." He would come in the cruiser right away.

When he arrived, she made him wait while she helped Peter into his coat and boots. Going across the road, Marjorie thought how young and thin the police chief was, how his crew-cut hair showed white scalp. She wondered why he didn't wear a hat. Henry Dodge stood in front of the barn staring at what she had not bothered to tell him because she thought he must have known. Whatever man or men had been there in the early morning hours could have left no tracks in the rain; whatever tracks they might have left would have been covered by the still falling snow. He kept staring at the ground, where, besides his own, there were three sets of footprints.

"Those are all mine," she told him. "It was too slippery to step in the old paths."

In the kitchen Henry Dodge drank fresh coffee and ate the fruitcake Marjorie had made for Forrest. He was the first man other than Forrest to eat fruitcake or even to eat with her in that house. Not all men were like her husband, she reminded herself. That she understood well enough even before talking to Henry Dodge, who seemed not to know what he should be doing. At least, Marjorie thought, he isn't doing it. She decided that she couldn't tell such a man everything, and she didn't. It was he who brought up the telephone calls, and though she wondered how he knew about them, she didn't say anything. She worried how much he knew and how he knew it.

Dodge said he could tell her nothing. A disappearance could be anything. Perhaps her husband had run away from something out of fear or anger. Perhaps he'd run to something. Lots of things men run to, Dodge suggested. Maybe he had just had an accident. Like a stage magician, Dodge explained the myriad possibilities while the secret lay silent, only barely concealed.

All during the time Henry Dodge was talking to her, his mouth kept twitching into a smile or a grin, as though he barely restrained some enormous joke from bursting him into laughter. Marjorie put more cereal into Peter's bowl. Because his long nap had delayed his lunch, he was eating twice as much as usual to make up for what he had missed. Marjorie doubted that she could do the same. Something awful, not a voice, more a half picture, was saying that she could never make up for what she had missed. In order to erase it or silence it, she had to get rid of Henry Dodge, so she began singing to Peter, singing the little nursery rhymes that he liked. In the middle of ''Humpty-Dumpty,'' the police chief left. Then Marjorie, having already called one policeman (despite anything that Forrest would have allowed her to do), called another.

To the state police she did not admit her fears, neither the smaller suspicion of Henry Dodge, nor the larger certainty about the town of Enoch. She explained only that she was worried and needed assistance. But when Trooper Thurston arrived, he appeared as a specialist brought in for a second opinion. Unlike the Enoch police chief, he wore his uniform. A tall man, graying over the ears like those men with the medical charts in the magazine advertisements, he seemed to accept her preference of him over Henry Dodge as his simple right and due, needing no explanation beyond itself. She was aware in a way she hadn't been for twenty years of the need of men for flattery and their ability to turn every attention or even request into compliment. Forrest was no alchemist. To him sucking at someone's teat was a child's need or that of a calf.

As Henry Dodge had done, the trooper went to the barn. There, she told him, the Enoch police chief had stopped. He had said he didn't want to walk across all that milk. It had embarrassed him to think of trodding through the pond of white, a pond she knew she would have to hose out before it became foul and rancid. Satisfied that there wouldn't be much in the milk room, Henry Dodge had gone to the other end of the barn, and had even looked underneath. Unlike Dodge, the trooper did not look for footprints, nor did he worry about walking through the spilled milk. Inside the barn he took notes in a little book, writing down Marjorie's answers as they talked. Now, from across the kitchen table, she watched him, too, eat Forrest's fruitcake and drink his coffee. She told him about the telephone calls, more because Henry Dodge already knew about them than out of any real confidence in the trooper.

As she sipped from her coffee she saw that the trooper was watching her, perhaps judging her practicality against the reaction he expected from a woman. She checked the living room and saw that Peter was playing with his marbles. Dropping them one by one into a small cardboard box, he would tilt it so the marbles rolled like the rapids of a glass river.

The trooper told her it might be a long time before she found out anything about her husband. For the first time in many years, maybe since she had found out about Peter, she had to choose a response, a reaction. With Peter it had been a gradual knowledge, like winter, and then Forrest was there to set the lines of her movements as surely and proudly as he walked the boundaries of his property each spring. Gone, he had left her to search out the walls for herself. She decided not to tell the trooper that Henry Dodge somehow had known about the telephone calls.

TWO
Spoiled Milk

8 / *Do This in Remembrance of Me*

January 1956

It was bitter cold. Marjorie didn't want to take Peter, but she could neither drive nor get a baby-sitter. Middle of January, folks said, time for the thaw. Unless that warm spell during the holidays was it. Unnatural, wasn't it? they said. They thought more about the weather than about Forrest. She supposed they could talk about the weather safely. People in Enoch were always safe. Clinging together, they warmed themselves in the heat of their own lies. She would make it hot for them.

Peter had eaten all of the cereal, a new kind with maple flavoring that he seemed to like. She refilled his bowl, thinking she should get some syrup from Clay Freeman. Normally Forrest would have called his cousin for the syrup, normally, when Forrest had been there. Already Peter had accepted his father's absence, though of course he didn't understand it. Thank God. Peter ate his second bowl slowly. There was plenty of time. She wanted them to be in the middle of their meal when she arrived, all of those smug citizens, eating their church dinner, stuffing their sanctimonious selves.

People in Enoch thought about Forrest, even if they tried to hide it. There was Henry Dodge telling her it was still only a missing persons' case. Persons, she thought, only they're not missing. They're hiding and being hidden right in Enoch. A small town could never be so small that it couldn't hide its own. Protective coloration, not the blue jays or grosbeaks that came in angry wrangles over the food she put out, but sparrows, small and quiet and in so many varieties she couldn't tell one from another. Sparrows that crowded along the windowsill ate the most simply because there were so many of them.

Perhaps they would never find the body. It would float down the river (she was certain it was in the river) until it reached the sea, over a hundred miles away. She wondered if a body could travel that far. Rapids and dams, one not seven miles downstream, could prevent that.

What she had to say at church would not be written out. Before his murder she had wanted to warn Forrest. Nowhere in their talk had she found place to voice her fears, so she had made up a letter. The more she had written, the more she had felt as if she were back in Miss Shelton's English class at Newfound High. Every communication has its own logic, Miss Shelton had said. You must find the logic of your message, be it business or personal, and pattern your letter on that logic. Oh how Marjorie had excelled in finding her logic. Miss Shelton had pleaded with her to go on to college, even to the point of assigning her to write a letter of application to the university. Marjorie had felt no desire to go to college, to become (as Miss Shelton had told her she should) a teacher, so for the first time she had not done what was expected of her. She had stayed home.

The logic of her letter to Forrest had a single conclusion: stay home. You have crossed these men, unfortunately crossed them with violence, and now they will respond in kind. In the end she couldn't finish it. She couldn't even sign it. "Love" had no part in the logic of the letter; "sincerely" was too weak. Thinking of Miss Shelton's class, she had remembered the warning delivered to Julius Caesar in Shakespeare's play. That had been signed "Thy lover, Artemidorus." The boys had snickered at that. But they were lovers, she and Forrest, not like in the movies, but in the classical way of Shakespeare's plays, full of respect and restraint. Caesar had not heeded the warning.

Even his wife's pleading he had ignored. He had gone out into the morning, and they had murdered him.

No one had expected her to marry Forrest Langley. She had not written any letter for that. She had sought no logic in her decision. Nor did she now regret marrying him any more than she regretted stopping her studies after high school. Writing a letter or searching for the logic of what she had to say to the people of Enoch would only delay her action. (No one had ever called her willful, though she knew she was.) Only Forrest had been powerful enough to combine desire and logic so that she never needed to act outside the boundaries of his constraint. And now he was dead.

Marjorie rinsed Peter's dish in the sink. She had already cleaned the cereal from the pot. Supper dishes didn't amount to much now. She found it hard to eat much except at noon. With Peter she ate a good dinner, before the day would begin to close in on her again. In the closet she took down Peter's wool jacket, a "car coat" the clerk in Newfound had called it. Beside her own storm coat was Forrest's plaid shirt. She had sewn it for him from cloth she got specially from the mill. Peter would never grow into it. It along with all the rest of Forrest's clothes would have to be stored in the attic.

In the attic were the trunks they had moved up from Newfound when they sold her mother's house. On the heavy closet rod Forrest had nailed to the rafters, Marjorie kept her off-season clothes. It was there she hung his shirt, next to the mink jacket he had bought for her a year ago. Slipping the mink off the hanger, she held it to her body. The lining, dark and shiny, was cold when she put it on. In the bedroom she changed into garter belt, nylons, purple dress of silk brocade, and the mink. Before going downstairs she took off the jacket so as not to startle Peter. Only after she had bundled him up and pulled his toque over his ears did she put it back on.

With one gloved hand she held tightly to Peter. He still wore mittens, big ones she had knit for him. He had not been able to master gloves. Between her house and Grimsley's it was dark. Past there a streetlight threw a parsimonious circle of light to the ground. The matching mink hat sat warm on her head. Though it was after five, she could wear the hat. They would know she had had to walk.

In the entry she took off Peter's mittens and toque and unbuttoned his jacket. Leaning against the wall, she slipped off her overshoes and set her hat on the top of the rack. The mink she kept on. She clothespinned her overshoes together and put them at the end of the rack. Peter's mittens and toque she stuffed into his pockets. Warm from the walk and the steaming radiators, she unbuttoned the mink jacket. From beyond the door came a constant noise, voices like flies in the barn on a hot summer's day.

The door to the vestry was thin and light. It banged against the wall. When the buzzing stopped, only a click of silver against plate broke the silence. She had imagined herself going to the lectern at the other end of the room and standing firmly behind it. But that had been when she had planned to write out her words and when she didn't know how she would get their attention. Not one of them was looking elsewhere.

"I know what you thought of my husband," she began. "Now I'm going to tell you what I think of you."

She named no names. She felt no need to name names or recount past offenses. She had only to go back a few weeks, and she could find all the wickedness any town needed. "And where will I find Forrest? He never took a thing from any of you except what he earned or paid for. How did you earn his life? How are you going to pay for his death?" She told them about the phone calls and about seeing her husband frightened. For the first time in her marriage. "And that must please your miserable hearts," she said. "None of you had the courage or honesty to talk to him directly. Only wait for him, a bunch of you, wait for him when he went to work. How appropriate—to take him in the barn he loved and you so hated him for. And the rest of you joined in silence as if you were at prayer."

As she talked the heat of the room and the inner heat of her own body met. The sides of her neck ran sweat; her underarms seemed awash. She would not remove the mink. Not one of them moved or spoke, but neither did they look at her. Her eyes swept their guilty faces, and they turned away. Her voice, she knew, would last if only she would not faint in front of them. She hurried on with her last thought.

"I came here with a hope and a curse. They make no difference. They were only words. But there is a truth I will tell you. There is an infestation in this town. The contagion will strike all of you."

Turning to the door, she found she was still holding Peter's hand. He was smiling. Out in the vestibule she threw off the jacket and put Peter's outside clothes on. It was not nearly as warm here. The sweat along her neck and down her body began to seem cold. She removed the clothespin from her overshoes and slid them on. As she was reaching for her hat the door to the vestry opened. Clay closed it quickly behind him, shutting out the sound of the wicked flies. She followed his eyes to the bench where her mink lay.

He put it around to still her shaking. "I'll take you home," he said. While he was getting his car, someone opened the door, but when whoever it was saw Peter, the door was pulled shut. Marjorie started to laugh, not loudly, but enough to shake her shoulders. Peter, too, in his cracking voice, laughed. When Clay came in, he stared at them.

"It's funny," Marjorie said. "I think they're afraid of me."

Clay said, "I shouldn't wonder."

"How's your wife getting home?" she asked.

"Duncan Hatch."

At the house she asked Clay in for a cup of coffee. She set the coffee on the stove and took Peter up to bed. She sang some nursery rhymes for him until he fell asleep in the middle of "Humpty-Dumpty." Downstairs she fixed two cups of coffee with cream and sugar.

"Clay," she said, "you understand I'm not crazy."

"I don't think you're crazy."

"They want to," she told him. "You're afraid I might be." Of course she knew it had been crazy to go down there, and she had flaunted her craziness in the form of the mink jacket.

"Thrust into this." He pointed vaguely with his spoon. "With the boy and the dairying—who could blame you?" He smiled. His spoon navigated nervous circles in his coffee.

Margorie thought of the boy who used to visit her before she had met Forrest. Like Clay, he spoke nervously with a soft voice. He was younger than she, but he pretended not to know. He talked to her about her plants and about movies, but he never asked her out. The furniture or her mother's money or even her age, all frightened him in some way. Though she was sorry he felt uncomfortable, she had enjoyed her small portion of power.

"They've always hated Forrest," she said.

"You really believe the town's involved in a conspiracy?" Clay asked.

His cup was empty. If she refilled it, she would have to talk some more, and she wasn't sure what more she had to say. "He sent money to Billy Harmes, a lot of money." She and Forrest had never talked about money. Everything she had needed, he had bought without quibble or question. "He sent money, and they killed him anyway."

Once again she listened to the arguments she had heard from Henry Dodge and the state trooper. There was no proof that Forrest had been murdered. No proof (fortunately, Clay emphasized) that he was dead. If Forrest had been killed, it was probably out of some personal, private grudge having nothing to do with Billy Harmes. Clay covered his empty coffee cup with his hand and rocked it on the table.

"People all went over to Grimsley's," Marjorie said, "to pay their respects. Who came here? The minister, the police, you, and Louise." She stopped. She was about to cry. "Of course, people expect old women to die."

"Are you frightened?" Clay asked.

"Why would I be frightened?" she said. So that she

wouldn't have to watch him, she got the coffee from the stove. He waited to speak until she had refilled his cup.

"Henry Dodge has been asking around for you," Clay said. She knew he wanted to soothe her, tell her Enoch wasn't a lawless community but New England, with a long history of punishment.

"Henry Dodge is a fool," she said. "The only person he's bothered is my hired man." She told Clay she trusted Jonas Cloudman. That man, alone in town, had come to work for her and agree with her. "Do you know of some reason I should be frightened?" she asked Clay, her voice soft with fear she hoped he wouldn't detect.

"If I could be of some help—"

She stopped staring at her cup and looked at him as if he were a cat that had just brought a snake into the kitchen. "Why, Clay, what could you do?"

"I can find out more than you."

She laughed. "At least you agree there's something to be found out."

"A lot of people are wary about this," he said. "That's never been my way. But you're wrong about Enoch."

"Then prove it to me."

"I just don't believe it," he said.

"For me, it isn't a matter of belief," she told him. "Won't Gladys be worried about you?" She watched him back his car out of the driveway. She wondered if her remark about his wife made him nervous. He would have to be firm if he was to be her ally, firm as Forrest had been. She needed help. Jonas Cloudman did fine with the cows, but he was as far outside the community as she was. As she cleared the table she decided that Clay would end up on her side because she was right.

The boy who used to visit her went to work for the florist where she bought her plants. He would take cuttings from different varieties, root them at home, then bring her the plant when it had gotten started. It gave him an excuse to come over. One day he had brought a spider plant with him. She was sitting in the living room with Forrest, and her mother let the boy in. Is this the boy who brings you plants? Forrest asked. The boy never came again. Marjorie had read in the paper that he had enlisted and a year after that he had been killed. She wrote a letter to his mother, but she wasn't sure where to send it. The list of gold star mothers had two with the same last name as the boy. She still had a plant from a spider of the one the boy had brought to her.

Now Forrest was dead.

In the kitchen she pushed the button to light the fluorescent tube in the stove. Forrest had liked that. Enough light to see the clock, he had told her; the rest I don't have to see. On the edge of the front door was the twin-buttoned night lock. She pushed the top one in. They hadn't locked the front door before. She didn't ever know the purpose of the twin buttons until Jonas told her what they were for. She had asked him to install a new lock, and he had told her she didn't need one. That night lock would keep any ordinary thing out.

Upstairs she checked Peter. He slept on his back, almost motionless. Earlier, as usual, he must have tossed. Marjorie pulled the covers over his shoulders and pushed the dark hair away from his forehead. Enough of his father's features were on his face to make her pause. She kissed his cheek.

She switched on the light in their room. The top of Forrest's dresser was, as it had always been, clean. Nearly a month ago she had pulled his closet door to. In there were empty clothes hanging above empty shoes.

Of course it had been crazy to go to the church. Not merely indecorous, but insane, an insanity to frighten them. She wanted them to be frightened as she had been that long week before they had killed him. And what else she wanted would demand craft, so for right now it was just as well that they thought her crazy. She undressed and turned off the light. She rolled over to Forrest's side of the bed and felt on the floor. When she found the safety catch of the gun, she clicked it off.

9 / *A Seeker of Truth*

January Thaw, 1956
No one Clay knew, except Marjorie Langley, wanted to talk about his cousin's disappearance. "She's the only one who has a theory as to what happened," Clay told his friends in the Down the Hatch.

"And that theory," Duncan Hatch said, "is as cracked as her going down to the church supper in a mink to deliver a sermon."

Something was wrong. Something had happened to his cousin, and every once in a while Clay wondered if people did know that Forrest had been killed and out of their hatred for him were shielding the murderer. Or out of their concern for the murderer himself. But he figured that was the kind of nonsense a woman like Marjorie, who had depended on Forrest for everything, would fall into the minute her husband disappeared. Clay had no excuse for wild theories, however odd his friends' silence might seem to him.

For a change it was warm enough to open the small windows of Hatch's lounge. The warm, wet air came in with the smell of spring, but no one was fooled. It was only the last week of January.

"Exactly the same weather we had New Year's," Duncan Hatch said. Tonight, like Zack, he was drinking a highball. As usual he had changed drinks with the shifting weather. "Two thaws this year. Almost more than we deserve."

Zack took a long draw on his cigar and blew out a vapor trail of smoke. "Figured out a way to take care of your distributor problem," he said to Clay.

"Supply," Clay said. He could distribute all the maple sugar he could make. The difficulty for him was in getting enough syrup. Later on it would get tough to find the time to boil it down. Maybe this year he could get Gladys to do some of that, but he doubted it. His wife hated the syrup business. Before too long he had to go talk to Marjorie Langley about tapping those trees. "I may get a good local source."

"I meant the distributor on your car," Zack said. "Don't you ever stop thinking business?"

It was the usual joke. Zack, who couldn't tell a joke without fracturing the punch line, could always apply old tag lines to new situations. At home Clay got the same thing about business from Gladys, but she wasn't joking. His three friends had businesses where people came to them. The big three, he thought: dining, driving, and dying.

"Parts salesman was in to the station Friday," Zack said. "He gave me the idea. I told him no matter how many wires we changed or spray we used, wet weather did your beach wagon in."

The salesman's plan, Zack explained, was to get an old boot or rubber and cover the distributor with it. The coil, too, the salesman suggested.

"Some car you got," Duncan said, "you need a rubber for it."

"Got to hide the distributor in an old boot," Davis Scales said. He took a Lucky from Duncan's pack on the table. "Should've had it Christmas. Hang your boot out for Santa."

Clay sipped his Scotch and soda. The sap would be running in another month. As sugaring time neared his life got busier and busier, his stomach got better and better. "I wish to hell I had had it for New Year's. I spent a few hours sitting down below my cousin's place waiting to start."

"That's another thing the parts salesman said." Zack grinned. "Stay out of puddles."

Clay finished his drink and slid it toward Duncan Hatch. "New Year's there wasn't anything but puddles. A man would have needed seven-league boots and a magic carriage to have avoided them."

"You were gone that night, weren't you," Duncan said.

"Coming back from Vermont with the last drum of syrup

in the state," Clay said. "You remember I was so tired the next day I couldn't even make it up here."

New Year's Day sleep had been the only escape from Gladys. She had made enough noise getting the boy ready for church to wake the dead, so it wasn't actually until she had left that Clay had fallen asleep. At dinner she wouldn't speak to him, only to the boy who sat in his high chair between them like a judge. The afternoon was a symphony of snarls as she listened to the radio and told him business was too much for him. That evening, too tired from the night before as well as from the long day, he had skipped going to Hatch's and had simply fallen onto the bed, hoping he would be fast asleep before Gladys came upstairs. As a result, it wasn't until sometime Monday that he had heard about Langley's disappearance.

"And now nobody wants to talk about it," Clay said.

Duncan Hatch brought a fresh tray of drinks to the table. "Henry Dodge been to see you?" he asked Clay.

Clay watched the three drinks come off the tray, knowing exactly what they would be. There were only three because Zack hadn't finished his highball. He might not finish even the one, though he would go through several cigars. In the summer the ratio of cigars to drinks would be reversed. Davis Scales had another beer. Every time Duncan went to the bar, Davis was ready for another beer. Every time Duncan's pack of Luckies was on the table, Davis tipped one out. Yet during the week he never smoked and scarcely drank more than a glass of wine. The highball Duncan Hatch drank this week would be replaced by a brandy and seven next, then a gin and tonic, or a martini. Clay himself drank according to his stomach, always of course Scotch and soda, only the quantity varying with business. All this he knew about his friends and himself. It was a comfort because even their changes were regular.

"What would Dodge want with me?" Clay asked.

Duncan explained that the police chief had been trying to see everyone who was out New Year's morning. Jonas Cloudman, who confided in Duncan because Duncan had not called

Dodge when Jonas was drunk, had told him that Dodge had given him a tough time.

"It's hard to believe Henry Dodge could give anyone a tough time," Clay said, "much less Jonas Cloudman." Clay thought of Henry Dodge as a man who did only enough of his job to stay cop.

With the gold double-action lighter he always kept with him, Davis Scales lighted one of the Luckies Duncan had left on the table. The lighter was a strange tool of his profession, Clay thought.

"Jonas would be remarkably easy to intimidate," Davis said. "After all, he had more access to Langley than anyone save his wife."

Duncan Hatch spoke quickly. "And it's not likely anyone in this town's going to form a committee to defend Jonas Cloudman. I hate to see him blamed. Man's had trouble enough."

The smoke from Zack's cigar tickled Clay's nose. With the cigar and the wet weather he would be sneezing and coughing half the night, but he didn't complain about the habits of his friends. "I don't think Henry Dodge knows I was on the road," Clay said. "Who else has he been to see?"

"Spare yourself some trouble," Duncan told Clay. "Don't let him find out."

"Particularly since you spent the time not a half mile from your cousin's barn," Zack added.

"I'll bring the car into the station tomorrow to have the boot installed," Clay said.

He had to get around on Monday. Getting syrup from Marjorie Langley could help his supply problem. Truth to tell he was a little tired of having to make so many trips to Vermont. He had to make sure things were still square with Ned Grimsley. Clay could pick up the goat's milk and see about running lines from his trees, too. He could see the two of them tomorrow while Zack was fixing the car.

If we're not careful, somebody's going to be blamed for it," Duncan said. He said Jonas Cloudman told him the police were worried about the case. Henry Dodge, according to Duncan, was upset because Mrs. Langley doubted his competence. The state police believed it was a serious crime, not the usual domestic quarrel that finally went too far. "And with her performance at the church supper," Duncan concluded, "she's accused everybody in Enoch, so I suppose they'll have to find someone."

"But they shouldn't start looking just because some hysterical woman went ranting at a church supper," Davis Scales said. "Clay, do you realize what she was saying?"

"What do you suppose she hoped to gain by it?"

None of them knew. Davis said it wouldn't get her any sympathy. In fact, although people had always excused her, by acting exactly with the same proud disdain her husband had she was now putting herself in his category. If she had had names to name, Duncan thought, she would have gone to Henry Dodge. Duncan wasn't sure if she herself even believed what she had said. It would be a wonder if anyone else did.

"If she's that crazy," said Davis Scales, "maybe he just left, went off to God knows where, like Grimsley always talks about."

"If she's that crazy," Duncan said, half seriously, "she could have killed him herself."

"She just wanted to show off the mink," Zack said. Clay laughed with the rest of them, though he had never known Marjorie to show off anything. Duncan brought over another round of drinks. This time, the last round of the evening, even Zack had a refill.

Clay did not think it could be laughed off. The purposeful ignorance of the town was, to him, just a way of lying to itself. Lies, though sometimes useful, demanded a price from the men they served, a markup far out of line with the product. After all, something had happened to Forrest Langley. Clay's cousin was not a mysterious man, yet there was a mystery about him.

That was another difference between him and his three friends. They always seemed confident about who and what was going on in Enoch, while Clay had to dig to find out. At home he told Gladys he was pleased to have three friends in the know. She said they ought to know about Henry Dodge. They put him in office, didn't they? What you don't seem to know, she told Clay, is that they're home six nights a week. Besides, no one, not even your three wise men, says anything about Forrest's murder.

The next morning, with his car at Zack's, Clay had to wait. He hated waiting, and he hated walking. When he had been on the road for the spice company, he had spent more hours than he cared to remember rolling tires down roads to find somebody with a pump and a patch. He had run out of gas so often Gladys wouldn't go anywhere unless she checked the fuel gauge. It wasn't that he was cheap; he just pushed everything, thinking he could make it. So he spent too much time waiting in gas stations.

A little after eight Clay left Zack's station. As he walked, the slush along the road leaked into the slit at the toe of his overshoe. He was not cold, and the wet did not bother him. He had been out in enough cold as a kid so that he felt permanently insulated by his youth. But now, not much over forty, he knew he had hated walking for forty years. It wasn't laziness. He put in more hours and energy than any two men in Enoch, save Forrest Langley. They had grown up in the Birches, where work came as naturally as walking, but in their jobs on the road they had learned to depend on cars. Even Zack, whose job was cars, didn't depend on them. In fact he was a bit offhandish about cars. Clay's work, as confused and unstructured as it was, demanded speed and efficiency. It never occurred to him to change his work, just to increase it.

Ned's wife met Clay at the door. Esther was a pleasant, homely woman who came to the house selling Avon. Gladys told Clay she felt sorry for her because of the woman Ned kept in Newfound and the father he kept in the house. Clay didn't think much about it. It was wrong, but it wasn't really his business. If she can stand it, I guess I can, he had told Gladys. Never, even when he was on the road, had he taken another woman. Nor had Langley, as far as Clay knew. Some of the salesmen picked up women in the hotel bars or even had regulars they visited. There are fools in every line of work, Clay had told Langley. Most men are fools, Langley had replied. Langley had never said anything to Clay about Ned's woman, who was, after all, his own sister, as well as Clay's cousin.

When Ned Grimsley heard Clay's plan, he said he wouldn't be hooked up with Marjorie Langley. Clay grew more enthusiastic about his idea. The more stubborn someone became, the more eager Clay got. It came from all his years on the road. Finally, Ned took him to the barn to put up the goat's milk Clay sold in Newfound. There he told Clay he thought they ought to agree what to say about New Year's Eve so they could stay close to the circumstances.

"See how clean it is?" Ned asked him. "You have to keep it clean or the smell will taint the milk. You can smell goat piss half a mile upwind."

Direct as he seemed, there was something circumspect about the man. Clearly he was holding something back. Clay said nothing.

"You going to take the milk with you now?" Ned asked.

"I'm walking," he reminded Ned.

But he was not ready to go yet, because the tall man had told him nothing except that he was awake to see Clay come out of Langley's barn the morning Forrest had disappeared. Clay didn't even know where Ned was when he was watching the barn, though he guessed Ned might have been in Newfound pretty late with Louise. Not that Clay was worried about anybody in Enoch accusing him of harming his cousin. They knew him too well. Still, there was something odd about Ned's silence, as though it weren't just Louise he was being quiet about.

Clay stood and moved toward the open door. "Just what circumstances are we supposed to stay close to?" he asked.

Outside the barn was bare ground turned muddy. Clay avoided the soft spots until he got back onto the snow.

"Just what it was you were doing in Langley's barn." Ned leaned his length against the barn and smiled. "In case somebody asks. Somebody's almost bound to."

"Not if they don't know I was there," said Clay. It was clear Ned wasn't going to volunteer any information. "I told you about the cloth to dry the points. You could have seen it in my hand."

"Was a hard night to see in," Ned said, still smiling. "Could have been anything yellow."

"What were you doing that night?" Clay asked as quietly as he could. He was not afraid of Ned, but there was no sense in getting a big man riled if you didn't have to. "Did you get up to take a leak or something?"

"Why, Clay," Ned said, "I told you. I was watching you."

"Let's just hope that there wasn't somebody watching you, because we don't know what circumstances he'd stay close to." Clay started off down the driveway.

"You bringing your car back for the milk?" Ned asked.

"First I've got to see Marjorie," Clay said. Then, to prevent any trouble, he added, "About setting up the collection system for her sap."

But the first person Clay saw at Langley's was Jonas Cloudman. He watched the short dark man cross the road, coming up from the barn, where, Clay figured, he had finished washing up the milking machine. As he walked along beside the elms that lined the driveway, Jonas moved swiftly, easily, but his upper body had a wooden clumsiness, as though he were carrying himself in his own arms like a load of kindling.

"Jonas!" Clay called. He puffed his way up the driveway. "She in?"

The small man looked up to the top of the tree he had stopped by. Clay's eyes followed his, as if they were looking for Marjorie in the upper reaches of the elm. He could see that it, like the other elms in Enoch, was dying.

"She don't go no place," Jonas said.

Clay asked Jonas how Marjorie was making out running the place. He said he had a project in mind that would bring them both a little money, and since Jonas would probably be doing the work, he ought to be in on it. Clay explained to him how they could run plastic lines from the maple trees down to the shed behind Marjorie's house. "Boil it down right there," he said.

"Could be," said Jonas. He looked across to the trees as if he were measuring distance.

Clay suddenly let his enthusiasm show, just as in the old days when he was on the road. "Won't take much to run all the lines together," he said. "Just like the bulk tank down in the barn. What do you think?"

"It's interesting," Jonas said. "But she makes her own decisions. Ain't any different than when I was working for him, 'cept I like her. No reflection on your family."

Nobody liked Langley. Clay mentioned that to Jonas.

"But you notice ain't nobody saying that." He shoved his hands into his jacket pockets. "No friends, no enemies. It's like he never even lived here."

Clay and Marjorie soon settled on the syrup business. She was eager to settle and even laughed with him, though her laughter had a cracked sound, as though she actually might be crazy. She asked him if he was sure they could make money. When he told her just to leave it to him, she began to tease him about taking care of her.

"I take care of Peter and the farm. You take care of Gladys and me." She turned away from him. "But who'll take care of you? Of course, with the money from my syrup, you can do anything you want." Her hand, hesitant for a moment, shielded her face. "Anything you want."

"You're frightened." He felt a fool to say what she must have thought would be obvious to him.

"Do you know of some reason I should be frightened?" Her voice trembled with fear.

"I can find out," he said. "I can find out more than you can."

She stared at him a moment, as if he were a cat that had just brought a snake into the kitchen.

She laughed, but this time her laugh had none of that brittle quality to it. "At last a man who agrees with me," she said.

"You said Jonas agreed with you."

"He works for me," said Marjorie.

Clay soon discovered that he didn't agree with her. Her hurt was real enough, but pain was not truth. She was telling him that his town had killed her husband and conspired to keep quiet about it and shield the killers.

Trudging back through the slush, he wondered if he should be more cautious than he was used to. Caution, so quick it was automatic, kept him from telling Marjorie Langley that both Ned Grimsley and Jonas Cloudman had been abroad that night. Jonas Cloudman, not even a neighbor, would have had to drive. Clay couldn't remember seeing another car. He had been so tired that he remembered very little except the damn car not starting.

Her agreeing on the syrup was a victory for him. He would have to wait to find out if the stuff would be as good as he thought, but he had confidence in it. He also had confidence that he could prove Marjorie Langley wrong about Enoch. After what he had learned from Cloudman and Grimsley, his first impulse had been to go to Henry Dodge. Apparently, though, Dodge already knew about Cloudman and perhaps about Grimsley, too. Talking to Dodge would reveal his hand, something Clay under any circumstances was reluctant to do. If Dodge came to him, he'd talk with him; otherwise it'd be better to work quietly.

Zack had his car all set. Around the distributor was a boot, its top cut off. The coil, too, was wrapped in old rubber. Zack told him the boot would have to come off each time they did a tune-up. Clay kidded him about more labor charges.

"You ain't even seen the bill for the boots," Zack said.

At the house Gladys was upset. It was past one o'clock;

why hadn't he called? His dinner was cold. He told her he had got the car fixed.

"If you were at Zack's all this time, you could have just gone over to Hatch's," she said.

He told her he'd go now. He didn't want to cause a fuss.

"Now your dinner's back in the oven heating up," she said. "You'll stay here."

He knew she got upset with his lateness, though after twenty years he thought she shouldn't be surprised by it. He depended on her to be there as he depended on the house. No more would he expect her to disappoint him than he could imagine the house disappearing one day. They were the tangible realities of his life, the solids he took for granted. Their stability, he was aware, allowed him to wander in the uncertainties of what he considered his real life.

Gladys brought him a glass of milk with his dinner. "Other people use the phone," she said.

He ate slowly. He didn't like to be hurried through a meal. "Other people have more time than I do," he said.

She wasn't listening. Sometimes in the middle of his telling her of his plans to enlarge the business, she would stop listening. It was a sort of approval. Now, however, no approval was indicated.

"Gladys?" he said.

She was crying. Marjorie Langley laughs, and Gladys cries, he thought. Her sobs were accusations of some sort, unanswerable. Neither the dinner nor his lateness could have provoked this. She always had to prepare him for her complaints by giving him her feelings first. The only way he knew to stop it was to go comfort her. He took a final forkful from his plate and went to her. Holding her shoulders, he asked her what the matter was.

"If you were just home once in a while," she said, "if you just had a regular job. And don't tell me we're any better off for all the running you have to do. You like doing it, that's what I think."

"All right," he said, "all right," trying to contain his own anger.

"Someone called for you," Gladys said. She turned around to face him. There were no sobs in her voice now. "They said to tell you to watch yourself."

"Who?" Clay asked. No one would do this to him.

"He knew my name, Clay," she said. She sank into the chair by the table, his unfinished dinner in front of her. "He said, 'Gladys, tell your husband to watch himself.' What's going on, Clay?"

Clay started to pace. In his stomach, bubbles of pain formed. "That's what I intend to find out."

"Don't get things stirred up," Gladys said.

Through his anger he could barely see her face.

10 / *Strictly Personal*

Jelly Enman lost his footing in the hot sudsy water and slipped to one knee. He grasped the smooth steel wall, wishing it were a neck. Jelly wished he could throttle Daryl Crockett. He wished he could have his son-in-law right here in the stainless-steel tank, could throttle him and press his face under the water so that when he was done, Daryl would just float there like a dead fish.

Jelly bit down on his lip. He would have to do something about Daryl before it got out of hand, before he or Daryl got out of hand. He knew that the job of cleaning the tanker multiplied his anger at Daryl, anger that should be directed at Sonny Rutherford, because it was the kid's job if he hadn't been late getting in from the run, and at Jack Niles, because the foreman could just as easily have waited until Sonny got back. You'd think, Jelly said to himself, that the bastard would have had enough of sending somebody in Sonny's place. After that fracas with Billy and Langley. Well, at least there ain't going to be anybody killed over this deal, not even Daryl Crockett.

Helping unload the tanker of bulk milk from Cabot's wasn't all that bad, not until you had to clean the thing. The unloading procedure was simple enough that even Sonny enjoyed it, but that was because, Jelly decided, it involved a lot of serious standing around. After connecting the truck hose to the dairy's tank inlet, you were free to stand there smoking cigarettes with the driver, making sure no leak developed in the coupling. Jelly had got restless waiting and had started making trips to the top of the tank, where he would loosen the cover and peer into the emptying tank. It wasn't difficult work, so it had given him too much time to dwell on that goddamn Daryl.

When the milk had all been pumped out, the tank had to be cleaned because the driver couldn't take it all the way back to Vermont with a coating of milk souring on the sides. It was the responsibility of Land's Dairy to clean the tank immediately or pay for a very elaborate and expensive cleaning when the truck got back to Vermont. When Jelly had told Jack they should wait for Sonny, the foreman had laughed and said that Jelly, short as he was, was more built for the job. So Jelly huffed and puffed his way down into the dark tank, and Billy brought him a droplight, which dangled in the hole, its light gleaming dully from the film of milk on the cylindrical walls. With the light off so that the bulb wouldn't break, he had first sprayed cold water to rinse the sides. The hose, thick and heavy as a boa constrictor, dragged behind him, pulling on him and reminding him of Daryl Crockett. Crouching in the darkness, he had played water throughout the insides. Next he had got out, secured the drain plug, and flooded the bottom with hot water, adjusted so that it was mostly live steam. Inside this giant dishpan his shoulders ached. With light and brush he crept through the tank, scrubbing every trace of milk from the sides. For though he detested the job, he was a thorough man. Sweat beaded on the backs of his hands and streamed, itching, down his face.

It wouldn't pay to let it get out of hand, like what had happened with Langley. Jelly wasn't sure that people would keep as quiet for him as they did for the other people, not just because they had a different position in Enoch, but also because if he went after Daryl, it would be family business. And family business, as far as Jelly was concerned, was strictly personal. He would not go today, not now when anger filled him as hot as the steam from his hose. He would take tomorrow off and drive down to Newfound in his own good time so that he could act like a cool rinse to Daryl Crockett's filth.

Jelly pulled the droplight out of the tank and opened the outlet. He climbed into the wet darkness and rinsed the tank with scalding water. Hunched, his feet trying to maintain purchase, he knew there were several ways to die in here, each of them horrible. His weight was against him. You know what happens when you overload one of those pumps at the dairy? the doctor had asked him. He would be lying then in the steamy water, gasping the suffocating air, while the sounds of his insides bursting echoed in the dark. At the top the droplight revealed the tank spotless and pure, as if it had never carried anything but water or air. When Jelly climbed down, he found Sonny Rutherford bumming a cigarette from the driver. Jelly was still angry, but he liked the kid, even if he was three-fourths gink.

"I'm going to tell you one thing right now," Jelly said. "It won't be me stuffed in there ever again. So you just make up your mind the next time a tanker comes in, you don't linger with Jonas Cloudman's daughter. You get your long-legged self back here and lay in that tank if you're going to lay somewhere."

Sonny set his hand down on the fat man's shoulder. "I don't mind, Jelly," he said. "It don't bother me a bit."

•   •   •

Three days later Sonny Rutherford was in the tanker. That was two Jelly owed him. One was telling Jack he'd be back to do the tanker instead of Jelly, and the other was telling Jelly that if he went down to Newfound and cleaned house with his son-in-law, he'd be fired. Any more fighting, Sonny's father had said, he'd fire the man, no matter who it was. Fighting wasn't Sonny's problem. Linda Cloudman, or more rightly, her father, was his problem. And Sonny didn't want to end up in the pool with Langley.

Sweat filled his eyes and ran warmly down his ribs. Sweat he did with Linda. And sweat worse when he thought of Jonas Cloudman, though he could no more stop seeing Linda than he could stop sweating. Finished, Sonny crawled out of the dark tank and saw Henry Dodge. The cop's face had a creamy smile, like vanilla ice cream starting to melt. It just beat the hell out of Sonny what Dodge was standing there for.

"I'm convening a little picnic," said Dodge. His eyes shifted to the upturned crates where the other men were sitting. "They already got you a seat reserved."

Sonny, taking a cigarette out of the shirt he'd slung over the trailer's bumper, waited long enough for the cop's smile to harden before he moved over to the gathering. Once there, he stood towering over all of them.

"Why does everything come back to that goddamn Langley?" Jack asked. He twirled his cigarette in the ashtray. "I'm getting sick of it."

Billy looked sick, Sonny thought, even with his eye healed and his grip nearly right. He looked sick every time somebody mentioned Langley, even though it was Langley done him and not the other way around. Must have figured they did it for him, Sonny thought.

"It keeps coming back to us," Dubber Handley said. He squinted at Jack, as though peering through a slit. "At least to you."

"People know where I was New Year's Eve," Jack said. With the back of his hand he wiped coffee from his lips. It seemed to Sonny a gesture of menace. "I didn't spend it cuddled up with you."

"We were all together," said Sonny.

"Oh, everybody knows where everybody was," Dodge said. He forced a little smile, this one the cut metal of a half-opened tin can. "And there's a lot of standing up for everybody. But you see I need to know the specifics, the pedigrees on all this stuff."

"Why?" Jelly said. The fat man asked as innocently as he might ask a farmer the butterfat content of his best milker. But Dodge didn't take it anything like that.

"Because I'm the cop, and I have to know what goes on, and I will know what goes on." He stopped for a minute, then sat down on the case that had been left for Sonny. "Look," he went on, "I don't care what happened to Langley or who did it. But if I don't know, it could turn out awful bad. I'm hired by the town, and I've got the town interest at heart. Now, if things start to get tough for me, they're going to get tough for everybody."

His voice lowered as he went around the group telling them why they ought to stick together. Jelly had asked him to go to the Newfound police about his son-in-law, which was why his son-in-law was in the Newfound jail instead of Jelly. And Sonny could be thankful Jonas Cloudman didn't get regular reports about the whereabouts of a certain pickup truck getting weak in the leaf springs. Jack, Dodge said, had done his part on the telephone and, being a modest fellow, wanted to stay anonymous. He was going on to Dubber Handley when Billy interrupted.

"What do you have on me?"

"Nothing, Billy," the cop said, his ice-cream smile returning. "It's only it was done for you, that's all." He got up, and Sonny thought he could hear the crease in his pants creak. "No secrets from me now."

After Dodge left, Jelly said, "One thing for sure, Dodge

don't know shit about this, and they ain't seen fit to tell him."

"People ought to stick together," Jack said. Then, the menace now in his voice, he turned to Dubber. "But you and Flora were alone that night, so you can just keep quiet around here about things you pretend to know, or maybe it'll be your name Dodge is looking up the pedigree for."

"I know enough not to make phone calls when I've got nothing to say," Dubber told him.

Sonny saw Billy's hand move at the same time Jack's did, but the foreman reached only for a toothpick. Billy's hand hung in the air while Jack tried to hold both cigarette and toothpick in his mouth. Sonny wondered if either of them knew what he was about.

Jelly said it was too easy to kill a man. He said he'd had all the guns he ever wanted during the war. Now he didn't even hunt. Taking guns apart and putting them together twice a day for the better part of four years would spoil the taste of the best venison south of Canada.

"Well, I'm glad I've got my thirty-thirty," said Jack. He spit out the toothpick.

"If I'd had a weapon two days ago, I'd've widowized my daughter. Course you don't have any daughters," Jelly told Jack. "Keep a weapon out of your house, because you can kill a man without strength or skill or without even meaning to, but afterwards he's dead."

"There's not a house in Enoch without a weapon," said Dubber. "Even Langley had one, and they didn't need it."

Then Billy began to explain about the bowling team. Sonny knew about it because Jack had gone to Sonny's father, who had asked Sonny to look into the details. What he hadn't realized until now was that Billy was trying to give one to Jack, as if to make up for the ruckus of sending the milk back to Langley.

"There's the five of us," Jack said. "It'd be one night a week."

"How much is it going to cost?" Dubber asked. He was drinking a half-pint coffee milk out of the cooler because, Sonny knew, he got those free.

"Maybe Flora ought to bowl in your place," Jelly suggested. "They'd probably let her take it out in trade."

"That might be all right," Dubber said of his wife, "but she'd be the whole week making up the money."

"It'll cost a buck," Sonny said. He leaned back and let his long legs slide into the space in the middle of the men. "A buck each time, including shoes. We'd start the end of the month in the Industrial B League."

"You getting a commission from the bowling alley?" Jack said. "Or are you figuring to be captain of the team?"

Sonny pulled his foot out of the circle. Just about the time he would begin to feel easy with Jack, the son of a bitch would turn cruel on him. Before he was foreman, Jack was always whistling away. He could tilt a forty-quart can on its side and spin it into the cooler, all the time smiling as wide as the path he made. Always had a good word. The job had soured him.

"Daddy asked me to look into it," Sonny said.

"I'll tell you what he's up to," said Jelly. "He's trying to save the company name. But I'll tell you no amount of success is going to improve our reputation. No bowling trophy is going to clear the suspicion that hangs over this place."

"Anyway it won't make any difference because everybody figures this is a place where your neighbors might get together one night and come over to cut your throat," Dubber Handley said. "Just the same I think Mr. Land ought to pay for our strings if it's his good name we're bowling for."

"Langley's throat wasn't cut," Jelly said.

After they'd all punched out, Billy's car wouldn't start. Dubber waved good-bye and pulled out of the lot. Sonny with a red and black tangle of jumper cables in one hand threw up Billy's hood with the other. Jack drove his car up beside Billy's while Sonny sorted positive and negative clamps. As soon as Billy's car started, Sonny pulled the cables from Jack's battery.

He told Billy he ought to let it run awhile, but Billy and Jack were talking as if he weren't even there.

"I only called once," said Jack. "And that's all I did." He put his hand to the black wave of hair at his forehead, hair as thick as Billy's. "You believe me, don't you?"

"I guess so," Billy told him. "But you shouldn't have to tell me. It's a terrible thing, because any name would satisfy Dodge and no name at all would please everybody else."

"I don't think folks are getting any fun out of this," Jack said. "Even if they're going to stay quiet, it ain't out of pleasure."

Sonny coiled the cables and made sure they were stowed under the front seat of his truck. There was one person who gave him pleasure and one name that he didn't want to think about if he got stuck somewhere with her.

11 / *Protection*

The school vacation at the end of February gave Jonas Cloudman additional cause to worry about Sonny Rutherford. Linda Cloudman, who each day for a week would be home when Sonny came for the milk, tried to reassure her father, but Jonas was certain what the boy was after. He's a long-legged gink with no more sense than a blind calf, he told Linda. She had said there was no harm in him. No, he'd replied, not in the way there is in Jelly Enman's son-in-law. Still, there ain't a man walking that don't have harm in him. He couldn't go beyond that with Linda. A phrase ran through his mind, something he'd heard Duncan Hatch say: A stiff prick has no conscience. If his wife were still alive, he could have her tell the girl. Of course, she'd be right there at home while he was off working for Marjorie Langley. He wouldn't have to worry about Sonny Rutherford had his wife been alive.

Climbing out of his truck, Jonas saw that the slush in Langley's yard was not nearly as deep as that in front of his own house. Marjorie had told him any of his work he found more convenient to do at her place he might go ahead and do. He had accepted that, though right now it might be more convenient to be at home when Sonny Rutherford came by. Jonas stepped with indifference in and out of the shallow puddles around his truck. He figured one more storm and one more cold spell before they'd be out of winter. He usually had a good sense of winter; a feeling, he told himself, for disaster.

He kept the lumber dry in the back of his truck. He had found it stacked by the loft in Langley's barn the night he had been looking for Sonny Rutherford. When he had asked Marjorie might he have it, he hadn't told her he had discovered it the night her husband had been killed. She could take it out of his wages, he said. Working regularly for her, he had more money than he'd ever had, even in the summers. He wished his wife were alive.

Marjorie outright gave him the lumber; dry, clear boards and straight two-bys. She told him to use Forrest's tools if he needed them, so he did that, too. You're a kind woman, he had told her. Oh, we're very much alike, Jonas, she had replied. More than you realize.

All of the work building the stake sides for his truck would be his, but other than the cost of the eyebolts he had had to buy, the frame was free. (Maybe because she was a woman, he felt he could accept things from her that he could never take from a man.) He set the two-bys in the holes, measured them, then took them out and cut them level. Setting them back up on the truck, where they stood up like guard posts, he measured the distances between them and carefully marked on each where the crosspieces would go. On both sides of the boards he put eyebolts so that he could string a tarp over the top and rope off the sections in between. The completed frames, one for each side of the truck, were almost too heavy for him to lift. By the time he had finished, his feet were soaked. He raised one frame to the truck's side and slid the posts into the holes. It fit like a lover. On the right side went the other frame. It got away from him and dropped too hard into the sockets, delivering a load of rust onto the ground. The metal under the rear fender shrieked and gave. A great rent appeared, revealing the white two-by that had pierced it.

Jonas swore only once, a long curse. He cursed himself, and he cursed Sonny Rutherford because he had been thinking of the kid when he dropped the frame. When he was done, he saw Henry Dodge pulling into the driveway. Since Langley's disappearance the town cop had come by a few times. Jonas turned his back to him and lifted the frame up. It had sunk so far down that his short arms couldn't raise it over the side of the truck. He eased it back into the hole. Up on the back of the truck he lifted the frame to the edge.

"Suppose you can help me gentle this thing to the ground?" he asked Henry Dodge.

The policeman, who had been watching Jonas, had to return his notebook to his pocket so he could take up the frame. Together they lowered it to the ground. "Did a job on your truck, didn't it?"

"Saved me searching out the rust, I guess." Jonas hopped out of the truck. He would have to store the frames in the shed until he could fix his truck. When Henry Dodge just lingered there, Jonas asked him, "How's your wife coming along?"

"Due next month, she says."

Jonas spat into the mud. "Marjorie's in the house," he said. Jonas lifted the frame from the other side until it towered above him. He handled it firmly and lined the two frames up against the shed. Henry Dodge was still there. Jonas wondered what the cop wanted, but he didn't ask. Before going home for his dinner, he had yet to repair the rollers on the barn door. Waiting for him at home was an afternoon's worth of chores before he had to return here for the milking. He was thankful that the girls did his milking for him. He left his truck where it was and walked down the driveway past Henry Dodge to work on the barn door.

The cop called him. He had waited until Jonas was nearly to the road. "I got to talk to you."

"Official business?" Jonas asked.

"All right," Henry Dodge said. He pulled his notebook out of his pocket while Jonas walked back to him. "I haven't forgotten you were out that night."

"Look, Dodge, there ain't a soul in this town talking. Did you expect me to be any different?"

"You working on his place, taking Mrs. Langley's money, of course I expected some help," the cop said. "Besides, it's the law. You got to help."

Jonas laughed. "You're the law," he said, "but there are people in Enoch that give you no more consideration than a broody hen."

"And you're afraid of them." Henry Dodge smiled.

Jonas thought it was poor excuse for pressure. "If I was afraid, I wouldn't be working here. Me and you and most everybody in Enoch knows how you got that job, and I'm willing to bet if it wasn't for your wife being pregnant, you'd be trading in that uniform for some working clothes."

"If I was to lock you up, be awful hard for you to work, wouldn't it?"

Jonas stepped back to his truck. Inside was a tire iron, lying beside the seat. He put his hand on the door handle. "I told you where I was that night, and that's all I care to say about my personal business. Other people's affairs ain't my business." He forced his hand to his side. "If you was to take me from my girls, you'd regret it every day you drew breath."

The cop nodded his head. "I thought there must be something you cared about," he said. "You come down to the office later on. Either we'll talk about some people or we'll talk about you."

Marjorie Langley came out onto the porch. "You take a

long time to get into a house, Henry Dodge. It's a good thing you're a policeman and not a burglar."

"He's being a cop today, Mrs. Langley," Jonas said. "After me again."

"There's no man I'd sooner vouch for than that one standing there," she told Dodge. "It's no help to me for you to be wasting the time of the one man in town that I trust to have on this place."

The cop closed his notebook and returned it to his pocket, where it formed an odd, square bulge. "I'm not working for you, Mrs. Langley," he said.

"No, but my husband's death seems to have given you a sudden promotion."

"Disappearance, Mrs. Langley, disappearance."

"It's given you cause to work, which the people who hired you never thought would happen," Jonas told the cop. "Could be they didn't know how much of a jackass you are."

"I know where I'll be seeing you," Henry Dodge said.

Jonas found himself wishing something would happen to the fool. He wanted him to slip on the rutted ice and go under the car or fall in such a way that his pistol would discharge. Jones was not much a happy man, but he despised to think he was a hateful one. If ever he were to do violence to a man, it would be to kill him, and Henry Dodge was too foolish to kill. What Jonas needed, he decided, was protection from his own fear, so he would go to the only man who had offered protection from the things that nipped his heels. No man would protect him from the howling in his heart. That was, of course, what drew him and Duncan Hatch together.

"Don't you worry about that man," Marjorie Langley said after Dodge had left. She went down to where Jonas stood by his truck and touched his arm. "You're working for me, and I take care of my own. It seems to be the only way around here."

He thanked her, and she told him she had no doubt about his loyalties. "You're a good woman to work for," he said. "If you ever have any doubts, fire me. That's what I'd surely do."

There was a stamina to her that he admired. He admired her going to that church supper full of mealy-mouthed drones, and keeping the farm going and tending Peter. So he told her she was brave because it covered a whole lot of things he couldn't tell her. Among them was that she was better off with Forrest Langley gone. There were things in the way of information he also wouldn't tell her because he had other loyalties.

Back at Jonas's house, Linda had dinner on. From the way she pranced around the table, Jonas knew she had fixed something special. The meal—chicken, potatoes, and green beans—was one she had cooked before. In fact they had it often. She poured his coffee, and the three of them sat down. Jane looked at her older sister and giggled. It must be the dessert, Jonas thought; she's gone and made a pie or something.

"Good potatoes," he said.

"I used a little cream instead of milk," Linda said. "There's some for your coffee, too." Her sister giggled again.

"Mr. Land'll be upset with you, skimming the cream right out of the milk we sell him. What's different about the beans?" he asked her.

"I did the beans," Jane answered. "That's a little cinnamon. Mrs. Bagley said you should try different spices."

"Oh, she did," Jonas said. Mrs. Bagley, Jane's home economics teacher, was a young woman his daughter particularly liked. "And what restaurant's she cooking for?"

Linda switched her head to him. "Jonas," she said, "there was nothing to do with the beans except throw them in a pot. She wanted to do something for you."

"Very sweet," he told Jane, "makes the beans sweet. I suppose you'll be cooking the whole meal one of these days." And Linda could be tending the animals, he thought, while Henry Dodge has me somewhere to give answers to questions he ain't quite figured out yet. The chicken was good, too, but he couldn't talk about it. "Where's dessert?" he said, trying to cheer himself up again.

"There isn't any, Jonas," Linda said. "I'll sit with you

for a cup of coffee, though.'' She went to the stove for the pot. Jane, instead of going off as she usually did, just sat at the table.

"All right," said Jonas, "tell me what's special about the dinner. Must be something the way the pair of you are carrying on."

"It's the coffee, Daddy." Jane said. "Linda made the coffee."

Before he could stop, it was out of his mouth. "Left over, is it, from what you fed to Sonny Rutherford?"

The coffeepot remained half raised when Linda turned. "Stop it," she yelled, "just stop it." For a moment she was a figurine arrested in midair, but she didn't smash to the floor. She set the coffeepot on the stove so carefully it didn't make a sound. Then she left the room.

Jonas went to the doorway and called to her. From the stove came the strong, good smell of the coffee. Finding his cup in his hand, he poured himself some. He called her again.

"She won't come down," Jane said. "She made it special." The girl looked across the table at her father, then got up and started clearing the dishes. "Did Mr. Dodge find you this morning?"

"He's just about cop enough to locate a man that does nothing but mind his own business and try to raise his family right."

"What did he want?"

"Just to ask some more damn fool questions," Jonas said. He sipped from his coffee. It was better than what he made. At the sink Jane had her back to him. She was shaking. "Your sister made some good coffee," he said.

Tears were on her face. "Oh, Daddy, why don't you just leave us alone!"

By himself at the table he finished his coffee, holding the last swallow in his mouth until it had no taste, just warmth. He finished taking the dishes to the sink and without any of his usual instructions left the house. He drove back past Langley's, through the square, to Hatch's, where a few customers sat at the counter. Duncan asked him to go downstairs to the empty lounge.

"You want a drink? Beer?" Duncan asked.

"I don't want nothing on my breath," said Jonas.

From the bar Duncan brought himself a beer and Jonas a glass of ginger ale. Duncan laid out his package of Luckies on the table. "There's nothing in your drink," he said. "What's Henry Dodge got to know?"

Jonas told him. "You can see the spot I'm in."

Duncan lighted a cigarette and turned the pack toward Jonas. "It's just that you were out that night, see. Worse came to worse I'd speak to Dodge, but that's not going to happen."

"It's going to happen if I don't tell him something." Jonas picked up the pack of cigarettes and read the label as if it were something new. He had never understood smoking. He replaced the pack on the table and spun it back to Duncan.

"Dodge only thinks he needs to know everything. Anybody else out that night?"

"Clay Freeman."

"There's a name you could give Dodge. Everybody knows about that because he had to go to Zack's forty-nine times to get his car fixed."

"Dodge didn't know about that when he talked to me," Jonas said.

"Then give him Clay's name."

"Freeman'd know it was me," Jonas said.

"Clay won't hurt you," Duncan said. "He'll just figure you were doing your duty. It's what he would do. Anyway, there's no law against getting stuck by the road or being out late at night either."

Jonas checked the clock. It was close on to the time he had to be in Dodge's office. "I wasn't thinking of that," he said.

Duncan Hatch slipped the cigarettes into his shirt pocket. "Now I don't care what happens down there, we're going to help you keep your family together." He reached over and squeezed Jonas's wrist.

No man ever touched Jonas. He knew that gesture made him more secure than the offer of help. "Just wish there'd be a way around Sonny Rutherford." Jonas would have to wait for Henry Dodge's questions before he decided whether or not to tell him about Clay Freeman's car. He imagined the cop writing that out in his notebook: Cloudman says Clay Freeman was parked by the bridge the morning of the disappearance. Jonas took a swallow of his ginger ale. He couldn't finish it because it reminded him of the final swallow of Linda's coffee. She hadn't come down or so much as looked out the window when he had left the house. The only person he could say he despised was Sonny Rutherford, yet he was treating his daughter cruelly and was about to betray Clay Freeman. Leaving the lounge, he thanked Duncan Hatch and drove over to Dodge's office. He knew what man he wouldn't name.

12 / *The Wages of Sin*

March 1956

When Ned Grimsley got home from work, he knew his wife was still awake. Never before had Esther waited up for him. Or at least, Ned thought, she hadn't let herself be caught at it. Regular nights, nights when he just came back from the shift, she'd be asleep. Now two nights running, nights that he had been at Louise's, she was up. Of course she had gotten up the night Langley had been killed, but that was coincidence. The night his mother had died, Esther had been up when he got home. He wondered if that had been when she started watching for him, adopting a duty his mother had never performed.

In the dark of the kitchen he stood listening to her move about in the bedroom above his head. Over two months ago he had counted out aspirins here as if he were preparing for something final. But Ned wasn't ready to die. What did she hope to accomplish, pacing around up there? He sat at the table, just sat without coffee or water or aspirin. If she had something to say, she could damn well come downstairs to say it. Bedrooms were not meant for arguing.

She had been stewing for a while. The night his mother died, Esther had said nothing about where he had been. As his wife, she had to stand by him and his father through the funeral, which, no matter whose mother it was, had been the worst funeral he had ever attended. That damn Treadwell had had to mix his ideas of Christian duty into the funeral service of a woman who didn't have any more to do with crime or sin than rabbits and eggs. And it was probably Treadwell who had brought it up in front of Esther in the first place, so that she couldn't deny even to herself what she had no business knowing.

He knew she was on the bed. Sitting there, getting up once in a while, she made little noises as if to call him upstairs. The Italian family he had known during the war used to whistle their children home after dark. He was no child to be whistled home. Ned went through the ell to the barn. The floorboards squeaked with the cold. Taking a bundle of straw he packed an extra handful into each of the rabbit hutches. The rabbits, huddled together, barely stirred. Finished, he blew on his fingers. Back in the ell he opened the refrigerator, where, lined up on the top shelf, there were a dozen quarts of goat's milk waiting for Clay Freeman. All was as it should be except that Esther was awake and sitting up for him.

In the yard, water from the day's melt had refrozen. Ned walked down to the road. Neither man nor light were to be seen. He thought of the crunching noise of his feet as an invitation for her to come down. What could she have to say to him? It had gone on for too many years to start talking about it now. He wasn't going to stop seeing Louise; in fact he would find it difficult to do anything Esther asked of him if her asking was the only reason to do it. He was glad the bastard who had told his father about Louise was dead. He was glad because he was sure that was how Esther had found out. The light in the bedroom went on, and he knew he must go in.

Her eyes, red-rimmed with soundless crying, dissolved the anger in him. How long she had been awake he could only guess. Down the hall slept his younger daughter and, farther down, his father. Ned would be quiet with Esther. He hoped she would be quiet with him. Lying on the bed, she spoke softly.

"I have to leave," she said. "Tonight."

He slipped off his pants and laid them over the chair beside his bureau, then he dropped his shirt by the chair. He didn't look at her while he took off his underwear. His pajamas on, he turned and saw her huddled on her side of the bed, her knees drawn up, her arms wrapped around them. She clutched the covers to her throat, hiding everything but the fierce terror of her face.

"I'm going, Ned. I have to get out of this house."

Tentatively, he sat on his edge of the bed. Everything up until now had seemed so solid. Now all was tentative, as though he had suddenly been thrust into her world, and she into his. He turned out the lamp over the bed. Together they lay in the dark. In the cold dark, he thought. She switched on the lamp and sat up.

"I need my clothes," she said.

When she stood, Ned rolled over to her side and held her. He spoke to her of practical things, of money and darkness and cold. She couldn't even drive a car. At that hour of night where could she go? She laughed, an awful laugh, and pulled away from him with a sudden energy. Standing in the corner, she shook with sobs. Once a big gray barn cat had started bothering his rabbits and had finally succeeded in getting into a hutch.

The doe, a New Zealand pinkeye who had four young in the cage with her, had kicked the cat to death. The tom had just had no place to escape to.

Esther was crying now. "Marjorie will have me. There's plenty of room at her place, and I can walk there."

He pulled her back to the bed. She fought, not hurting him but struggling to stay on her feet. When he had her on the bed, he covered her with his body. Again he switched out the lamp. Her body tense, she lay quiet under him. The house was cold and quiet. He relaxed his grip on her wrists and let his weight settle on her.

No crowbar of a woman was going to pry into his business. Marjorie Langley could do all the prying into her husband's death she wanted to, but Ned would see to it she stayed out of his affairs. In the morning all would be over with Esther. Then he'd prance right over and take care of Marjorie Langley.

"My God, my God, even Carol knows," Esther said. Carol was Ned's youngest daughter. "She's ashamed. In this town she's ashamed." She rolled and was on the floor. She stood before he could get off the bed.

"Stop this, Esther," he said. "Or you'll have to go to the hospital."

"Like they did to Pete Zakrzewski? Would you do that too?"

"You'll wake up the old man," Ned said.

"I don't care about him," she said. "I don't care about any of you men."

He wrestled her back to the bed. She wouldn't look at him. Like him, she must have been thinking he would have to go to sleep sometime, and with her wildness up she probably thought she could outwait him. He wondered if she could. He thought if he relaxed, she would let down a bit, keeping herself just keyed up enough to frighten him. Frighten him? Was it all bluff, deliberate, played out?

"Go to sleep now," he told her, "while there's still some night left."

The pain ripped from below his ear, across his throat, to his chest. His hand went to his neck, and she was out of the bed. As he got up she slapped his face. On the same side as the scratch, his eye stung. He grabbed her and hugged her to him.

"Margorie Langley's right," she said. "You men think you can live any way you please. Do people the way it satisfies you to do them with no thought of your wives or daughters or common human decency. Well, Marjorie's living on her own, and she has Jonas Cloudman and Reverend Treadwell hopping to her."

"I don't give one sweet damn about Marjorie Langley," Ned said.

He would just have to wait now. She had never fought him; no one fought him. But the crazy spell of pulling her little shawl of the world together over her shoulders and going out into the night seemed to have passed. She wouldn't fight him again. That must have been a quirk in the transition from the wildness. She would probably sleep through the morning when she got back to bed. Gently he turned her toward the bed. She stamped on the top of his foot. The pain had just begun when she did it again. He let her go and sat on the bed.

"If you do anything more," he told her, "I will hit you."

"You won't stop me," she said. Her fat body filled the corner by the closet. Her arms across her chest, hands holding her shoulders, made her look cold. "I know how you stop people."

"What are you talking about?"

She gave a little laugh and shuddered. "Oh, I can't stay here. I can't." Behind her the door slowly closed.

He got up and pulled the door to so that it caught. Ache from his right foot made him shift his weight to his left. He wondered if she had broken one of the tiny bones in his arch. Metatarsal. He began to think of the bones of the foot. In college he could name them all like saying the alphabet. Below the doorknob was a key with the loop at its shaft broken. He turned it until the lock snapped home, then he got into the bed.

When Ned got up, he didn't speak to anyone. In the kitchen he grunted at the old man rocking by the stove, poured himself a cup of coffee, then just held the cup in his hand while he stood staring out the window. The sky was clear. Stalks of grass sticking up through the crusted snow bent with the wind. Cold outside, too, he thought. In like a lion.

He left the cup, still full, on the counter next to the sink. After milking the goats, instead of going back into the house as usual, Ned drove down to Hatch's. There he sat at the counter and ordered coffee and English muffins. He finished a second cup of coffee and another order of muffins before he left. After paying Duncan Hatch, he said, "You certainly were right about that son of a bitch." Then he went straight to Marjorie Langley's and drove into her driveway, not leaving the car in his own yard less than fifty feet away.

In the time he sat there, he realized it was a good thing Cloudman was elsewhere. Five minutes passed, and still he sat in his car, waiting for her to come out. He couldn't shout to her, not to a woman. He pushed open the door and stretched his long legs out onto the wet ground of her driveway. Still there was no movement from her house. At his knock she opened the door. The kerchief wrapped around her hair made her look younger than she was. Like me, Ned thought, looking younger than I am.

"I don't see your hired hand around," he told her.

"Are you looking for Jonas?" She stood in the crack of the door.

He didn't answer her question. Instead he talked about the burden of farming, running a place on your own. How hard it was for a woman. The pressure of things and the lonesomeness could prey on a woman's mind, make her say things she didn't mean, do things she didn't intend, hurt people she had no business hurting.

"You already have a woman on the side," Marjorie told him. "I wouldn't even want to play first fiddle for you."

He told her he'd go into her barn before he'd go into her house.

"Maybe you did, last New Year's."

"Whoever did, did the town a favor." He hadn't wanted to talk about Langley. Forrest Langley didn't matter anymore. He was just dead. Ned hadn't come to talk at all, but to tell this bitch to stay out of his business and out of his life. "I warned your husband," he said, "and I'm warning you." The door shut, and eyes stinging as if the mesh of the screen had been pressed down on his eyeball, he got back in his car.

That night Ned left the mill after working just two hours of his shift. The lead man asked him if he was sick. Yes, Ned said, you can call it that. When he entered Louise Langley's apartment, he saw the television set on, its perimeter of light glowing in the darkened room. Before making coffee, Louise switched off the television. Sitting at her table in the kitchen, he wished she had left it on. He wanted to talk about something other than Esther or Marjorie Langley, though that was all he could think of to mention.

"Where'd you get these cups?" he asked Louise. She had served their coffee in small gold-rimmed cups with straight sides such as he had seen in Europe. "We haven't used them before."

"Forrest and Marjorie gave them to me," Louise said. "Marjorie ordered them from Boston, from Jordan Marsh. I was going to save them, but—do you like them?"

"They're fine," he said. He wished he hadn't brought up the cups. From under the sink he got the whiskey and poured himself a small glass.

"Why are you bothering my sister-in-law?" Louise asked. Her brown eyes looked straight at him as though he were only a face on her television screen.

He wondered if Louise was suspicious, jealous, and as rapidly as that thought disappeared, he wondered how she knew about his visit. Marjorie Langley must have called after he had gone to her place. "The amazing thing," he told Louise, "is that I've already started thinking of the place as hers."

"Because you're sure my brother's dead?"

"Because there isn't another woman in the town of Enoch who on her own holds property in the form of a working farm," Ned said. Nor could he imagine such a woman.

"I'm on my own," Louise said.

"That's different," he answered. "You're single." He sipped some whiskey to warm his stomach.

"Marjorie's single," Louise said. "Isn't she?"

"She's what she wants to be," Ned said. "That's what I hear from my wife. How Marjorie's got Jonas Cloudman to do her beck and call, a regular drone. If Jonas Cloudman wants to work for a woman, that's his business, but what went on at my house, in my bedroom, last night was nobody's doing except Marjorie Langley's. She was to blame." He swallowed some whiskey and washed it with coffee. The mixture tasted green and burned at the same time, reminding him of army coffee.

"You don't work for a woman," Louise said.

"I'd kill myself first."

"You don't think you work for me, do you?" She asked as if he hadn't answered her already. "You blame Marjorie for Esther finding out about us?"

"Her and the minister," Ned said. He wished she'd be quiet. He just wanted to get in the bed and feel her warm thighs against his.

"Marjorie told me everybody in town knew about us."

"That may be," said Ned, "but everybody in town's got enough sense to keep their mouths shut about things that don't concern them."

"Like what happened to my brother?"

"If that's what's bothering you, Marjorie's got two or three good men working on that for her."

Louise finished her coffee. "Then she doesn't need you over there telling her what you're going to do. And you can spare me your sarcasm." She took her gold-rimmed cup to the sink, where she rinsed it before setting it, upside down, on the counter.

Ned put his hand out as she walked back, but she skirted around him and went toward the bedroom. He drank off the rest of the whiskey. In his cup the coffee seemed like a great draft of medicine. "Spare me," she had said, an expression he figured she'd learned from the television. He dumped the coffee in the sink and refilled the delicate cup with water to rinse the whiskey from his throat. It was city water, warm, tasting of metal.

Louise came back wearing her quilt robe. "Good night," she said.

He stared at her. He would hit her if she started in like Esther. "Is this it?" he asked her.

She came no closer than the end of the counter. "You were very drunk when you left here New Year's Eve," she said.

He flung the cup to the floor. "Everyone in town except the cops and his relatives knows what happened to Langley."

13 / *Lessons*

March 1956
For the first time in his life Clay Freeman sat on the passenger side of his own car. Beside him behind the wheel was Marjorie Langley. From his pocket he took a thick set of keys, raised them in the air suspended from a single square-headed silver key, and shook them. They chattered like miniature bells.

"This is the ignition key," Clay said.

Marjorie opened her right hand and accepted the keys, which jumbled together in her palm. Reaching into her hand, Clay started to rummage through the keys. She pushed his hand away and told him she would find it. With a search governed more by feel than by sight, she discovered the square-headed key and held it up to him.

"Ignition key," she said. She smiled in satisfaction and continued smiling at Clay's alertness, a brightness in his eyes such as she had seen in no man's face for three months.

"Put it into the ignition slot," he said.

He grabbed the shift lever, pulled it toward them, and pushed it up. The red needle stayed at *P*. He told her to try it. She repeated his actions. The red needle was still at *P*.

"Good," he said. "Always start in park."

"Why, Clay?" she asked. "It'll start in neutral, too, won't it?"

"It's just better," he said. He glanced at her, but she was concentrating on the key.

As soon as the motor began to turn, Marjorie backed off with the key. Then she turned it again, and a whirring cried from the engine. Clay covered her hand with his so that together they could turn the key, holding it down until the motor caught. Clay switched it off and told her to try it. When she started it, they exchanged smiles.

She tried the various switches and knobs on the dashboard, clicking the signals and shining the lights on her own garage doors. Clay told her to turn off everything except the heater. Reaching over her knee, he pointed out the emergency brake pedal on the left wall of the car. From the dashboard popped the silver lighter, red hot, onto the back of Clay's hand. He held his hand to his mouth. "Jesus Christ," he said. Then they both said "sorry" at the same time. He replaced the lighter in the hole in the dash. And neither one of us smokes, he thought.

Clay had her back the car down the length of her driveway using the mirror. As she pressed the accelerator to get onto the road, the tires spun on the sand, then hit the tar and squealed across to the far lane. Black marks of burnt rubber lay on the road. Marjorie laughed. Clay told her to drive to the other side of the river.

The sun was bright, warm for March. Down on the flats the snow cover had shrunk and settled. It had peeled back from the edge of the road. Above the winter-old crust stared weed stalks, dry new eyes for the spring. The steel bridge that spanned the river clanged, and its grill floor whined with the tires. Marjorie tightened both hands on the steering wheel. Clay told her not to worry, it was only the bridge.

At the top of the ridge she stopped the car, moved the shift lever to *P,* and got out. "We've come a long ways," she said as Clay joined her. Clearly visible on the hill across from them was her large barn. The house and garage from which they had started stood beyond the road. With her eyes Marjorie traced the route down the hill and over the flats.

Clay was squinting, shading his eyes. Bunched around his shoulders, his bulky coat made him look as though he were in pain. "Yes," he said, "about a mile and a half."

Back in the car Marjorie turned the key she had left in the ignition slot. Again from the motor came the crying shriek. She pounded her fist on the steering wheel. "Damn."

Lightly Clay hit the dashboard. "Damn," he said. He smiled. "Try it in low this time."

She brought the gearshift lever down until the red line was on *L.* Coordinating brake and accelerator, she brought the car back onto the road. The car jumped forward, then nearly halted. It went through that sequence three more times before Marjorie got it smoothed out. At the stop sign she turned left.

She drove a little faster on the highway. The spacers in the cement sounded a steady rhythm, the rapid beat to a song without melody. On the opposite side of the narrow valley was the village.

"The church needs painting this year," Marjorie said.

Clay said nothing. He too was looking across the river. In front of the church the square was filled with snow. Even from here it looked dirty. Clay saw that the car was in the middle of the road. "Bring it back," he said. She did so, smoothly, and he told her to pull into his driveway just down the road.

Marjorie pumped the brakes, crammed the wheel to the right, and, at Clay's word, pressed the accelerator. The car spun into the driveway and kept going, nose into the snowbank. Clay fell over, his head in Marjorie's lap. She laughed. Righting himself, Clay looked away from her, to the snowbank in which the fender was embedded. She backed the car out, then, without a word from Clay, drove up the drive to his house. While Clay went into the house to tell his wife they were going to Hatch's, Marjorie turned the car around.

"That was good," he told her when he got back in the car. He was amazed she had done it alone.

They drove back across the river, up through Enoch, to the restaurant. She waited for a car to pass, then turned left into the plowed area of Hatch's parking lot. Directly in front of the big window was a space between two cars. She aimed for it.

"Brake," Clay told her.

She pressed down hard on the pedal, and the car accelerated between the two cars. Clay's foot crushed against hers as the bumper and grill broke the window. The tires caught at the base of the building. Clay reached over and pulled the key from the ignition slot.

Marjorie Langley wondered if she'd ever learn to drive. At school she'd always been quick. She was barely over forty, far too young for senility, too young even for the change of life. She shook her head at that. Few women would ever go through a change such as hers. Too many women didn't truly change; they just did more.

Clay had said his car was insured, but that didn't matter. She had told him to have Zack fix it and send her the bill. Money just wasn't a problem. All those years Forrest had worked for money, they had hated him for it. Now it wasn't a problem either. Just as she had lived with a fear that was no longer a problem either. She brought the gun downstairs.

Had the accident happened elsewhere, she'd have sent the car to Newfound to be fixed. She didn't want to do business in

Enoch, even if it wasn't her car; but with the restaurant torn open like a hidden package by a willful child, they all knew her mistake. Of course, she would have to pay for the window, too. She only wished a few of them had been in the path of the exploding glass. Having Zack repair it, obviously Clay's choice, would bring Clay a little closer to her, something she would have found difficult to arrange. She wanted to have someone close. Jonas Cloudman just wouldn't do.

From the top shelf of the cabinet over the sink she took the clip for the rifle. Jonas had asked her if she was going to keep it loaded in the house. I don't know, she had said. Should I? He had held on to the rifle, patting his palm with the barrel as a man will drum his fingers on a table. You going to shoot anything in the house? Nothing is going to get into this house that will need to be shot, she had said. Then I'd keep the clip up, out of reach, he had told her. I don't much fancy guns myself. Taking three shells from the box on the high shelf, she filled the clip and put it in the rifle. Henry Dodge still had Forrest's shotgun down at his office.

Upstairs Peter was napping, though soon he would be up. Marjorie went to her bedroom to dress herself in her hunter's clothes. Out of season, she thought. Like a trophy, the mink still hung in the closet. She took out a single hanger with both the gray slacks and the flannel shirt she'd bought in Newfound. She left her dress on the bed, as Forrest always had left his clothes, she thought. In the hall closet hung her plaid wool jacket, the mate to Forrest's, a little smaller. She waited in the bedroom for Peter to rise.

In the narrow three-quarter bed he lay like a single flower in a box from the florist's. He was nearing the age of the boy who had come to see her before she met Forrest. Under the dark green blanket he hugged his bear, the third or fourth one they'd bought him. When Peter first stirred, she touched his shoulder to wake him. Now he was an easy-waking child, though before he had been difficult when he got up. Marjorie caught herself, drawing back so quickly that Peter clutched for her. She had always thought of him as young, but now she was thinking "before" for him too. Now another infancy was over.

She helped him to dress. Buttoning his shirt, fastening his trousers, that was about all she had to do, though of course she had to select his clothes and decide whether it was cold enough for his coat or jacket. Men, she had noticed, had little natural sense of timing. In winter they wore one thing, in summer another, regardless of the weather; or they were fooled by an extra-bright day. Responding truly to the way things were was how she functioned, was how most women must function if they weren't bamboozled by the men they lived with.

In back of the house they walked in snow, here and there stepping down to their knees. The undulated surface of the snow hid the holes and rocks that were the true floor of the field. In midwinter Marjorie and Peter had crossed on top of the snow, not breaking through, but those days had passed. Soon the snow itself would be gone.

Jonas Cloudman had piled four bales for Marjorie near the edge of the field. He had taken them out when Clay Freeman was running the plastic lines to tap the trees. If he asks anything, Marjorie told Jonas, tell him I need a recreation to take my mind off my problem. The stack was in front of a small rise that acted as a backstop. She walked to the pile and unfurled the roll of paper she had been carrying. On the topmost pile were two flat rocks. She reached up and sat the rocks on the two corners of the paper. It was brown butcher paper Clay had gotten for her from a supply company in Newfound. I know them from when I was on the road, he had said, with Forrest. He hadn't asked what she wanted it for. The paper blew out against her, so she tucked the bottom between the first and second bales. A piece of the stiff straw stuck under her fingernail.

Standing thirty feet from the bales, she neither leaned nor rested on anything. There was an awkwardness to her raising of the rifle, as though it stiffly resisted her; but once it was up, she stood in perfect control. She looked back over the stock to check Peter, who held his hands like a pair of earmuffs over his ears.

She smiled at him, turned back to face the bales, and squeezed off a shot as Jonas had shown her. She thought it was appropriate to squeeze and not pull or yank the trigger, appropriate because squeezing made the gun seem more natural.

Her shoulder and collarbone were sore from having shot before, particularly when she had pressed the gun too close to her neck. Right after the shot she began to smart. She didn't mind the jolt—the kick, Jonas called it—because she expected it as part of the shooting. Yet she shouldn't be too conscious of expecting it. Else you'll shy, Jonas had said. Sharp, like the pains of labor, the kick of the gun came, but she accepted it; it seemed as necessary as the contractions. The soreness afterward was just her weakness and wouldn't affect her accuracy. Jonas had said she could fix a pad to her shoulder. She had told him she couldn't go around wearing a pad all the time.

It was a new target. The single hole from her first shot was within the black-lined man's form, in the lower body. She didn't walk up to check closer but worked the next shell into the chamber. Before she fired, she looked at Peter, who was standing in the same place, his hands still over his ears, smiling now.

Behind the bales ran the plastic lines carrying clear sap from the maples. The veins fed together and finally gathered in a shed behind the garage where Jonas kept the fire going, boiling the liquid as it turned darker. Not too dark, Clay had told her. Just a little darker than the golden hair on a newborn girl. That's your fancy grade. Last-run sap may get a little darker. Marjorie had said, My hair was a honey blond, but it all gets a little darker with time.

After she had finished firing, she took Peter up the hill a ways. There she found a union in the plastic tubing and pulled it open. She tried getting the sap flow into Peter's mouth, but he pulled at her hand until she let him take the tube and suck in the cold, clear liquid. It's going to be boiled anyway, she thought. He handed the tube back to her, pointing the nippled end at her face.

"Momma," he said.

She let the liquid fall into her mouth, then bent to reconnect the tubing. As she did she saw a man at the edge of Grimsley's field begin to walk up the hill. She raised the empty rifle, not to her shoulder, not aiming at him, but just enough to show him what she held. The man stopped. She walked Peter down past the bales and, leaving the target behind her, went across her field.

Ned Grimsley waited until Marjorie reached her house, then walked over to the bales to see the target. Along the length of the paper in the outline style of dressmaker patterns was the form of a man. Ned stared at the paper man, holes torn in his head and body. "Suffering Christ," he said.

"And this year, your busiest time of year," Gladys Freeman said, "you're out teaching a woman to drive." She had been reading to the boy while Clay looked through the paper. He didn't so much read as look through it, his eye catching here a sale, there a death, somewhere else a cartoon or news item. This search for the fortuitous relaxed him. He was annoyed with his wife's interruption.

"She pays," he told her, the paper still a sheet over his face.

Gladys plumped down on the couch. "That's not an answer. It would be worth my soul to ask you to drive us somewhere during this season."

"Well, maybe that's not all I'm doing." He lowered the paper, though he kept it spread in his lap. "You know, whether you want to think about it or not. There's something big gone on in this town."

"Yes, and now that Henry Dodge has accused you of it, you think you belong square in the middle of it, just as if you had killed your cousin."

"Henry Dodge just brought it to my attention," he said.

On the file cabinet in Henry Dodge's office sat a heavy porcelain hot plate. Large bubbles rising from the bottom were visible in the Silex. The glass itself was filmed with dirt of the sort Clay had seen on old milk cans at the farms where he picked up syrup. Sometimes, near summer when the first haying was done, the cans felt sticky, not from syrup but from the accumulation of things that grew in the hot air of the barn. He'd tell the farmers, Give me the syrup in clean cans, but they were always afraid he wouldn't return them.

Clay had refused the offer of a coffee. He'd sat watching the crazed surface of the cup Dodge held in both hands while the cop tried to frighten him. He had told Clay he had expected him in on his own, but with the testimony given in the very office they sat in, he'd had to call him in.

"You know what he called it?" Clay asked. "His goddamn evidenciary file."

"A little learning is a dangerous thing," Gladys said, "especially when it all comes from *Dragnet.*" She laughed, a healthy, full-throated laugh. With her head tilted back, her long neck was exposed. A beautiful long neck, Clay thought.

There had been nothing in the file folder Dodge had put on the desk except sheets of soft, yellow paper with Dodge's penciled handwriting. He'd told Clay he couldn't see them, though the inky signature at the bottom had been plain enough. Laboriously the cop had written down what he called Clay's statement.

"Well, did he accuse you?" Gladys asked. She was still smiling from her laughter.

"He told me the prosecutor did that. Besides, they haven't even found Forrest yet." Gladys looked at him, expecting more. "You know what really burned my ass? He made me go get the cloth I took from the barn that night." Dodge had stuck the dirty yellow cloth in a manila envelope as if it were the only piece of physical evidence he had. "He also made a big deal of us being relatives."

"You are relatives," Gladys said. It wasn't the cloth she wanted to talk about.

"It was Jonas Cloudman's name on the statement," Clay said.

"Dodge wanted you to know who turned you in," said Gladys.

Cloudman had been abroad that night and had seen Clay's car. That hadn't surprised Clay. What had surprised him was that Jonas had talked to the cop at all. When he'd asked Dodge about it, he'd been told it was a police affair. Then Clay had asked the cop why he was bothering with him. It's my job, Dodge had answered.

"He better not have had any reason for picking me," Clay told his wife.

"You don't think it might be dangerous to spend so much time with Marjorie?" Gladys stretched her legs out along the couch and stuffed a throw pillow under her neck.

He let the paper slide to the floor, where the pages fell into disorder. There were people who had suggested hers might have been a hand on the knife, but no one suggested an accomplice. "I'm being deliberate with Marjorie," Clay said.

"You're too blind to see what's going on. You'd just better hope she's not being deliberate with you," Gladys said, "because your purposes might make for something troublesome."

As far as Clay was concerned, both he and Marjorie wanted to learn the same thing: Who had killed Forrest. Why he wanted to know was not easy to say. To prove wrong Marjorie's theory of his town gone mad was less personal than what he felt, though certainly he felt no desire to avenge his cousin's death.

Gladys broke the silence. "I hope you're not over there for what people call the obvious reason."

"I'm not Ned Grimsley," he answered. He kicked the confusion of papers aside. Ned was under some illusion he could escape the realities he had been linked to since birth, realities Gladys scoffed at in her disdain for Enoch. Clay also believed, though he didn't tell his wife, that there were no hard and fast rules about the obvious. Too many shades confused the figure and the background, and patterns could be made from almost anything.

Gladys swung her feet to the floor and leaned, elbows on knees, toward him. From around her ear a wisp of hair, ruffled by the pillow, turned gray in the lamplight. "You know, Clay," she began, as though she were explaining something to the boy, "before New Year's everybody talked on and on about this thing. Now everybody's quiet, and the women are either ignorant or afraid. Except for Marjorie Langley."

Quickly he glanced at her. "Talk is unreliable. And in Enoch so is silence."

"That rifle of hers." Gladys rubbed her cheek against the sleeve of her blouse, allowing the sheer material to caress her skin. "You don't think she intends to shoot somebody—at least to be able to shoot somebody? Even if she hasn't decided who it's going to be."

"It's a bluff," said Clay, "a colossal bluff, like some of the games we used to play on the road."

"Games on the road, Clay? These aren't games on the road." She spoke sharply. "You'd be further ahead if you just concentrated on the business you left the road to do."

"Supporting you and the boy takes up most of my time as it is," Clay said, the sharpness in his voice, too. "I've explained about Marjorie." He watched sadness come into his wife's anger. As it does so often with women, he thought, because they expect sadness as their position in life and get it too often. He watched, with a feeling that kept him sunk in his chair. Below the tearstained cheeks, fists clenched and formed balls of fury.

"It wasn't Jonas Cloudman on the telephone," Gladys said. "Either time."

14 / *Syrup Turns to Candy*

From the bottom of the kettle rose large bubbles, the size of half-dollars. Clay Freeman smiled. "It's ready," he said, "and it's beautiful." He frequently talked to himself while he worked in the room off his garage. He talked about what he was doing, his observations. "It's grained," he would say. "Must be near two fifty," and he would stick in the candy thermometer. His other thoughts of Ned Grimsley, Marjorie, Jonas Cloudman, were broken pieces like the returns of crystallized maple leaves, hearts, and stars he would collect from his outlets each week. These things too he thought about and spoke of in slowly considered phrases. "Need more jars from Duncan." "Letting them break." Clay took a ladle with a narrow, beaked mouth and dipped it into the boiling golden syrup. As it flowed back into itself he pronounced it ready.

It was light out now. He had gotten up early to finish this batch so that he could distribute it this afternoon. He saw ahead of him not the endless repetition of individual steps, pouring, cooling, grouping, packaging, sealing, but rather the whole process as completed, separate from its component acts. He had planned to leave by noon. Now he had pushed the time back to one, and at that he would have to skip his dinner.

When they had been on the road, he and Langley were both known as early risers. Other salesmen quoting all the clichés about their ambition were in fact stunned to discover Clay and Langley had grown up close by each other, for they were as unalike as cows and trees and knew it. Their fathers were alike, though. Clay used to tell people that. When we were growing up, he would say, there were two mean men in the Birches. One of them was my father, and the other one was his. The odd thing was, Clay thought, they weren't even brothers.

Clay seldom thought about the differences between him and

Langley because he thought himself different from most men and accepted that difference as natural and right. In the same way he considered his father's treatment of him as the best the old man could do. He had me chase up and down New Hampshire and Vermont all during the war to keep him supplied with bananas, Clay told Duncan Hatch once. He told me if I couldn't fight, at least I could forage. Well, I might as well have gone out in my shed and tried to invent bananas as buy them anywhere, and remember I had connections with stores in every town and crossroads in northern New England. And when you did bring them, Gladys had said—speaking to Duncan, but using that "you" as a shorthand indictment—he'd look over every fruit for a spot of black; whether it was spoiled or ripe didn't even matter. Or if one of the hands was still green he'd comment on that. The most that ever came out of that man's mouth was "Suppose it was the best you could do." Langley's father was never much on talk. He would just laugh at Forrest. And the two of them were dead now, dead within a week of each other, as though the meanness that ate through their bodies had finished the corrosion at the same rate.

Along the counter Clay aligned his new molds. They were made of thick rubber, some dark black and others soft brown, nearly the color of the boiling syrup itself. Nailed in the middle of the counter was a hot pad on which Clay set the kettle. Ladleful by ladleful he filled the stars, the maple leaves, and the round forms he called simply "cakes." He was not a sloppy man, but he moved quickly and soon drops of maple syrup were hardening on the counter, the spaces between the depressions in the molds, and even on the apron he wore over his shirt.

Hot though it was in his room, he kept his shirt buttoned and a tie cinched at his neck. He had taken off his cardigan, and now that he had ladled the kettle empty, he reached into the pocket for a mint Life Saver. The sharp taste of the candy competed for a moment with the rich sugar smell of the room before it settled for a solitary existence in Clay's mouth. Clay never ate the maple candy he made except to sample its quality.

Clay knocked the lid off the forty-quart can next to him. He dipped his sample glass into the syrup, then put it into the rack on the counter for quality comparison. A row of small jars each filled with syrup slightly darker than the next stood on the counter. The sample jar he had taken from the newly opened can nearly matched the lightest-colored standard at the end of the rack. "Almost pure fancy," Clay said. "I knew that sandy hill of hers would bring out some beautiful syrup."

With the kettle on the floor, Clay lifted the can just enough for a sheet of syrup to pour into the kettle. Sweat beaded on his brow, not from the heat of the stove but from the work of lifting the syrup. He sat the full kettle on the burner. "An hour more," he said aloud. "The old man could lift one hundred pounds in each hand without a streak of sweat. Well, I can do the same. It just looks harder when I do it."

He plugged in the iron so that it would be ready when the candy had hardened enough to be packaged. They liked those new packages down in Newfound. That's how he'd gotten into the A&P. Packaging, Clay, packaging's the thing now, the manager had told him. Then he had asked, When you going to move out of that backwater you live in? Some town; when a man's neighbors take a disliking to him they come by and kill him.

Next Clay had stopped at the little store he had serviced all through the thirties. The owner, a man Clay had known for twenty years, started in about Forrest; and Clay had told him they hadn't even found the body. Maybe they won't, the man had said. One of your farmers may have chopped it up for silage. Someone in Enoch will break, though. You wait and see. One of you will break, or you'll all come to hate each other and take care of the rascal yourselves. Bring me a jar of the cakes, too. I like the packaged candy, but a lot of folks come in expecting to see those little twenty-cent cakes. Clay had told him not to put them in the sun because they'd turn on him. Why don't you get some jars with dark glass? the man had asked.

Because all your old customers wouldn't find those little twenty-cent cakes they come in expecting to see, Clay had told him.

He hated the easy, ugly assumption they made about Enoch. They pretended a sort of smug horror, but underneath it were the giggles and smirks, as if they'd learned about a raided stag party at some club, a police report filled with salacious details. Details were exactly what was missing in this instance, the only certain detail being that Langley had gone out early to do the milking and hadn't been seen since.

The candy in the molds had hardened so that Clay could pull back the rubber and have the pieces come out golden and perfect. The rubber itself had a soft, warm feel, though Clay thought they came out too slowly. Of course, this way none of them break. The metal cupcake trays, which used to be his only molds, came last. Each of these he banged once on the counter, and a dozen of the old-fashioned cakes splashed out on the counter. But he was right—two or three from each tray were broken.

Of course they were right in thinking Forrest dead. He wasn't the kind of man you could keep around, even for money. Things could have begun that way—an attempt at kidnapping, though no note ever came. Clay reached underneath the shelf for the plastic bags he packaged the figures in. He stacked them next to a pile of cards, each of which said:

CLAY FREEMAN—THE CANDY MAN
Ridge Road—Enoch, N.H.
"The sweets of a New England Spring"
__oz. of pure maple sugar. __¢.

The numbers had not been filled in. He began by putting nine maple figures into a bag, then with a black marking pencil writing "eight" before the ounces and "seventy-five" before the cents. He folded the plastic over once at the top. Maybe a note had come, he thought, and no one had said anything. But Dodge couldn't keep his mouth shut if that were true. Still, maybe

Marjorie hadn't told him, maybe she was dealing with the state police and fooling Dodge and everybody else. He ran the plastic across the hot iron, sealing the package.

All of these ideas that more than one person was involved made the ugly assumption that the people in Enoch were rotten, because even those who weren't in on the murder knew about it, and still kept quiet about it. In town he had heard all sorts of theories, everything from suicide to an insurance murder planned by Marjorie. When he told people outside of Enoch what the town said, they just snorted at him. The manager at the A&P asked him if they all got together once a week to invent a new story. No one in Enoch or out of it seemed able to accept the simple idea that one man, either riled or drunk or both, had gone to the barn New Year's and killed Forrest Langley. Probably hadn't even meant to, said Clay.

He had forgotten to weigh the packages. One by one he took them from the open box and laid them on the counter. The white of the scale was broken only by a yellow seal from the State Bureau of Weights and Measures and the black needle that went to 7½ oz. with the first package. The next package registered the same. Hell, he said, and arranged the rest of them back in the open box. Just my luck some inspector will find one of them short, he said. Well, I've been short before, and I've been shorted a good many times. When he got done with the figures, he started on the cakes. They were easier; he just stacked them in the gallon jar he had gotten from Hatch's Diner.

Who went up there? Could walk in on him in the barn? If there was someone. The absence of a body was not as puzzling as the absence of some logical person to imagine in that barn the same morning Clay had been there. Somebody wait for him? Surprise him? Clay excluded middle cases; either Langley went out of that barn on his own or he went out dead.

As he filled the gallon jar he checked off the names of the outlets he would deliver to today. He had figured pretty close how much a batch of sugar would make so that each day's route would be something he could reasonably handle. Though Gladys never believed it, he really did plan to be back for supper most nights, but he didn't work an eight-hour day. He had never set that limit on himself because if you were in business you couldn't, not if you were going to get ahead. Gladys just said, You've been a working fool since you grew up on that crazy farm, and I'd be crazy to think you'd ever change. But don't expect me to like the way you do things.

Even if he couldn't picture someone in that barn ready to tackle onto Forrest Langley, he could think of a thousand schemes that would draw a man out of his house and barn before breakfast. Insurance, of course. It was a hell of a lot faster and easier way to make money than milking cows would ever be. Forrest had always wanted to make money and had been willing to make the sacrifices attendant on turning an honest buck, as they had said working together in the thirties. They had had that in common. That and quitting the road (or the company) to come back to Enoch to make it on their own. Oh, they knew how to live all right, the good hotels and the best steak, but it never went beyond that. So insurance didn't make a lot of sense. Nor could Clay grant that his cousin would leave that farm for Marjorie to run. Could he be on it still, staying indoors just waiting? Clay just laughed at that idea as he screwed another lid on a full gallon jar.

Whatever had happened to her husband, Marjorie did not know about it. Her changes indicated too strongly that she believed Forrest to be dead for Clay to think that she had her husband hidden somewhere on the farm. Nor could she fake all of that hatred had she murdered him. He had known her long enough to dispute the commonplace view of their marriage. But her changes and her anger combined were not enough to convince Clay that she was right about the town of Enoch, because that would mean that many of the people in it were keeping a secret from him. Things like that just didn't happen.

Perhaps Ned Grimsley wasn't the only man in Enoch who had a woman on the side. It would be a strange town if he were, and Clay figured that made more sense than Marjorie's idea that an actual group of men had gotten together like some vigilantes out of a Western, or a Southern lynch mob, and murdered her husband. People said she'd become unhinged since Forrest left. Maybe because she knew exactly what had happened and where he'd gone. Make as much sense as me with a woman, Clay said. What woman? Crazy as Gladys's ideas.

What made more sense than that was the thought that he had just had it. Twenty years of living in a town that hated him so much that a festering grudge was the only recognition it would give to his accomplishments may have been just enough to push him over the edge. And sane or not, he just decided—on the spur of the moment? drunk for the first time in his life?—to leave, the same way he'd gotten fed up with his father for the fiftieth time and finally headed out the door and down the road. Clay knew that feeling, but walking away from your father's home was a far way from walking away from life.

As he carried the jars like sleeping babies in his arms, Clay began to wonder if his was more a search for truth than for facts. The boxes of packaged sugar shapes were easier to load than the jars. Those he would take down to Enoch to the supermarket where he marketed the goat's milk from Ned Grimsley. The gallon jars mostly went to restaurants and the little corner stores, where they sat next to cash registers. Later in the spring he would put them into the gift shops in the mountains and in the state tourist shops. That was always his best volume. When he got to Hatch's Diner, he found his jar had been removed from the counter.

"Sell them all, Duncan?" he asked the owner.

From under the cash register Duncan brought up the jar, over half full. "They turned white on me," he said. "Couldn't have them looking moldy in the restaurant, Clay."

"I'll credit you for them," Clay said. "Did you have them on the counter?"

"No, in the window. Figured I'd give you a good display, right next to the high school basketball schedule."

"They crystallized—right there in the sun. You can't keep

them out in the open like that. I ought to have them in dark glass, but then you couldn't see them at all.'' He made out a slip, and Duncan paid for the ones he had sold. The crystallized cakes Clay gave him credit for would just go in the pot tomorrow for the next batch of sugar, though Duncan didn't have to know that. Clay didn't tell his friends all his business.

"You coming by Sunday night?'' Duncan Hatch asked.

"Far as I can see,'' Clay told him. He was looking forward to a night in the lounge.

"Sure is a lot nicer having you come in this way,'' Duncan said, "instead of in through the window with your chauffeur-driven car.''

Driving home, he saw lights on at Grimsley's and Langley's both, as though the two were sitting up watching each other in a dark standoff. He turned down the hill, over the frost heave at the bottom, and started across the flats to the bridge. Then he stopped the car. Behind him up on the hill was Langley's barn. The field was empty now, but it hadn't been the last time he had been stopped here in the dark.

But that night, he told himself, had been cold, rainy, with mist so thick he couldn't see the barn. Tonight in the spring the sky was clear, and a man might see all kinds of things, even, if the brow of the hill didn't shadow it, Langley's house itself. The thickness of New Year's Eve had hidden things, and what a man saw on a night such as that might not be the truth at all.

What he thought he had seen told him nothing he wanted to know. Or told him all—if he was willing to stop with the simple answer to a simple question, though Clay knew himself well enough to doubt he would be satisfied so easily. He hit the steering wheel with the heel of his hand. There was nothing easy about his ideas, his revelation. So simple it was he didn't know what to do with it. Most of all he didn't want to believe it, and for the first time in his life, he wished he weren't right. And the more he wished it, the more certain he became that he had seen three men dragging the body of a fourth across the fields to dump it off the bridge.

A car eased up beside him. It was the town cruiser. Henry Dodge, leaning across the seat so that he nearly disappeared, rolled down the passenger window.

"Having trouble, Clay?"

Clay turned to the cop. "No, just stopped."

"I thought your car might have died on you," Henry said, "like it did back in the winter. Back New Year's Eve."

Clay looked down the road to the steel bridge that led home. "There's nothing wrong with the car." He switched the ignition on and started the motor. "I just stopped."

"Ought to use your blinkers, Clay, dark like it is here."

"It's not that dark," Clay replied.

When he got home, he was late for supper. He didn't want to explain to Gladys why he had stopped by the road. He didn't want to talk about Dodge's sarcastic warning. And he didn't want to tell her the names of his three friends who had killed Forrest Langley.

For once she brought his reheated meal out of the oven without a word of reproof to season it. She didn't even mention the phone calls.

THREE
A Dark Necessity

15 / *The Dead You Will Have with You Always*

Full of melt the cold river was flowing swiftly in late March. From around the cement footings that held up a steel bridge, the current, pulsing with its own strength for the first time since the new year, swept the winter debris downstream. Limbs and roots from along the shore, paper and a few old bottles, and great quantities of mud slid into the water and formed inchoate masses that blobbed into further entanglements until freed once more by the constant current.

Not far from the bridge a large, mucusy body moved from behind the boulder where it had been lodged for months. Cold cloth stuck close to it, closer it seemed than its very skin, which was puffy and distended. The pants and jacket stained dark by the water marked the body as human as it rolled along the bottom. A few yards downstream it hesitated, then stopped completely. Above the jacket was a round protuberance without feature except for dark hair that waved in the current like water weeds. The flesh of the cheeks had been eaten day by day in microscopic nibbles. When the current moved the body again, small pieces of skin scraped from the limbs as they dragged along the bottom. With momentum the body rose to the middle of the river and floated eyeless in colloidal suspension with the muck of the river.

Around the body and loosely connected to it was a length of quarter-inch rope, now a grayer white than the flesh had become. The rope, sturdier and more durable than flesh, seemed attached accidentally or through habit, rather than with any plan or purpose. Occasionally it snagged on a rock or root and momentarily held the body back, but the onflowing current soon freed it for the journey downstream.

On the ridge paralleling the river, Clay Freeman drove his car, the rear deck loaded with maple sugar. He had just had an argument with Gladys and was on his way to Newfound to deliver candy there. He would never strike a woman. Gladys could not understand, Clay thought, that when you were in business you didn't get to take off every weekend, particularly when you were right in the middle of your busy season. Nor could she understand his double involvement (driving and buying) with Marjorie Langley, a woman she said might be crazy. She may need help in overcoming her problem, Gladys had said, but you were only her husband's cousin. You just let Timothy Treadwell take care of those sorts of things, she had told him. That's not the sort of stuff I'm concerned with, he had said. I hope not, she had answered. I just hope not. He hadn't told her how urgent he considered it to stay close to Marjorie. After that phone call, it would just rattle Gladys. Besides, he believed he knew what her objections to Marjorie Langley were.

In a broad, shallow valley the river formed a serpentine series of sandy turns, coming back on itself while trying to escape its past. In the summer, sand as golden as that on any resort beach formed in the middle of the bottomland. Now in the spring flood the surging water overflowed and made connections with its own coils, forming dangerous pools of cold, murky water. The body from below the bridge followed the circuitous path of the river, never passing over the sandy banks, nor yet rising to the surface.

High on a ladder against the open side of his house Jonas Cloudman was approaching the peak. One broad path down the clapboards was already white. Linda did the trim around the windows while her sister was inside picking up the house. Linda was glad to be outdoors, and Jonas, who hated detail work, was glad to give her the pointed sash brush for the red paint she had selected. Always before he had painted the whole house white, not bothering with trim. It'll bring it to life, Linda had told him. So to please her he had bought the gallon of red and the extra brush and told her to go ahead.

The wood, dry and gray, drank the paint up so that Jonas could scarcely do two clapboards before having to dip his brush into the can again. He had painted it for his wife before she died because he wanted her to see one thing complete. She had been delighted with the white, which she had said made her feel proud. Later in bed she had asked him if the next time they could paint the trim, but he knew the paint would outlast her, so he just turned his face to the clock ticking on the bureau next to him. He hated the paint and was glad to see it wear away to a lifeless gray dirt color. Only when Linda asked if she could paint the trim did he realize that he had left it to weather all the years since his wife had died.

Jonas knew that Sonny Rutherford would be over for her tonight, after supper. What he didn't know, what she wouldn't tell him until after dinner when they sat with their cups, drinking the coffee he now allowed her to make, was that she was going to Newfound with Sonny to a movie.

Beyond the meanders of sandy shores the river stayed to itself, sinking deeper into a valley that narrowed slightly between ridges. The current moved powerfully here, and the twigs and sticks and debris it carried flowed swiftly with the water. Just below the Birches, the final section of Enoch, spread the town of Rumford, a community of shacks and farmhouses so forlorn that it was difficult to distinguish the lived-in from the abandoned. The river ran east of the settled roads, but in the summer the boys walked over to fish and swear and swim and fight. It was yet too early for them to fish there.

•   •   •

Back in Enoch from the side door of the Langley house came Marjorie in a fawn shirtwaist dress. It was a simple dress, decorated only with a tiny bit of embroidery—bouquets of flowers on the collar points that she had done herself the previous week. The wet warmth of the day made her smile as she pulled Peter out onto the porch beside her. He smiled and kept hold of her hand.

"The air is sucking up water from the earth," said Marjorie. "You'll only need your little jacket today."

"Li'll?" Peter said. He looked at her, just barely having to tilt his head upward.

"It's warm. We'll see if we can find some frog eggs."

He let go of her hand and jumped to the edge of the porch. Reaching down under the boards, he pulled a handful of clay-like mud. "Chugrump," he said.

"Come inside for our jackets," Marjorie told him. "Leave your mud on the ground."

Peter hopped to the edge again and shook the wet clay from his hand. He had to do it twice because the first time his fingers forgot to open. He stood up and walked back to the doorway where his mother waited for him. Putting his arm around her back, he went into the house with her. On the fawn-colored dress appeared a shapeless mark of clay.

The two of them in tan poplin jackets walked beyond the garage into the field. The boy's head came barely to his mother's shoulder, but he matched her strides over the wet and soggy ground. Past the stack of hay bales where she practiced shooting, Marjorie turned right, and for a while they walked along the fence that separated Ned Grimsley's farm from their property. Over a little rise was a depression before the trees started to join the forest along the ridge. Lines with flowing sap ran down the hill and across the field to the shack where it was boiled into the last of the season's syrup. By the depression a pond spread into the weeds and small chunks of snow yet left over from winter. Marjorie took Peter's hand and keeping on the pond side herself, walked him around the edge.

"They look like jelly," she told him, "a cloud of jelly."

The edge of the pond was indeterminate and fell or advanced almost with each step they took. Peering into the water, Marjorie hoped they would find something. In past years she had heard the peepers here, and later in the season, when the pond receded, it was easy to spot bullfrogs in the evening making their declarations. From her jacket pocket she took the mayonnaise jar she had brought to keep the eggs in. Then she spotted them.

From the safety of his tractor Ned Grimsley watched them, the stunted idiot boy and his crazy mother, as they crossed the field to their house. One of these days they'll all have guns, he thought. It was too wet to plow, would be for a while longer. It didn't pay to rush things. In this hilly land, you rush things with a tractor, you end up with the damn thing on top of you. Plowing was meant to be slow. He grinned. He knew what plowing meant, and he hadn't done any of that lately either, though Marjorie Langley couldn't have known that. In a weak moment he had wanted to go to her and say, I haven't had anything to do with your husband. Whatever's happened to him, happened without my hand in it. But, he told himself, he hated her too much for that, nor would he tell her what he did know or even suspect.

He had pulled all the lines on the spark plugs before he had seen Marjorie and stepped back because at first he couldn't tell what kind of danger or threat she had passed to the boy. Now he snapped the deep socket into his ratchet and fitted it over the end of the spark plug. Turning the selection to "off," he freed the plug. Then, accompanied by the rhythmic clicks as the ratchet returned, he spun the plug out. It stuck in the deep socket so that Ned had to tap it until it fell into his hand.

"Damn near burnt right up," he said, inspecting the bent electrode.

He pulled the rest of the spark plugs out of the block and from his pocket took the new ones individually wrapped in their cardboard boxes. Holding each fresh plug eye-level, he slid the small blade of his jackknife between the protruding electrode and its contact. That done, he turned them back in their holes finger tight, added a quarter-turn with the ratchet, and snapped the wire connector over their heads. He worked quickly, pleased with the smooth, expected way the job went.

Suddenly he jerked back, looking about, his arm across his chest like a shield. In the open field between him and the Langley's was no one, only the breeze blowing sweet moisture from the wet earth. His hand fell and hung limp by his side. At work, in the noise of the machines, he felt no fear, but he hated work at the mill. With a little money he could go away, to Italy where he had once been happy. It didn't take much to live there. Come summer he might have put enough aside, sell Clay Freeman enough goat's milk or something, so that he could go. Now that his mother was dead, there was no longer any reason for him to stay on with a cranky old man who before long would start to wet himself and a wife whose kindness had reversed and a daughter who seemed to know just enough to make him feel uncomfortable every time he told her what time to be home. By July he could be in Italy, where it was warm and a man could live his own life.

Pulling the snaps from the distributor cap, he unscrewed the points and condenser. Clay Freeman said he had had to dry out the points on his station wagon so often he felt like a tune-up machine. If he kept going over to see Marjorie Langley, Ned thought, he'd have to be some kind of mechanic. Clay was always like that. He'd do business with a snake and never notice the scales. Ned used the screwdriver to reset the snaps as he closed the cover on the new ignition set. The sun on his back felt good, secure. Come July, he thought, I won't care if this bitch runs or not.

Along the line of trees at its new, spring shore, the river flowed rapidly, dragging its accumulated burden downstream, the sticks and debris bumping against the trees and floating into each other. Below the surface churned the mud and stones, made almost animate by the power of the current that rolled them in halting, reluctant movements along the bottom. Like a large slow fish, the body drifted in active suspension between bed and surface, maintaining in its rises and falls a constant downstream momentum. The flesh of the body was a paler color than the belly of a bass, and though the head was smooth like the face of a horn pout, it was neither dark nor horned. Bits of garbage adhered to it as secretions will accumulate around a grain of sand or other piece of offal in an oyster. No coating, however, formed pearls around these attachments, and the water relentlessly washed the thing clean as it moved downstream.

In Rumford the valley broadened, slowing the spreading river. The few houses that had been here had been moved some twenty years before, so that no one stood in the warm afternoon to see the large, fishlike body begin finally to bob to the surface. It would appear only for a moment before settling into the dark water once again. On a small point of the shore, suspended from a tall maple, was a tire swing that kids used to leap into the water, but no kids were there this day because Saturday or not, the water was still too cold to swim. Had they been there they would have wondered at the body bobbing near their swing, for they knew there were no fish that large and white in the river.

At the dairy the men had a late dinner. They had wanted to finish up early, but Sonny still wasn't back.

"Might as well eat," said Jack.

"Can't dance," Jelly said.

Billy's paper filler lay in steam-cleaned pieces waiting to be reassembled. He took the cigarettes from his T-shirt and lit one. "Get me a coffee and a grilled cheese," he told Dubber Handley.

"And tell Flora to slide the meat between the bread on my hamburger," Jack said. "Married to you she might forget that sort of thing."

"She told me next time I got a hard on we should freeze

it," Dubber replied. He pushed through the double swinging doors to the kitchen.

"I thought it was frozen," Jelly said.

"So's that story," Billy muttered, quietly enough so that no one else heard.

While they waited for their dinners, they talked about the bowling league they were going to join. Since there was nothing else to do on Sundays, they had decided to bowl on Sundays, until Jack had found out that the league was all set up for Wednesday.

"How many of us have to be on the team?" Billy asked. Jack told him there were five on a team. "There's only four of us here. Who's going to be the fifth?"

Jelly coughed a bit. "Sonny," he said. "He'll be the fifth, and his father can be substitute."

Dubber brought in the tray of sandwiches. "Sonny's father don't want to bowl regular? I thought it was his idea."

"It was Billy's idea." Jack bit into his sandwich. "God, there is meat in this one, but it's only about the size of yours," he told Dubber.

"You should know," Dubber said.

The laughter in Jelly's throat choked on a swallow of coffee.

Dubber asked if Mr. Land was providing uniforms for the bowling team.

"No," said Jack. "And he ain't tucking you in at night either. And in case nobody told you, don't bring Flora. We might want to stop on the way home for some relaxation, if you know what I mean."

Dubber scratched his head. "I was just thinking if Mr. Land wants us to bowl so as to keep up the good reputation of his business, oughten he to help us along a little with the expenses?"

"It's our reputation, too," Billy said. "It's our reputation mostly. Nobody thinks Mr. Land did anything to Forrest Langley."

They were quiet a moment, as if someone had asked them to pray. Hands quietly raised the remains of sandwiches to mouths, and coffee cups were gently set on the tray so that there was no telltale click. From the front pocket of his white bib overalls Jelly took his lighter and cigarettes. When he lighted his smoke, he turned away from the other men as though there were a breeze blowing.

"You know what I wish?" he said. "I wish the cops would take that son-in-law of mine and lock him up and throw away the key."

"Nothing you can do with Daryl?" Billy asked.

"Nothing you can do with these kids," said Dubber. "Sonny's the same way. Most of the trouble around here comes from kids."

Once again they were silent until Jack said, "Take this crap back in so we can finish cleaning up."

"Can't finish until Sonny comes," Billy reminded him.

Jelly stood up and pointed outside. Around the building came the red truck Sonny drove, milk cans banging into each other as he jammed on the brakes. Without waiting for the truck to stop, he ground the gears into reverse and backed to the loading platform, bumping it just hard enough to send the cans back against the restraining chain.

"Let's go," Sonny shouted, "I've got a date tonight."

All the men except Dubber helped to unload the truck. Dubber, after taking back the dishes, started to work on his machine. Gradually the others came back to their own, Billy to reassemble the paper filler, Jack to clean out the pasteurizer. In the back Sonny and Jelly dumped the milk from the last run. They all finished about the same time.

"Who you going with?" Jelly asked Sonny.

"Linda Cloudman."

"Better not let her old man find out where you're going," said Dubber, "or you'll be buying tickets for three."

Sonny laughed. "Don't need no tickets at the picnic grounds," he said.

"Jonas Cloudman finds you down by that dam, you'll be just one more skinny drift log, floating down the river," said Jack.

Billy grabbed Sonny's arm. "You going to bowl with us Wednesday?" Sonny nodded his head. "Why don't you try out the alleys so you can tell us about them before we go."

"Might do that," said Sonny, "but I ain't skipping the picnic area."

Before leaving the limits of Rumford, the river ran into a dam built back in the thirties in the midst of twin disasters of flood and famine. Now the sluiceways of the dam were open to allow the full river to disgorge itself. From the road a short drive led to an upper parking lot away from the green picnic tables provided for the families of Rumford and Enoch and Newfound, though they seldom went there. Those who did were teen-agers who drove at night, carefully keeping their bottles of beer in their cars, only occasionally leaving white telltale signs of their activities in the bushes a ways from the overlook where people did come to show their children the river. From its spring high the water level would gradually diminish, revealing the naked sides of the riverbanks. On this Saturday there were no picnickers, and when the workman left to drive home to New- found, there would be no one there until Sonny Rutherford brought Linda Cloudman parking after bowling three strings in Newfound.

In the grease pit at his garage Zack replaced the muffler on Duncan Hatch's car. The anodized metal of the new muffler reflected dull gleams from the droplight, the smell of oil and exhaust and grease fouled the air, and Zack told his helper to open the bay door to let some of the fresh air into the station. After tightening the nuts on the U-clamps, he grabbed the tail- pipe and shook it to check for rattles. Satisfied, he climbed out of the dark pit, made out a new inspection sticker, and glued it to the windshield. Then he backed the car out and, leaving the door to the stall open, wheeled the car to Hatch's Diner. He told Duncan it was quiet as a snake.

Davis Scales had had a funeral in the morning, and in the afternoon a body to prepare. It was three o'clock before he started with the makeup, and he knew he'd have to have the body upstairs in the good light before he could finish. He took the body up on the elevator and finished the rouge. When he was done, he hurried to his bedroom and changed his clothes. In his cardigan sweater and gabardine pants he drove over to Hatch's Diner.

After the lunch hour was past, not so rushed but longer than a weekday, Duncan Hatch went down into the storage room and began to lug up the gallon jars of mayonnaise and catsup he would need for the coming fish fry. The supplies were stored in a cage, a chicken-wired frame in the middle of the cellar lit by a single bulb. It looked like a prison cell. Upstairs he helped his chef clean out the Frialators so that the french fries and fried fish would carry no taint of rancid oil.

In the late afternoon the three of them, Zack with his cigar, Davis with one of Duncan's Luckies, and Duncan himself positioned so he could watch the counter, sat in a booth. Little laughter came from the group, and it was not only that Clay Freeman wasn't there, because he was the subject of their conversation.

From the center of the river a strong eddy pushed to the right bank. It carried the body from the bridge, tumbling now in the sunset so that red streaks mottled its smooth white surface. Only one piece of clothing still adhered to it, a pair of sturdy gray pants encircled by a brown belt, visible only from the back, where it was not covered by the swollen guts. Near the shore the flow of the sluiceway pulled it out of the eddy and drew it toward the dam, but it snagged on a low branch and swirled even closer to shore until it lodged between a rock and a cement platform at the base of the dam.

There on the west bank darkness came, and the red mottling disappeared, leaving first a ghostlike white aura, then only a dark shadow against the dark water. Later, when night was on both shores, an animal walked down through the trees to the edge of the swiftly moving river. Along the shore it came, shying from the water, then returning in an uncertain zigzag pattern. Near the dam it saw the body lodged next to the cement platform. Sitting on its haunches, it looked around before running a semicircle so that it could approach from the other side. On the platform it growled, a low and threatening rumble, and approached the body. Again it growled, then tore a hunk of smooth white flesh from it. Out of the hole rose a putrid gas that smelled of rankest decay, a lurid foulness stored for months under the clean and simple water. The animal with the meat in its mouth hurried back into the trees.

Out of the truck Sonny seemed even taller. Illuminated by the light on the sign for the dam, he seemed, as he unhooked the chain that barred the road and slung it across the road, to be one long shadow that ran into shadows. When he got back in, the light from the dashboard showed garish purple on his face and the face of Linda Cloudman, who sat beside him. Past the entranceway the boy stopped the truck, but this time it was the girl who got out, walked back to the metal post, and stretched the chain across the road again.

The parking area that overlooked the dam was dark and deserted, the only light the glow of the cigarette that Sonny dropped out the window of his truck. They moved together, the tall lean shadow and the shorter, smaller one, held each other and only gradually changed positions. A light breeze came from off the river, bringing with it an oddly warm scent. Linda moved to her side of the seat and turned on the radio. Sonny's head moved to the window while he slapped the lighter into the dash with the palm of his hand. When his cigarette was lighted, Linda spoke to him. From under his seat he took a long chromium light attached directly to a square battery, and they both got out of the truck.

The light beamed on the wet earth and growing ferns along the path as they descended. The odor of death, stronger than freshly manured fields, stronger even than hen houses or billy-goat urine, came powerfully at the foot of the path. Linda held the boy's forearm. They stopped walking. After a moment, he pulled her to the cement platform and played the light slowly along the shore. When it got to the river, the light formed little mirrors until it reached the huge, stinking whiteness caught by the rock. It looked like an enormous piece of mucus shaped accidentally by the water into the temporary form of a man. The face was featureless save where a chunk of flesh had been bitten out between what might have been cheek and neck. The body itself was perforated like a weathered and rotted board cast off and forgotten. The eyes were gone completely, eaten away by countless microorganisms of the water. The two lovers ran back up the hill.

16 / *Down the Hatch*

Sunday night Clay Freeman sat with the three murderers who were his friends. The body of his cousin that had lain so long in the river had broken free. Surely now would come the answers to the questions that had festered since New Year's. An end to the ugliness, he thought, an end he hoped to hear the beginning of this night. And not only answers, but action.

Davis Scales, who always drank the first two beers of the evening rapidly, was killing his third. Sitting under the silver-sparkled letters that spelled out Happy Easter along the wall, he looked about with small, dry eyes. Clay wondered if he had been up too late with the body the night before.

"At least it's a good thing he wasn't found Friday night," said Duncan Hatch. He seemed as comfortable here in his lounge as most people were in their living rooms. In a sense, Clay thought, it was his living room. "Or Reverend Treadwell would have had to preach on that for Palm Sunday."

"In my church they don't much do that," Zack said. He puffed his cigar and looked around the table. Clay was surprised to hear him mention the Catholic Church.

"Not a bad idea," Davis Scales said, "because now we'll have to listen to it for Easter. It's been just long enough since the business at Mrs. Grimsley's funeral that he's probably forgotten and will plow right in with another message for us all."

Duncan Hatch loosened his tie. "I don't think he's forgotten the unpleasantness with Ned Grimsley. Treadwell may be thickheaded, but he's not thick-skinned."

"Say, what's going on between Grimsley and Marjorie Langley?" Davis asked.

"Ain't nothing going on," said Zack, "Clay's got the corner on that market, ain't you Clay." He poked Clay with his big hand. His pokes always hurt.

"Grimsley blames her for that business of the funeral sermon," Duncan said. He took one of his Luckies and spun the pack around to Davis. "And for the other losses he's suffered."

Davis took one of the cigarettes and lighted it with his double-action lighter. "Meaning Louise Langley." He waited for Duncan to nod agreement, then smiled.

Clay sipped his Scotch and held his glass midair. He wondered why Davis had mentioned her name. "Marjorie believes he may have killed her husband," he said. He set the glass back on the table. His fingertips went back to the top of the glass and made a web to the rim. "But they're both mistaken."

"Don't get that going again, Clay." Davis Scales tapped

his cigarette in the ashtray with such violence he nearly put it out.

"Kids all moving away now," said Zack, changing the conversation. "I come up here, but I stay in touch with the family in Newfound. Still, I feel more a part of Enoch than I do down there. I've been here most of my life." He drew in on his cigar and let the curling smoke slowly out of his mouth. "When our children go, it'll be to another state."

Clay finished his Scotch. "On the other hand, you take me. I traveled all over the place. You couldn't have made me settle if you'd've nailed my feet to the floor. Still, here I am and likely to stay."

"When you're here," said Duncan. "Christ, you're still gone as much as you are at home. Guess Gladys must have gotten used to your being away a long time ago. Kind of convenient." The other men laughed at that, and Duncan went on. "I mean a guy like you, gone all the time, could have his little flings wherever he wanted and nobody'd be any the wiser."

Davis Scales broke in. "Not like Ned Grimsley. All the time thinking he ought to live where everything is done at leisure—crap. That man was so regular in his habits he came to time in everything he did. Even that."

"Which was why he got caught," said Clay, "and not anything to do with Marjorie Langley nor Timothy Treadwell." He wanted to come back to the murder. There seemed no other subject to talk about, if he could just figure out what to say. After all, it wasn't as if he didn't know something. In his empty glass swirled the ice. "But you can have your pick of women," he told Duncan. "You don't have anyone to answer to."

Duncan looked serious. "I lost my taste for women after my marriage, that is for other women, and I can't seem to reacquire it. Of course, if you take someone with children, like Marjorie Langley, they might look for someone right away. And she's going to have a child all of her life."

"Jonas Cloudman's got children," said Clay.

Davis Scales smiled. "But who'd ever have Jonas Cloudman?"

Duncan was still serious. "Jonas is a good fellow, and he's having an awful time with his daughter. A man ought to be left with sons. Somebody ought to speak to Sonny Rutherford to sort of back off."

"I wouldn't be surprised but about a hundred people have already spoken to him," Clay said.

"May not make any difference now," Duncan said. "Sonny was in here this afternoon, saying ugly as that blob of flesh was, floating in the river like a creature from a horror movie, he'd face ten of them before he'd face Linda's father."

"They ran away from the smell as much as from ugliness," added Davis Scales.

Clay imagined the body white like the fetus of the destroying monster, himself rooted, unable to flee. It turned out Linda Cloudman had phoned the police. Sonny, being struck in an inspired way by an uncharacteristic practicality, wanted nothing to do with the body. He was still baffled by that when Linda put another nickel in the phone to tell her father where they were and that they must wait until the police came. So many police came that it was after midnight before Sonny backed down the access road and drove Linda home.

"Cloudman must have been in a tear," Zack said, a smile forming as though he enjoyed the idea.

"Only because he didn't know they'd stopped at the dam on the way home," Duncan went on. "After a fashion he'd accepted their going bowling, but the parking he hadn't bargained for. I guess he consoled himself with the thought that if they were walking when they discovered Langley, they couldn't very well have been doing other things."

"What did they find in the body?" Clay asked Davis Scales. "Was there anything to excite Henry Dodge?"

The undertaker pulled a cigarette from the pack on the table and lighted it, blowing the smoke out into the middle of the group. "They couldn't even tell who it was. Lucky to identify it as something human."

"Are you telling me," said Clay, "there was nothing they could tell about the murder? I mean the condition of the body—"

"The body was intact," Davis Scales interrupted, "but even if it hadn't been, no one would have known what caused something—say the head—to come off." He took a neat drag from his cigarette and inspected it as he exhaled. "Bullets would be washed away, cuts could have occurred along the bottom, or on rocks, as could bruises. Only a broken bone—you have to realize, Clay, the very flesh, what was left of it, fell off the man like a tender piece of meat that's been stewed too long. Things were gone, eaten away. You couldn't even be sure it was a man."

As Davis described the deteriorated condition of the body, he and Duncan chain-smoked a couple of Luckies, adding to the smoke from Zack's fresh cigar. Clay's eyes, reddened and itching, began to tear, and his throat became dry so that he had to take an ice cube into his mouth and let the cool water trickle slowly over the irritated membranes. In his stomach was a large fist of gas that rose slowly and closed about his heart, threatening to squeeze it until it burst like a prankster's water-filled balloon. Davis told them that once Mrs. Langley had come and identified the body—actually the trousers on the body—she had had it removed to a funeral parlor in Newfound.

"So you couldn't really tell how he'd been killed?" Clay asked.

"Might have been suicide for all I could see," said Davis. He wasn't smoking now. Duncan brought a new round of drinks, and Davis started in on his new beer. "More than likely it was suicide."

Zack and Duncan chuckled. "That would take care of it for Henry Dodge and everybody," Davis went on, "and the way his wife acted, why you might have thought she had known it all along. Many people—men more than women—will hold back their grief until the day of the funeral, out at the cemetery when they'll do something completely off base. That's when they try to jump in the grave, though that's usually a woman. But this woman was as cool as you please. 'That's my stitching,' she said. 'He could have had new trousers, but he just was fond of this one pair, so I had to patch them. Young's from Newfound will be up to get the body.' "

"Just like that?" Zack said. With his cigar he tapped the beat of the words "Young's will be up to get the body."

"Well, you can see why the poor bastard would jump off the bridge," said Duncan. "Now that he's gone, she's been taking out her spite on the town. It's only a wonder she doesn't pick at the boy."

"Wouldn't surprise me if they ruled it suicide," said Davis Scales.

Clay's intestines seemed full of gurgling mercury; it weighed him down and pressed against the bends and creases of the tender tubes of his guts. His heart was firmly gripped. He asked Duncan to get a glass of straight seltzer and pushed his drink aside when the seltzer came. For a moment he thought he was going to vomit; then the first gas climbed up his throat and fled in a rich belch.

"You guys are full of shit," Clay said. "When you grow up where we did, suicide doesn't even cross your mind. . . ."

Duncan looked carefully at him. "Clay, are you trying to tell us something?"

"Isn't a soul could tell you guys anything," Clay said. "My stomach's so bad I can't even take your soda water. Feels like Vesuvius inside there, so gentlemen, if you'll excuse me." Clay slid out of the booth.

Duncan laughed. "It seems to have come on of a sudden. You aren't getting hot flashes on us, are you, Clay? Or are you getting hot for a little widow down the road?"

"Who only just found out that she's a widow," said Zack.

Davis Scales waved his hand in the air. "Oh, she must have known all along. She's had Clay and Cloudman and Timothy Treadwell up there regularly ever since the new year. One to take care of the place, one to take care of her soul, and one to—what do you take care of for her, Clay?"

"Right now I'm teaching her to drive," Clay answered.

His three friends sat on the bitter edge of their teasing. The faint accusations that underlay what they joked about had some scent of truth to them, and Clay could have understood if they felt they had some power because of that. It was the sharpness to their taunting, a knife blade keenly poisoned, that cut into his feeling and left the stinging of an open slice in the flesh. He hadn't been able to say what he knew because he wanted them to tell him. And all they had told him were lies.

The bedroom was dark when he got home, and he left it dark when he woke Gladys up. He could hear her turn to the nightstand between their beds.

"Don't turn on the light," he said. "I talked to Davis Scales about Forrest's body."

"Did you settle anything?" In her emphasis on "you" was the same bitterness she used for anything connected with Langley, especially his widow.

"He's dead," Clay said. "It's a fact now." Truth in a town like Enoch seemed a readily available commodity. Meaning or justice, though, they back order and never deliver, just switch you over to another line of goods.

"I'm sure the interested parties, what few there actually are, had already guessed that." She shifted her pillow on the headboard so that she could more completely lean against it. "Some didn't have to guess. Some knew all along the simple fact that he was murdered."

He didn't want to tell her how right she was. "The body was in such bad condition Marjorie had to identify him by the mend of a tear in the back pocket of his trousers. Funny how cloth would survive the water better than a human being."

"Marjorie, huh," she said. Then her voice softened. "She wasn't spared even that."

"According to Davis, it was a mess right from the start." Clay palmed his shoes to the floor as he talked. Dodge and a state trooper and even a county deputy, all were there waiting for the coroner to come to pronounce the thing dead. That was the one law they understood and agreed on. That done, they could proceed to any action their foolish hearts suggested, but stench had overcome them. They had stuffed Forrest into a canvas body bag and had taken it in the back of Sonny Rutherford's pickup truck to the nearest place, which happened to be Davis Scales's funeral parlor. "They couldn't tell a thing from the body, not even that he'd been murdered." Clay one-handed the buttons of his shirt.

"People already knew about the murder," Gladys said. "Except for you and Henry Dodge, who are the only fools in town trying to find out about it. Finding the body is an embarrassment. Better it had washed all the way out to sea where the salt could have eaten away even his bones. It would have relieved all of you from having to think about the man."

Pulling off his slacks, Clay, wearing only his underpants, stretched out on top of his electric blanket. The cold settled on him. "At the lounge," he said, "the three of them said Forrest committed suicide. There was part of a coil of quarter-inch rope found with him. They said he must have tried to hang himself from the bridge and slipped and drowned."

In the dark he could hear Gladys turn her head on the plumped pillow. "That's crazy," she said.

"Worse," he said. He raised his legs, skimmed off the underpants, and went under the covers. "The three of them are the ones who killed him."

The lamplight gleamed brightly off the cream on Gladys's face. "If you know that, you'd better do one of two things," she told him. "Either you'd better go to Henry Dodge first thing in the morning, or you'd just better forget it."

Clay twisted the dial on his blanket. "Good night," he told his wife. He left the lamp for her to switch off.

17 / *Of Death and Life*

Monday morning it was raining when Clay pulled into Langley's yard to take Marjorie for a driving lesson. In the garage Jonas Cloudman was storing the plastic tubing from the sap collection network, the various lengths and connections spread about him like a puzzle of blood vessels. Sitting beside him was Peter Langley, who as Jonas pointed to them, would select pieces and hand them to Jonas. As he got each one the boy smiled, a smile, Clay thought, that was not simply the random smile of an infant but a real reaction to the world outside him.

"Morning, Jonas," said Clay as he walked into the garage. "See we're just about done with the syrup business this year."

Jonas held the length of pipe in his hand. "The last batch was pretty much down to B. Marjorie said I could take what I wanted and sell the rest to you."

There wasn't much Clay could do with low-grade syrup, no outlet where he could get rid of it. He certainly wasn't going to add it to the mix of grade A and fancy he used for the sugar. Most of his outlets wanted only the best. "You keep it all," he told Jonas. "I have enough to keep me going through next winter."

"Wait, Peter," Jonas said to the boy, who was pointing to pieces of pipe on the floor. "He don't cry when he stays with me now," he told Clay.

"See you're putting a coat of paint on your house," Clay said. "Kind of early to be painting isn't it?"

"Day like today, you'd think so," Jonas said. He turned and put his piece of pipe with a stack of others of the same length. "But I like to start early, and with Linda helping I'll be done in good time."

"What's your hurry?" Clay asked.

"Just a minute, Peter," Jonas said, as though he had acquired Marjorie's way of speaking to the boy. "That goddamn cop came by my place and said it was tax time. 'So,' I says. 'Well,' he says, 'you ought to be careful not to let any paint touch your house less they raise your assessment.' "

Clay looked up at Jonas, whose brows lowered over his wide-open eyes. "He won't let you alone, will he?" said Clay. "But I bet he's running around chasing himself trying to figure out what you're up to."

"That's why I painted the front first," Jonas said.

Clay laughed. Jonas joined in with him, and a moment later to the astonishment of both men, Peter was also laughing. "Maybe," Clay said, "he's catching on to the way things work around here."

"Leastwise Henry Dodge is not a major problem," Jonas said.

Clay didn't know what Jonas meant, though he didn't feel he could ask the small dark man. Some time ago he had put out of his head the idea that Jonas Cloudman could have murdered Forrest, but that had been when he was thinking of individuals and checking them off one by one like stops on his delivery route. Eventually he would discover the one he had missed and thus solve the problem, at least at a factual level. Yet now that he had, accidentally as it were, intuitively, landed upon the facts—what he was quite certain were the facts—he didn't know what to do with them. About Jonas Cloudman, however, he was sure the man was as innocent as he himself.

"Dodge won't quit," Jonas said. "These young punks today don't quit, but I'll tell you something—I know how to make Sonny Rutherford quit." He chose a section of plastic piping from the floor and propped it up with the others of its length.

Peter, who had been waiting to hand him a section, began to sniffle. Jonas, still dark from his last remark, looked at the boy. "You been waiting your turn, and then I cheated you out of it. Well, I'll tell you, Peter, that's the way it seems to go most of the time in my life." He took the next section from the boy and smiled at him as if they had both made a small and slightly embarrassing breach of etiquette.

Slipping into a raincoat, Marjorie came out on the side porch. She said she had seen Clay pull in, but she had had to finish cleaning up the kitchen. "You think it'll be all right in this rain?" she asked Clay.

"You can't make the sun come out every time you want to use your car," Clay said.

Jonas stopped working with the piping. "Can't make the sun come out anytime, and don't you forget it," he said.

Marjorie smiled at him. "Jonas has become a man of many ideas, but we love him just the same."

"Hand me that long one over there, Peter," said Jonas, pointing to some piping in the corner. "We've got to get this done before your mother comes back."

"I'd like to take the other car sometime, Clay," Marjorie said as she slid behind the wheel. "After all, it's the car I'm going to be using after I get my license."

"It's a stick shift," said Clay, pointing to the car in the garage. "You'd better learn on this first before you go onto something else."

"I'd like to get used to it, Clay," she said. "Next time we'll take it. I'll have to have Jonas fill it with gas or start it up or whatever, because it's just sat there since Forrest was killed."

He told her that would be fine. She smiled at him and started the car as he had taught her. Though she smiled often now, Clay had noticed the hitch in her voice when she mentioned her husband, as though Forrest weren't dead, the discovery of his body somehow reviving him in his wife's mind. She backed across the road smoothly enough until she had to brake and straighten the wheels, those actions each being done separately, stiffly. Still, she smiled, and Clay wondered at her unnatural happiness that found satisfaction in grief and pleasure in difficulty.

"Turn down the hill," he told her.

She slowed the car by dropping the shift a gear. "Is this right?" she asked.

She was an attractive woman. Looking at her face, Clay realized how carefully she had applied her makeup. More than the makeup, though, was the glow of craziness, the wildness of a woman who could put on furs and deliver scornful jeremiads, which shook him like a fever chill of the heart.

"Don't lower the gear until you start the hill," said Clay. "If you slow too much before you take the corner, someone will run into you. Anyway, you need the speed to take the corner."

Awkwardly, as though she were raising some heavy unfamiliar object, Marjorie brought the shift lever up, watching to make sure the red line moved back to D. The very motion of taking her eyes from the road and looking at the transmission indicator was made up of several discrete movements, so it was a surprise to Clay when they took the corner evenly, with some speed, and continued down the wet hill. He could see her stiffen when she changed gears, though nothing showed on her face until at the bottom of the hill she went back into drive as naturally and effortlessly as he could have hoped for. As the car, no longer held back, accelerated, she turned to him and smiled. At about thirty-five miles an hour they went through the deep puddle. A hundred yards down the road Clay's car stalled out. He couldn't restart it.

Marjorie began to laugh, a sound neither rueful nor humorous, not quite hysterical. Being with this woman frightened Clay. She's the only woman who makes me uneasy, he thought. Something, living with Forrest all those years maybe, that makes her take the odd turning or choose the off thing.

"I've got to dry the ignition," he told her.

She put her hand on his forearm. She had stopped laughing. "Clay," she said. "I very nearly killed you."

"I'd like to kill the son of a bitch who designed this car," Clay answered, "if ever I could lay hands to his throat."

"But I am serious."

"So am I."

From the glove compartment he took a yellow cloth and went out into the rain. With the hood up like a metal umbrella he leaned far into the engine. He was wrestling with the rubber boot Zack had installed when Marjorie came by his side. As soon as she saw the boot she laughed anew, though this time there was more humor in it. Clay turned to her, his frustration melting whatever reserve he had left. Then he laughed.

"Can you do anything," she asked, "out here in the rain?"

"No," he said. "Let's sit in the car. Maybe it'll dry itself."

"Does this happen often?"

Inside the car she laughed again, her laughter fracturing for a moment the monotonous rhythm of the rain on the roof. Leaning against his door, Clay turned to her and smiled. He told her the boot was supposed to keep the thing dry. It had worked since January.

"Yes," Marjorie said, "and it's hardly rained at all since January."

"How long did it take to dry when you were stuck here last January?" she added.

He shifted in his seat. Gripping the steering wheel, he pressed himself back into the cushioned upholstery. "Then I just had to wait until it got colder," he said. "It's not likely to get colder this morning."

"I'm glad this happened," Marjorie said. "Because even though Jonas told me about your car, I wasn't sure. Jonas says he's going to kill Sonny Rutherford."

"I doubt it." Clay relaxed his hold on the wheel and turned to Marjorie. "There's been enough of that here already."

"Jonas's isn't part of mine."

Clay told her Jonas had never liked anyone dating his daughter. It was common knowledge that the man was hard on all the boys, and of course one of the wildest would come after Linda. But Marjorie said Jonas's anger was something new. "He can't talk to her about it. He's not planning to kill the boy; it's all fear, just fear running through him turning dark as syrup."

"Has he talked to you about it?"

"Round about," said Marjorie. She fiddled with her coat collar, then cracked the window open. "Stuffy in here. Jonas's always so direct about everything that I believe he doesn't want to come upon this, so he either talks far afield of it or says, 'I'm going to kill that kid!' "

"He says that?"

"He said it once, that's why I worry about it."

"It's likely the boy will give him cause," said Clay, "if the girl is willing." He twisted in his seat to catch a look at Marjorie's face. After all, her a woman and with a murdered husband, it wasn't something easy to talk about.

"She won't have to do more than she has." Marjorie looked out the window at the field, her field, where the low white mist was slowly rising against the rain. "It all depends on how much he finds out. And on how much he allows himself to learn. If he was clever, he wouldn't want to know any more than just to keep her from harm, but Jonas is more like me. He's not clever."

Clay had some inkling as to what she was talking about. "Well, what little I know about Sonny Rutherford, I wouldn't go telling Jonas. There wouldn't be much way you'd have of stopping a man like that once he got his mind set on doing something. It surely wouldn't pay to lie to him."

"That's what I said."

"What's that?"

"You wouldn't stop him."

He switched on the ignition. "I'm going to try this again," he said. "Maybe you're right. Next time we ought to take your car, especially if it's raining." The motor turned over, caught, and died. On the second try he got it running and told Marjorie to drive back to her place.

"It's okay," she said when she got out of the car. "You're safe now, Clay."

"You've been awfully quiet about this," he said.

She looked back in the car before he had a chance to slide over behind the wheel. "There are many in town who are quiet because they don't want to know. Of course, there are others who are quiet because they are murderers or friends with those who are."

"I'm not quiet," said Clay. "I just don't know anything to tell you."

She smiled at him. "You're sweet, Clay. You really are."

She leaned in and kissed him, her lips full on his mouth. It was neither the quick peck of friendship nor the automatic kiss of marriage, but the warm press of romance. Instantly he wished he could tell her what she wanted to know, give her the names of his three friends. But that would prevent him from learning the more he felt he had to know before he could be satisfied. Not accepting her kiss merely as his due, he wondered at her. Naturally she wouldn't see herself as part of a mystery, whereas Clay saw her and Jonas Cloudman and Ned Grimsley all as people whose purposes were hidden, whose behaviors were unpredictable. He wondered why his three sad friends had felt they must disturb the regularity of life in Enoch. He himself, he knew, was an open man, as ingenuous as Sonny Rutherford, though with enough age on him not to think it sinister to be cautious. Wonder and delight from Marjorie's kiss filled him. In his sidelong glances when he got home was a surreptitiousness that Gladys immediately perceived.

"If you're looking for your supper," she said, "I threw it out. Warmed-over fish is no meal for you. I did save this." From the burner of the stove she took a heavy soup pan and brought it to him. Before he saw it, he recognized the delicate smell of oysters in the buttery milk.

"That'll be fine," he said. It was his favorite, a taste acquired when he had been on the road. Sitting at the small table wedged under the window, he remembered that oysters were nearly out of season. Only April had an *r* in it.

"I fixed the fish because you said you'd be home on time," Gladys said as she ladled the stew into his bowl. On one side she set his coffee, on the other, a box of oyster crackers. As she had since the boy was born, she sat down opposite him, cradling her cup in her hands and waiting for an answer.

"The car got stalled," he began. He brought a spoonful to his mouth, the liquor from the oyster barely visible in the stew. "Marjorie ran it into a puddle, and then, of course, I still had to go to Newfound with a load of sugar."

"Do you get enough for these lessons to pay for the wear and tear on the beach wagon?" Gladys asked.

He spooned an oyster to his mouth. He tried to make the oysters last so that the last of the liquor went into the same spoon as the final oyster. "Is there more stew?" he said, glancing not at her but at the pot still on the burner. He turned to see her nod her head. "Stalling out doesn't cost anything," he told her. "Zack already put the boot on."

"You didn't go to Henry Dodge," Gladys said, "to tell him about them."

"What makes you so sure?"

"I heard a story today," she said.

She told him she'd finally visited Esther Grimsley, who had told her that Ned was frightened. Ned was frightened of Marjorie, while Dodge worked at annoying Jonas Cloudman. Meanwhile the murderers sat fat and sassy in Hatch's Diner. Gladys reassured Clay that she hadn't told Esther their identity. It was just a figure of speech, I guess, she explained, a lucky figure of speech. There were a lot of people in town frightened because they didn't know anything.

"Even Henry Dodge doesn't have access to all your privileged information," she reminded Clay.

Clay chewed the soft sweet belly of the last oyster. The

liquor too was gone. "And you want me to tell him what I know?"

"What I told you," Gladys said, taking the pan from the stove, "was to either go to Henry Dodge or forget it." At the sink she ran cold water into the pan and scrubbed the ring of milk from the side. "It doesn't much matter if you do tell him, because he's their man anyway. He and everybody else in town knows how he got that job."

Clay clunked his bowl into the sink. "You think they're going to get away with this?"

Gladys swished the bowl clean and spiked it in the rubber drainer. "If anything's to be done, it'll be done by someone like Marjorie. That's why you'd just better stay out of it."

18 / *Do You Love Me, Peter?*

Easter Sunday, April 1, 1956

The lilies in the church gave off a mild, sweet scent. Along the rails in front of the pulpit stood the plants, straight and open. Behind them sat the minister, lost in his white robes. The back of the church too was crowded with lilies, more than a hundred all together, Duncan had told Clay.

After the meeting with his friends Clay had been a week in doubt. He had gone to Treadwell, hoping he might write a sermon to stir the innocent and move the guilty. He had been loud in his encouragement, but silent about his friends.

"I have chosen for my text this morning," began Treadwell, "the question the Lord asks his disciple, 'Do you love me, Peter?' "

Clay looked at the congregation. There was no sound save a cough from Ned Grimsley. Of course, he couldn't see their faces.

"The third time after the Resurrection that Jesus revealed himself to his disciples," Timothy said, "he found them fishing early in the morning. They were working men and men who needed to eat. They were also frightened men, afraid of what might be done to them because of their association with the Lord. Jesus came to them and told them they were to catch fish and helped them cook breakfast. Fresh fish—a far cry from one of the men's pancake breakfasts." Timothy smiled. Clay, who supplied the syrup for those breakfasts, grinned. "But maybe not so far as from here to Galilee. After breakfast Jesus three times asked Peter, 'Do you love me?' " Timothy looked over the congregation. Clay looked too, and for the first time he saw that there, sitting at the aisle edge of one of the front pews, where no one usually sat, was Marjorie Langley. "Do you love me, Peter?" Treadwell said. And again, "Do you love me, Peter?"

There was movement in the congregation, the kind of shifting in the pews that showed ease rather than discomfort. " 'Then,' said the Lord, 'tend my sheep.' Each time Peter answered, 'Yes,' and by the third time he was getting upset because Jesus kept asking as if he doubted Peter, each time Jesus said, 'Feed my sheep, take care of them if you love me.' Now," said Timothy, "this was not just Jesus' charge to Peter, it was the very definition of love."

Soon Treadwell as usual was talking about Cyprus or India, saying there is always hope. There is, Clay thought, always. Soon the minister spoke of the Last Supper and betrayal. Then he told a personal story about some cousin in Massachusetts who wouldn't look after his mother. Clay wondered what effect his words had had on the minister.

From the choir Clay could hear the rustling of bulletins against the robes. Through the windows on the right came the sun, stained bright and hot. Perceptibly, the sermon changed.

The tone of the minister's voice when he said "love" and "tests" and "trials" was desolate. Davis Scales sat with his family in the ease and dignity all of the Scales had. Only a tilt of his shoulder betrayed Davis's displeasure with the minister. Duncan Hatch, sitting in the Harmes pew, twitched. Clay knew he too had sensed the drift and current of the sermon.

"Nor will it comfort us to think that Peter was a coward. No, Peter was a man like ourselves, and the only comfort comes from the hope of God's love. When the priests and officers came armed with clubs to arrest Jesus, Peter stood up to them. He drew his sword and cut off the ear of one of them. In physical courage he was not lacking, but when he was asked if he was with Jesus, he denied it. Even when they recognized by his accent that he was from Galilee, he said he didn't know what they were talking about. The sword of truth never left his scabbard because he lacked trust in the power of love.

"In the night in the garden when Jesus asked them to watch with Him, they fell asleep. One of them betrayed Him, and a group of men took Him away. They let Him die alone and shut themselves up for fear. But when He came back to them, they were renewed and given strength, and they went on to found the church in His name. 'Greater love than this hath no man, that he lay down his life for his friend.' With the evidence of Christ's love before them, they became new men. And Peter, who in his denial had failed the Lord, was thrice asked 'Do you love me' and three times was told, 'Tend my sheep.' "

Now as Clay swept his eyes over the congregation he was no longer thinking of their reaction but of his own, of making the trust and faith and hope and love into the justice they could do, that they ought to do, that he believed they would do.

"The death of a single man may bring light and life into the world, for it was not only Jesus who was resurrected but his disciples."

Clay shut out the words. No longer did he look at the backs of the congregation. Nor did he think of their reactions. He stared out through the windows, seeing only colors. When the service ended, Clay discovered that his arm, laid along the top of the pew, had fallen asleep.

In the doorway Clay listened to Treadwell speak to his parishioners. Timothy's face glowed, though few said anything except "Happy Easter." Marjorie looked him in the eye and told him that he had courage. The Grimsleys said nothing. But Davis Scales spoke to Clay.

"What about Judas Iscariot?" His voice was cold and dry.

"What about him?"

"What happened to Judas?"

"He hanged himself," Clay said.

"There wasn't much hope for him, was there?" said Davis. "Nor love either."

19 / *Man on a Tractor*

In back of the house Ned Grimsley attached the spring-tooth harrow to the tractor. After securing the three-point hitch, he leaned against the green paint of his John Deere and looked west to his land. It dried easily, this land, and its dark soil was ready to be turned over. On the other side of the fence ran the plastic tubes that carried clear sap to Langley's shed, where it was boiled down. Over there too stood the awful stack of hay bales. Ned mounted his tractor and threw the hydraulic lever on the dash to raise the harrow. The sun on his back warmed him as he sat on the old cushion that padded the metal seat spring behind the big rear wheels.

He drove down the incline to the level land he planned to plant. When he got to the flat area, Ned put the tractor in neutral and lowered the harrow so that the tines could pry into the ground. A sudden flock of grosbeaks, a stream of yellow and black, flew over him and settled in the trees of the hill opposite. He set the tractor in gear, raised the throttle lever, and made his first pass. The ground, soggier than he had expected, held the tractor back. Big chunks of earth fell off the cleats of the tires as they turned. Ned shoved the throttle lever higher, racing the motor against its governor, then cut it back. He made another pass before he saw Marjorie Langley.

She was without the boy this time, but she carried the rifle and the hateful sheet of paper. He had just begun to turn the tractor into the next pass when he saw her, so he sat there between the wheels, watching her. Like a boy hunting squirrels, she carried the gun easily, with one hand gripped around its neck. She wore boots and did not seem to mind where she stepped.

When she was even with him, he completed the turn and made another pass to the end of the field. He stopped there and watched her walk up to the bales of hay and fix the sheet of paper with the hand-drawn image of a man down its length. Idling roughly, the tractor vibrated the seat so that Ned appeared to be slightly palsied as he watched her. The woman walked back from her target, turned and raised the rifle in a single motion, and squeezed off a shot. The thin paper, struck at its center, remained flat against the hay. Ned pushed the throttle lever and started back across the field.

Looking behind him, he saw the teeth bite into the earth and reveal its wet dark interior. Steadily the metal of his seat sprung him above the two wheels. Facing forward he saw Marjorie Langley fire again at the paper man. She ejected the shell and turned to watch him. With her hair secured under her kerchief and her face struck by the side, she was a pretty woman. Despite himself Ned smiled at her.

When he saw her raise the rifle, he hunched down and jammed the throttle lever. Past the plowed section he remembered to raise the harrow. He looked back to see it up and the woman standing with her rifle shoulder-high and aimed at him. The governor slowed the motor until he got to the incline; there he began to get some power. Partway up the hill the wheels stuck, and as quickly as you could watch it, the tractor spun on its axle, turning the man upside down and driving him with the full weight of the tractor headfirst through the spring teeth of the harrow.

20 / *Candlepins*

"That's a son of a bitch of a way to go," said Jelly. "What'd you get, there, Jack? Is there a sleeper behind the seven?"

Jack Niles stepped aside so that they could see down the alley, and Jelly wrote down the score. After years of writing dates and weights, Jelly had earned a reputation for both accuracy and neatness, so when they had first gone bowling, he had simply taken the chair at the scorer's table and no one questioned him. Though with the lowest average, he bowled in first position; his occupancy of the chair gave him an authority he had not had since Jack Niles took his foreman's job.

Billy Harmes was sitting at the edge of the bench beside Jelly. He bowled in second position. "She called the ambulance right away," he said, "but I guess it wouldn't have mattered when she called them."

"No," Dubber Handley said, "she didn't call the ambulance. His wife did."

Billy took a cigarette from the pocket of his T-shirt. "Okay, but she called his wife. Mrs. Grimsley probably said she'd call the ambulance. Mrs. Langley probably knew it wouldn't do any good to call anybody."

"With the feelings between those families," Jelly said, "it's an outright wonder she called anybody. It's a wonder she just

didn't leave him out there for someone to come upon un-
awares."

"She ain't like that," said Billy. "When her husband beat
me up, she came out to help me into the truck. With him standing right there, too, glowering at her. I do believe if it hadn't
been for her, he'd've come at me again."

Dubber Handley gurgled a little laugh. "This ain't the same
woman," he said. "This is a woman with a gun."

Jelly wrote down the score for Jack Niles's second frame
and went up to bowl. There had been considerable disagreement
as to who should write down his score. Sonny, being closer to
Jelly than anyone, thought he should do it, but Dubber pointed
out he couldn't add so that anyone could tell it from multipli-
cation or spelling. Since no one much wanted to give Dubber
any honor, he was eliminated, and though it was okay for Jelly
to keep Jack's score, the reverse wasn't true, so that left Billy
Harmes. Besides, Billy made neater figures than even Jelly did.

"Did she have a gun with her?" Jack Niles asked. He sat
in Billy's place on the bench.

Sonny Rutherford stretched his long legs under Billy's chair
at the scorer's table. "Linda told me she took it out most every
day. She said her father told her Mrs. Langley would practice
at some hay bales."

Jack Niles said, "Jonas Cloudman's going to be practicing
on you if you don't stay away from his daughter. You're just
going to be one long piece of winter meat."

"But did she have it with her yesterday?" Billy asked.
"When Grimsley—"

"They didn't find any bullets in the body," Dubber interrupted, "though God knows with that spring-tooth harrow they
must have found holes enough."

"Turn a man into a goddamn saltcellar," Jack Niles said.

Jelly rolled a spare in his first frame. He was, for a change,
having a good string. Billy crossed the box with a diagonal line
and blackened in the upper half. On his next ball Jelly bowled

a strike. Though his average was the lowest, he got more marks then the others on the dairy team. If you could keep your balls out of the gutter, Jack had told him, you'd be a hell of a bowler. Jelly told him he could remember the days when Jack couldn't keep his ass out of the gutter.

"You know," Jelly said when he sat back at the scorer's table, "Henry Dodge will be wanting to make something of this. Something of its own or something connected to Langley, I don't know which, but I know the silly bastard'll try."

"What's he think," Sonny Rutherford said, "Marjorie Langley pushed the tractor over on the man?"

"Not that she wouldn't have wanted to," said Dubber. "That's your third ball, ain't it, Billy?"

"No, it's his second," Jelly said. "This ain't the bottle operation here, Dubber. There are other folks can count beside you."

"Counting's one thing; adding's another." Dubber sat twisted on the bench, one leg crossed high on the thigh of the other. He watched the alley, swiveling his head back to talk.

Jack lighted a cigarette. Both of his arms were stretched out along the top of the bench. "Maybe this time the fool won't try to connect it back to us," he said.

Dubber Handley snorted. "He's just trying to make a name for himself, and he can't get any closer to the Langley case than he could to a wild horse."

"Wild horse!" Jack laughed. "Henry Dodge's so foolish, he couldn't sneak up on a lake, even if it was winter and frozen a foot thick."

"Too bad on the split, Billy," Jelly said. He turned to the others. "Billy just punched out the middle and then put the next two balls through the same place." He wrote the 4 down for Billy's frame. "Come on, Sonny, you're up. See if you can bowl on the high side tonight."

Gangly Sonny was an erratic bowler. He owned both the high and low strings for the team. One night right after they had started the team, he had bowled 138, but that included a zero frame. The following week, using the same style of running to the left side of the alley and heaving the ball in a great loop that half the time caused it to bounce on the alley surface, he rolled a 56. If we were money bowlers, Dubber had told him, that wouldn't even get you a ride home. I got my truck outside, Sonny had answered him, and I ain't going home.

Billy lighted a cigarette and gave one to Jack. "Could she have," he began, "you know, done somethin' to the tractor?"

"Not her," said Jelly. "Jonas Cloudman. He knows enough to do it and enough so's you wouldn't know it later. Or he could have slipped over later and fixed it back again. Ain't no way Henry Dodge would outfigure Jonas Cloudman."

"Except the man ain't devious." Jack sat forward on his bench. "I ain't saying it was an accident. Though God knows better men than Ned Grimsley have been pushed into the ground by tractors. But if she thought he had something to do with what happened to her husband, she'd've found a way to harm him."

"Everybody's been so quiet about her husband," Dubber Handley said. "I suppose she figures they'll be the same about this."

"What to hell is there to say?" Jelly asked. "It ain't like anybody knows anything in Grimsley's case."

"She was there," said Billy. "She knows."

When Sonny changed places with Dubber, the tall boy gave him a little goose. Dubber kept going to the alley, then grabbed a ball as it rolled up from the machine, and turned to Sonny. "Someday you'll go too far, bub," he said. "I may not be the man to do it, but I hope I'm around to see it." He turned and sighted his bowl. He was the only one on the dairy team who used the spots. And he was the slowest bowler on the team. He was also the only one whose average kept improving.

"Understand Clay Freeman's going great guns with that maple sugar business of his, now that he's tapping on the Langley place." Jack snickered.

The men at the dairy liked Clay Freeman, not in the way most everyone in Enoch liked Billy Harmes, in that he was always on the right path and helped other folks and seldom had a bad word for anyone, but because Clay had all the pleasantries of a salesman who wasn't trying to sell them anything. He would, they thought, just as soon give the stuff away as sell it, as long as it was moving. But of course, unlike Billy, he was still a target for criticism.

"Understand it ain't only trees he's tapping up there," said Jelly. He wrote down Dubber Handley's score for his first frame. "I guess he's getting a little right there at the house. Jonas Cloudman ever say anything about that?" he asked.

At the mention of Marjorie Langley's hired man, Sonny sat up and stopped playing with his fingers. "He don't talk much about her," Sonny said. "I ain't heard him say anything about the two of them, except about the syrup business or learning to drive."

Jack said, "Not that he would say more than two words to you anyway—'get' and 'out.' " Jack grinned and clasped his big hands together between his legs.

Jelly wrote down Dubber's second frame. "I don't believe Clay Freeman would be that foolish. I've never known him to be pussy happy." He covered the score sheet with his huge chest and clutched the table to him so that Dubber, who had been leaning over, was shunted back. "You can check my goddamn adding later. You know within a half pin what you got all the time anyway." He looked up and saw the alley in front of him empty. "Come on, Jack, let's finish this string off."

Jack began rolling the final balls of his string. The men watched him. He usually had a good first ball, then chipped away with the next two, seldom getting a spare but almost never wasting a throw. Below his name was a row of 8's and X's. He picked up the spare in his ninth frame.

"We got a chance to beat them," said Billy. He looked up and saw that Jack had heard him. "Just bowl your usual, Jack," he said.

"How do you know Clay Freeman's getting some?" asked Sonny.

"The only other man up there's your future father-in-law," Dubber Handley said. He reached over and grabbed Sonny by the leg. "You two planning on a double wedding ceremony, father and daughter, widow and gink?"

Sonny took the hand from his leg and twisted it back against Dubber's thin and hairy wrist until Jelly told him to let go.

"Has somebody seen them?" asked Sonny, "that's what I meant."

"Ya," said Jack, "and maybe Ned Grimsley's been watching them, which is why he ain't too handy at driving tractor anymore."

"Throw your ball, for Christsakes," Jelly said. "People in this town already know more than they want to, without somebody sitting trying to learn more. Or figure out more."

Jack threw a strike, so they had to wait for him to bowl again. It was the first match the dairy team had won. Out in the parking lot Sonny stopped Jelly for a light. They watched Jack get into Billy's car and the two drive off. Dubber had to go somewhere to pick up Flora. Sonny looped his arm around the side mirror of his truck.

"You figure Clay Freeman is tapping Mrs. Langley?" he asked the fat man.

"You got to figure a woman like that might want a man who'd speak to her as if he thought she was something more than a cow or a machine."

The moon was down, and from the dark parking lot the sky looked full of stars. Sonny flicked an ash from his smoke and looked back at Jelly.

"I like Clay Freeman," said Sonny. "I wouldn't want to see him into trouble."

Jelly took a drag and set his hands on his hips. "You went on home now, you'd save yourself some trouble. End of the year that girl'll be out of school and on her own."

"Ain't everything waits for a guy," Sonny said.

"She won't wait, maybe she ain't worth hurrying for. Jack hurried a woman, don't you know."

With his right hand Sonny removed his cap and, still holding the cap, ran his nails along his chin. "Ya," he said, "I
thought of that one too."

"Let me ask you something, Sonny. You think Jonas
Cloudman could have misrigged that tractor?"

Sonny laid his cheek on his arm. Jonas Cloudman had had
to wire and shim every piece of equipment in his yard, and,
hired out, he had done enough regular fixing to call it a job.
"He could have," Sonny said. "He's got the smarts, but I don't
believe he would."

"What I'm saying is whether he did or not, he could."

21 / *Confession*

Marjorie Langley stood in the square of sunlight that formed in
front of the sink. After Forrest was killed, she hated doing the
dishes. She supposed she had always hated washing them,
though she had never thought to complain. To whom would she
have complained? Lately she had begun to use the time to think.
Because there were fewer dishes dirtied, she let them accumulate all day so that she could stand in the midmorning spring
sun and think. She thought about Ned Grimsley's death, Jonas's
hatred of Sonny Rutherford, and her husband's murderers. She
wondered if she should be afraid of the town.

All during the long week between Christmas and New
Year's she had been afraid. Afterward she had had no time for
fear. Not quite true, she reminded herself, for she had loaded
the rifle and set the lock on the door. Only later had the gun
become anger. She wondered if they would try to hurt her for
that. Men did that, she knew. They were never content to let
things reach an equilibrium, a point of rest, a balance.

From the corner came the sound of a truck shifting gears. With pieces of scrap wood Jonas had given him, Peter had built a barn and loading platform to which he backed a toy stake truck. Had Billy Harmes come back for Forrest, perhaps that would have been just. But the boy wouldn't have, hadn't. Of that Marjorie was certain.

She wished she were certain about Ned Grimsley. Enmity, acre after acre of it, lay between them, though enmity wasn't murder. The glasses done, she put the dishes into the soapy water. Never knew there was a plan to cleaning dishes, Forrest had told her one night. It's not a plan, she'd answered, it's just the way they're done. She hadn't killed Ned. It was an accident.

If Clay knew something, he'd tell her. He wouldn't let them hurt her. On the window ledge sat a ring keeper, her wedding band and diamond tight over the upright post. Margorie grazed it slightly and set it rocking like a cradle. *If Clay knew something*—she feared he might not, because no matter how friendly they were to him, he, like Forrest, was from the Birches. He was an outsider as far as they were concerned.

A dish gleamed in the sunlight. She let them air-dry. No more toweling dry, for what did it matter if they sat in the dishdrainer until noon? Jonas said little. Even if he heard, he said little. Maybe if she told him how it had happened, he would warn her, if warning were necessary. About Sonny Rutherford he talked to her, talk that frightened her with its revelation of the part of Jonas that could flash out of his small dark frame. But telling Jonas would create a sort of obligation, and Jonas didn't like obligations. Clay, even without the explanation, would feel the obligation. Already did feel it, she knew. If she knew so many things, she said to her vague reflection in the last dish, why didn't she know who had killed Forrest?

A warning of what could happen might help Jonas, even if when he talked he seemed to think of himself as beyond help. If only my wife were alive, he'd tell her, never completing the sentence. But then, thought Marjorie, he probably knows what happened anyway. Knows and says nothing to anyone. The fry-pan done, she took the ring keeper from the shelf, held it a moment in the sunlight, then returned it, her rings still on the post. She wouldn't tell Clay. She'd tell Timothy Treadwell. If it was to be anything like confession, she might as well go to a minister, a minister and an honest man. It didn't occur to her just to keep it to herself.

A little before noon Jonas Cloudman came into the house. She asked if he was coming back after lunch. She wanted to visit the parsonage awhile and wanted him to watch Peter. Lately, Linda had baby-sat some for folks, including the minister. Jonas preferred when she sat for Marjorie, because that gink was never here, nor did he pick her up in his truck, pirate flag flying from the radio aerial, when she worked for Marjorie. Goddamn marauder was what Sonny Rutherford amounted to, marauder. It was only a hope that by talking to Marjorie Langley he could keep himself from laying hands on that harebrained boy. Hope was about all she had to go on, too, he guessed. He wondered how she felt about Grimsley, a man Jonas wouldn't call innocent even if he hadn't a thing to do with killing her husband. What man could you call innocent? Clay Freeman, maybe, though what he was up to with his cousin's widow might give pause to think, Jonas allowed, considerable pause to think. So he told Marjorie he'd be right back without even a second cup of coffee, and on the way home he took pains to think about Marjorie and Clay Freeman.

In the kitchen, food was already on the table. On his lips was his wife's name. Linda, her face fresh washed, came in from the bathroom.

"Sit down, Jonas," she said, "it's all ready."

It looked like Sunday. Sundays with his wife had been quiet, for she had asked him to do no more than milk and feed up. At first he had rattled around in all that loose time. Then he had gotten used to playing with the babies or going for a walk or just sitting with her in the parlor listening to whatever she had turned on on the radio. Now the radio, always playing softly, was in the girls' room, where he seldom heard it. And he had gone back to filling up Sundays with his chores.

"Is this a holiday?" he asked his daughter.

"This morning I had to see Reverend Treadwell," she said. The amount she put on her plate showed she had more appetite. Lately she'd eaten no breakfast at all. "Instead of rushing back, I came home for a while." Linda looked up at him, her ponytail sweeping her shoulders with the motion. "I'm going back to the academy after dinner."

"Your mother'd be proud of the table you set," Jonas told her, "even to the coffee." Up at the school Sonny Rutherford could swing in with his blatting truck right at noontime and take her off to the sandpits. But she had come home to fix him his dinner. Jonas smiled at her. One thing in this world he had never cause to doubt was this girl's love. "Where's that from?" he asked, knowing she wanted him to.

Linda picked up the small blue ceramic creamer. Inside was white glaze, the color of the cream she had nearly filled it with. For a terrible moment Jonas imagined it a gift from Sonny Rutherford, then the girl said, "For baby-sitting." She said the Treadwells had given it to her. Out on a tray it had come when Mrs. Treadwell had brought coffee for her and the minister. She had told them, "That's a pretty creamer. Even Jonas would like a creamer as pretty as that." And they had given it to her.

Jonas lingered with his coffee. With the money he was making she could fix up the inside of the house, put something into the girls' room. Make it look nice, just as they'd painted the outside. "I earn my money," Jonas said. "I don't care who sees it."

She said she might not be there after graduation. She began to clear the dishes to the sink, carrying fewer than usual with each trip. "I might go away, Jonas."

From behind his shoulder she poured more coffee into his cup and moved the creamer beside it. "I don't know what you mean," he said. He turned quickly in his chair, catching a few drops of hot coffee on the back of his hand, when she jerked away. "I don't know what you're talking about."

"College," she said, "or a job or something. Something like that, Jonas."

He drove her back to the academy, remembering when he got there that he hadn't drunk the coffee she had poured for him. On the way he had wanted to tell Linda that he thought Marjorie Langley was going to visit Clay Freeman for some business Gladys Freeman would have closed accounts on, but Jonas didn't gossip, even to his own children. Something else had stopped him, which he thought just as well because when he got to Marjorie's, he believed she was indeed going to the parsonage. She did.

After lunch, Clay started boiling syrup. He had always found it hard to work while he was talking with somebody, at least when he was talking seriously with somebody. For so many years talking had been work, had been the source of his income and the satisfaction of his accomplishments, that now it was difficult to make sugar and conversation simultaneously. Making the sugar was only a means to an end, and even now he more enjoyed taking the giant jars of cakes and cardboard boxes of wrapped maple leaves into a store to cajole the owner until he accepted these with a promise of more in a week. It was the great power of salesmanship that was, for Clay, so much more fascinating than the mere production of candy. That any woman could do.

Opening the back door, he stood outside while the syrup came up to heat. Across the valley he could see the ridge and Langley's farm, its white barn bright in the morning sun. The trees, well leafed now, hid the river, though he knew it flowed slowly but still high. Only in August would the rocks begin to show. Down where it curved around Langley's land, the lower pasture in which grazed some forty Holsteins, the green of the water weeds would touch the surface. Higher up on the mountain was the Birches, almost directly behind Langley's place.

He had left it all behind, Clay thought, all but the meanness. He had had to take that with him. Maybe, he thought, that's what got him the land and the barn and the house, and in the end it had killed him.

Back inside, the syrup had boiled over, forming new rivers along the porcelain sides of the electric stove. Clay pulled the pot from the burner, cursing as he did so. He got the paint scraper from its place on the shelf, but the syrup had not yet hardened, so he replaced the scraper and left the sweet mess on the stove. As the burner cooled he set the pot back on it and watched the bubbles rising from the bottom. Quarter-sized, they were nearly big enough. In a little while he would be able to pour it into the molds, making dozens of maple leaves.

Clay thought he would see Marjorie first. Dangerous she might be, but not to him. Well, she wouldn't shoot him. And Gladys wasn't worried about her shooting Clay. He knew what she was worried about. Of course, like so many times, she was half right.

The syrup flowed into the molds and over the molds because Clay filled every form to overflowing. Between the leaves grew drops and even whole thin lines that might have been stems had they been placed at the base of each outline. Instead they were random, erratic, and the result was that they looked as though someone had come along after the molds had been filled and dribbled the dregs all over the surface. At least, Clay thought, it won't be wasted. The candy dripped a golden contrast to the heavy black of the rubber molds.

When all of the cakes and leaves and hearts and stars had been weighed, packaged, and sealed, Clay drove his station wagon around back, and opened the tailgate like a giant mouth. He filled the cargo space with his wares. Though there were three resorts in the White Mountains that he had to reach (and it was already past noontime), first he was going to go to see Marjorie Langley. What he had to tell her, he had decided, would be less than what Gladys had asked. The tailgate slammed down on his load, and without saying good-bye to his wife he left the house. On the way down to the bridge he pushed the button on the dash to lower the window in the tailgate so that he could have some breeze blowing through the car. When he got to Langley's place, the only vehicle in the yard was hers, and he wondered where Jonas Cloudman was.

FOUR

Sorrows

22 / *Visitors*

Clay had not planned to sleep late. Had he gone home after returning from the mountains, he still would have been late. But when he had stopped to tell Marjorie that Ned Grimsley was not her husband's murderer, she had made him promise to return. And when he had returned, he had noticed how carefully she had chosen her clothes, the muted red of her lipstick complementing her blouse.

All the years on the road not once had he betrayed Gladys. Not once had she spoken a word of jealousy. Now with reason she was suspicious. His allegiance was confused. After he had made love to Marjorie, he had told her the names of his three friends who had killed Forrest. Though he had added explanations to conditions, he still couldn't judge his betrayal.

Now a male voice in the living room woke him. Gladys was gone from the bed. The shade was white. It was even later than he had thought. His clothes just on, he met Gladys as he opened the bedroom door. He was thankful that she hadn't yelled to him. Henry Dodge was in the living room.

"Thought you might be up by now," the cop said.

In full uniform he sprawled in the armchair as if he expected a servant to bring him a drink. Gladys, nobody's servant, noisily slid dishes from the breakfast she and the boy had eaten into the sink. She could hear and be heard. Clay noticed Dodge didn't have his little notebook out. Nor was there evidence of it in his shirt pocket. He had come, then, unofficially, empty-handed except for a potentially frightening sociableness.

Leaving the cop alone in the living room, Clay went to the kitchen and set an egg to boiling. From the refrigerator he took a quart of milk, shook it to blend the cream, and poured a juice glass full. As he passed by the sink Gladys grabbed his belt loop.

"What's he want?"

"To be bigger than he is," Clay told her.

She let him go.

In the living room Dodge started talking about the Red Sox. Fourth last year, Clay thought they had ought to do better than that this season, particularly if Williams hit over .300 again. Ted Williams, Dodge said, is just about over the hill. Besides, the Yankees were hot again, and the Yankees stay hot.

"You want to know what it is?" the cop asked. He leaned forward in his chair. "Pitching. The problem isn't we don't win games. The problem is we lose them, lose them because we don't have the pitching. The last great pitcher we had was Babe Ruth—and the Yankees got him." Clay was about to say that the Yankees had turned Ruth into a hitter to win games when Dodge changed the subject. The milk in Clay's juice glass went down in tiny sips.

What Dodge wanted to talk about was Ned Grimsley. In detail he talked about Ned Grimsley, the man's affair with Louise Langley, business that had started when Henry Dodge wasn't old enough to know what it was. Nor did he now, Clay thought, though it was obvious the cop had had his ears filled by some-body. Dodge had discovered Grimsley's hatred for the town, his argument with the Langleys, even the fact that his wife had threatened to leave him.

"Sounds like you've done a thorough investigation," Clay said. "I'm sure I couldn't have told you half as much." Nor would I, he thought. Outside, gallons of syrup waited to be turned into sugar, a batch that would keep him busy all day. And he wanted to be busy all the day, watching the bubbling syrup thicken, thinking about last night. Thinking of Treadwell asking him if he was frightened of Marjorie made him smile. The only person to be frightened of last night had been himself, not Marjorie. In the kitchen Gladys began to wipe the plates and set them in the cupboard.

"You can tell me about Marjorie Langley," the cop said.

Only when he turned back to Dodge did Clay realize he had glanced out to the kitchen where Gladys was pulling knives through a dish towel. Dodge reached to his shirt pocket as if to pluck out the notebook that wasn't there. It seemed he wanted Clay to say something specific, something Dodge might already suspect but wanted confirmed.

"Ned's death was accidental," Clay said. From the kitchen came the sound of silverware being dropped into the tray in the drawer.

"Maybe," mumbled Dodge. He said there were a lot of details to know in a town like Enoch, a lot of information. Only recently had he learned of the connection between Marjorie and Clay. A moment of silence for Clay to ask how he had learned passed. When the moment was gone, Clay said that Marjorie was his cousin's widow.

"You know, Clay," Dodge said, "I don't like things to look bad." Clay thought this was a young man with old ideas. "She makes me look bad. Not that something's wrong." Now Dodge looked out to the kitchen, his eyes staying there as he talked. Enoch, according to Dodge, had a lot of hitters, more than might show on the roster. Even Marjorie was a hitter, maybe more than people knew. What it all needed, though, was organization. What it needed was a pitcher. "I intend to be the pitcher, and I can throw curves as well as fastballs."

Clay had played baseball. He knew it wasn't the pitcher who controlled the game. It was the man behind the plate, who could see the whole field, and if that was what Dodge wanted to do, he ought to be catching.

It was after one, and Jonas hadn't returned. Marjorie wasn't even sure what chores he had planned for the afternoon, though she was certain he had mentioned finishing something up. Besides, his "see you later" was never casually dropped, but always a firm promise.

The last record from *Madame Butterfly* dropped onto the turntable. Because Peter watched the television set now, she had the phonograph on less often. She would look at him, not the screen, so that she could see his smile, the giggles that creased his smooth face with lines. But at night, waiting for either sleep or a visit from Clay, she listened to her records. Sometimes he called. Only rarely did she; then it was usually something about driving or the maple syrup. Nothing from her courting with Forrest had been like the waiting to hear Clay's voice. It must have been, she thought, what that boy from the florist shop had felt. Were she twenty years younger she might well be as giddy as he. No, she thought bitterly, her situation would spare her that.

The night Clay had first come to make love to her, the marks of his struggle were more visible than the expressions of his pleasure. But there were expressions of pleasure. Clay in bed was a far different man. Unlike Forrest, who was the same embracing her as he was tending the farm, methodical, concerned. Except Forrest, in unfamiliar territory, was for once unsure of himself. Whereas Clay was all confidence. It was only the planning of it that raised moral tangles to make him twist and squirm.

At the phone she thought she hadn't talked to Clay since he had told her about the murderers. And about Ned. Today she would take care of Ned. She hoped he had done something about those others. At the very least he should have gone to the police. She spoke Jonas's telephone number to the operator, her voice dry from a long hour's silence. There was no answer, though Marjorie let it ring until the operator came on the line again.

On his bed lay Peter, fully clothed, his eyes wide open. Marjorie watched while he put on his sneakers and tied the first knot. Putting the bows in, she told him they were going visiting. He tried the word out, coming close enough to please himself into a grin. There would be something in that house, she told him, something he would like to eat.

"My, he looks tall," Esther Grimsley said. "Has he started to grow again?"

"It's the shirt." Marjorie smoothed the collar on Peter's shirt. She used little starch because the stiffness irritated the tender skin of his neck. Had Forrest's, too. "I used to keep him in jerseys all the time."

Esther said she had kept her daughters in jerseys. The youngest one, the girl still at home, was always in jerseys and always climbing trees. In the kitchen where they stood was the hot and slightly alcoholic smell of bread baking. Down the sides of Esther's neck ran sweat, shiny on her skin. Her floral print dress, faded and frayed at the hem, bore a white mark of flour at the belly. Without an invitation to sit, Marjorie remained just inside the door.

Peter let go of her hand and wandered to the counter. A finger whitened with flour went into his mouth. At the dry taste he made a face. The two women laughed, Esther saying he'd have to wait for the bread to come out of the oven, then she'd give him a nice slice spread with jam. Then she called her daughter.

"Take him outside to see the goats," she told the girl. "Our goats climb trees," she told Peter. Then she said, "I'll call you when the bread's ready to eat."

Through the window Marjorie watched Peter walking close to the girl, though not taking her hand. The girl, like her father, cast a long shadow. The thin tines of the harrow still attached to the tractor forced Marjorie's teeth together, an ache at the back of her jaw. The girl began to outpace Peter, who had to run. They both ran toward the apple trees. At the last minute the girl slowed so that Peter reached the tree first. Marjorie decided she was not like her father. Peter was like neither Forrest nor her. In the crotch of the apple tree stood a small brown goat.

"Why did you come?"

Esther sat in a ladder-back rocker by the stove. Her voice was flat and cold. Marjorie wondered where Ned's father was. The old man Grimsley, everyone called him. The widower. She knew Esther had cleared the house.

"Where's—" To finish the sentence Marjorie's eyes went to the old man's chair by the stove.

A backward wave of Esther's hand indicated the second story. "He can't hear," she said. "Why did you come?"

"I decided I would before I thought about why." Marjorie thought how they always met in kitchens, these people, over coffee. When she had visited with Hatchy—funny she hadn't thought of that nickname in years, and now Hatchy's husband was a man she wanted dead. What would Hatchy think? Hatchy, who had always wanted to have a cocktail, a grasshopper or something else sweet and colorful, never served Marjorie coffee. Still, when Marjorie would get home again, Forrest would ask, How was your visit? Coffee and visiting, that's what women in Enoch did. The men—well, some of the men drank coffee. And visited, like Clay. She started talking to Esther, talking rapidly while the heavy woman kept in continual motion in the rocker. None of it came out right, in order, logically developed as Miss Sheldon had taught her, as she had always thought of as her forte. Everything was falling apart, the murderers, and Clay, and standing in the field with the tractor turning. She had come to see if there was something she could do, to explain, to ask Esther's pardon, to share the widowhood they both so violently possessed. As it all fell apart, it all crumbled out of her mouth until she found herself still standing, shouting, "I didn't kill him. I didn't kill him."

Tears were on Esther's face and in her eyes. "I thought you knew," she said. "Sit down." Her lips turned up in a smile that met the tears that ran down her cheeks.

"Knew what?"

Esther explained that when she had talked to Marjorie before she thought Marjorie understood that Ned had stayed downstairs New Year's morning, vomiting, milking the goats, doing any number of foolish things except going to the Langley's barn. Marjorie realized she had spoken of Clay's telling her Ned was innocent. But that was all she had said about Clay. She hoped it was all she had said about Clay. Her two secrets—her bumbling lover and his knowledge of her husband's killers—she wanted to keep.

"All of my anger pointed the gun at him," Marjorie said.

"I was never angry enough," Esther said. She pulled a chair away from the table for Marjorie to sit on. Already her heavy arms were freckled from the spring sun. "I never told anyone about him, no one but you, though I guess everyone else in Enoch knew. They must have thought I was the only one who didn't know." Her arm raised up to her forehead as if to ward off a blow. Marjorie thought she was again going to cry. "But even I knew."

"I liked Louise," Marjorie said. She remembered when Esther had come to her after fighting with Ned. No more, Louise had said, no more. Tell her I won't see him. I've already told him.

"Once I got angry," said Esther, "and even then I didn't leave. It didn't even occur to me to make him leave."

As they talked, without coffee, Marjorie was amazed at how similar they were. Married to men as different as Forrest and Ned Grimsley, they should have been different. But their marriages had made them alike. As had their widowhoods. Despite the fact that Esther had always taken a casserole to the potluck suppers and sent fresh bread to the bake sales, as Marjorie hadn't, they were alike. Although Ned Grimsley most of his married life had carried on an affair and now Marjorie had taken a married man for a lover, the two women were alike. Their frankness was warm, pleasant, though Marjorie did not mention Clay or his secret. But Esther shared with her almost joyously, as Hatchy had. The seriousness Forrest had, the sullenness of Ned Grimsley, somehow became funny. They laughed at their husbands. And by the time the big woman got out of her rocker to set the bread to cool, Marjorie understood her. Understood and agreed.

"Keep your anger," Esther said. "They deserve it, and in a place like this, it's all we have." Then she called the girl to bring Peter in for his piece of bread. While he ate it, jam stained the corners of his mouth. The two women laughed, and when he finished, he laughed too.

Because Jonas did not come back to work, Marjorie had to go to the barn to milk the cows. As she was starting, Clay arrived. While he helped her attach the cups of the milking machine to the teats, he told her about Henry Dodge's visit. "Visit," Marjorie thought, it's always a "visit." Probably that's the word they used New Year's. Let's pay him a little visit. Clay hadn't left when the phone rang, so the two of them learned from Dodge why Jonas hadn't come to work.

23 / *Penance*

Jonas Cloudman carried no weapon late in the afternoon when he left his place. The dogs in the yard had looked up from the mud of their sleep when he strode by, neither speaking to them nor grazing their rumps with his boot. In the absence of attention the dogs had looked up, stretched to their front legs, ready to howl before they recognized the short dark man who went off as if there was nothing between himself and his destination except a few moments of filthy time. Nor did he think of weapons as he drove down the road toward Land's Dairy with his elbow slung down outside the window. He looked casual, like a tourist in the wrong vehicle, a salesman in the wrong clothes, but it did not matter to Jonas Cloudman, who for a long time had thought neither of clothes nor vehicles, and who now thought only of the single thing he cared most about.

It was an irredeemable loss, a destruction of the future more than an event of the past, that flooded his mind. Carefully he had rebuilt his faith after his wife had died, wonderfully he had found hope in his daughters. Now the horror of his wife's death revisited him with the destruction of the twin tablets on which he had rested his life. He plunged into a falling where there was no up. All movement in time was descent, and so he thought not of what had happened but only of the emptiness into which he had moved.

Death had once cheated him, had ripped his life apart and left him to mend it anew. But death fled. He could not lay hands upon it. This thing was not death, it would not flee, but grow daily into the future, a part of Jonas's life that no amount of mending would repair. No great distance away was the father of this horror, he who had crushed faith and hope as carelessly as he flipped his hair or drove his truck or draped his gangling self over a chair. In his falling Jonas knew only to clutch him by the throat and take him down into the abyss.

At the dairy Jelly Enman refused to clean out the tanker from the creamery. "Sonny'll be back in time," he told Jack. The foreman, pulling a cigarette from his shirt pocket, raised his eyebrows. "Tell you the truth you can fire me if you think I'm going to get into that sweatbox again."

Jack puffed on his cigarette and looked away from the fat man. "It's a good thing he'll do it for you because I ain't nothing afraid to walk down the hall and put my knuckles on Land's door. And don't you ever forget it, because one day there'll be something you don't want to do, and Sonny ain't going to make it on time to do for you. You know if that truck goes back dirty, Land'll have to pay for it. And you know just about how goddamn much Land likes paying for something like that."

"I told you what I know," said Jelly. "I know you ain't

going to find me inside that tank. You and Land and anybody else can split that up, deal it out, and play four hands around." Jelly undid the strings of his yellow rubber apron and slid out of it. "I'm going home," he told Jack.

When Jonas Cloudman got to the dairy, he saw no one except Dubber Handley. Often Dubber would stay around, still on the clock, if there was someone else to confirm it, even if that person was just Sonny Rutherford. Dubber was an expert in bolt scrubbing, nut counting, grease checking, and any job that would stretch a minimum of motion over a maximum of time. This afternoon he was counting cardboard caps to be certain there would be enough for the next day's runs. There were (and he knew it) thousands.

Jonas Cloudman didn't speak to him but to the walls and machines, the scales and holding tank. In a place usually furious with noise his sudden voice ricocheted sharply about. Dubber had to stand up to see the short man next to Billy's machine, very carefully keeping his distance from the equipment. Dubber looked around behind him to the garage area where the Divco delivery trucks were parked next to the tanker. The driver from the creamery was out front in the dairy bar eating an early supper.

Turning back to Jonas, Dubber said, "He's working on the truck. I don't guess he'll want to see you."

"What's he doing," Jonas said, his voice even lower than usual, "trying to fuck it?" His hands were fist tight. They were dark with sun and grease and work and the angry blood that raced so close to the skin that it seemed almost to burst.

Dubber was silent except to point his finger at the tanker and say, "He's washing it out." The long shiny tank looked like a snake among the rabbit-bodied Divcos. Dubber wrote down the number of caps he had counted and walked down the hall to sit behind the brown veneer door on company time.

The years since his wife's death came on Jonas as double toil. He knew if he didn't finish now, without a moment's thought, he would just lie down and never move again. He could be no more than one of his dogs whose spine had been broken by a car, and even the dog had tried to bite the tires of the car that hit it. It was a terrible thing, Jonas thought, when all a man had left in him was no more than the bite of a broken-backed dog.

From inside the tank came noises of the long-handled brush knocking against the smooth inside skin of the truck. Stripped to the waist, Sonny was in her, just the droplight next to the hose dangling in the hole. Slowly from on top of the truck Jonas pulled the hose back so that he finally held it by the nozzle. Reaching over to the wall, he tightened the cold-water valve, then shot open the valve for live steam. Instantly the hose in his hand came alive, spurting steam and jumping with a violent energy. Jonas yanked the droplight from the tank and threw the live steam in. With the hose held between his legs he bent over the hole and sprayed the steam, smiling as if the raging in his heart had been metamorphosed into some sport.

The roar of the steam overcame the noise of screams, and soon it was the only sound in the garage area of the plant. White mist from the hose filled the tank. It was thick and choking with steam. On Jonas's face as he knelt over the hole was an expression of fierce concentration beaded with sweat. After a while he realized he couldn't fill the tank with steam, so he spun open the water valve. Water, hot from the steam it mixed with, gushed from the hose.

Lowering the droplight so he could look into the tank, Jonas saw that the water had just started to rise. From the tank came the fetid smell of human sweat and excrement. Jonas didn't look for Sonny. He couldn't wait for the tank to fill. He felt suddenly cold and tired. Cutting the steam and water off, he yanked both the hose and droplight from the tank and slammed down the hatch. After he tightened the wheel he stood astride the tank for a moment and looked not at it, and thought not of the body it contained, but stared through the open doors to the road that led back to his house.

They would come for him now, and just as Henry Dodge

had threatened back in the winter, they would take him from his daughters. There would be no one to protect the girls, and he knew this town. They would come for them at night, killing the dogs first, then breaking into the house. The girls would not even be able to fight back. For God's sakes Linda would still be, Linda would still be, she'd still be fat with the child. And they'd take her. And they'd take her sister. All this while he was in prison waiting to be hanged by the neck until dead, but they'd tell him about the girls before they'd hang him so that those could be his last suffering thoughts. He leaped off the tank and fled to his home.

24 / *The Truth Will Set You Free*

Sunday, May 6, 1956
It wasn't good, and Clay knew it. Sitting at a round table in the middle of the Down the Hatch, he knew it because despite the shape of the table the other three men all seemed to be on the other side. Smoke from Zack's cigar rose in a steady stream that created a vaporous mark upon his face. He hadn't said much, and Clay suspected that he, though amongst the three the least clever, had guessed or deduced Clay's purpose and so waited for what he might call the real conversation to begin.

Duncan Hatch had been talking about Jonas Cloudman. "The man is absolutely set on going to prison," Duncan said. The tray on which he had brought the drinks sat empty in the middle of the table. Duncan pulled it to him and shielded his chest with it. "Prison is no place I want to ever be," he said.

"I can't imagine why any man would want to," said Davis

Scales. He twisted the big signet ring around his finger. It was from the mortuary school and, Clay thought, didn't look any different from a high school or fraternal ring. Davis pinched a cigarette from Duncan's pack of Luckies. "Of course, it'll just be luck if he doesn't hang."

Clay said, "Ned Grimsley used to think that just living in Enoch was prison enough." He waited for one of them to pick up either side of that statement. No one did. "But I suppose he never was in a real prison, so maybe he just didn't know what it was like."

"Jonas says he hates the waiting," Duncan Hatch said. He set the tray down beside him and leaned it against his chair. "And he's afraid they may try to put him on Pleasant Street."

In the darkness of the lounge Clay thought about Pleasant Street. He had never visited the mental hospital, but he imagined it as a dark place. Going past the red buildings with thin iron fences, he was always reminded of dungeons. The prison, on the other hand, just looked like a prison, at least from the outside. It was certainly no place he'd want to go; however, he hadn't killed anybody. When you'd killed a man, there weren't many choices. Even when you'd only seen it done or knew who did it, Clay thought, the choices weren't all that varied.

"Does his lawyer want to put in an insanity plea?" Clay asked. He was still trying to play the conversation where he wanted it. He had stood in a good many muddy Vermont driveways discussing the weather and the Red Sox while he waited to get to the price. The price here was immeasurably higher than any syrup he'd ever bought.

"Cloudman wouldn't have to face a trial if they put him on Pleasant Street," said Davis Scales. There was an impeccable cut to Davis's clothes that Clay envied without coveting. Impeccable was not a word that would ever be applied to Clay, and he knew it. Davis Scales seemed so casual about it as to be oblivious to Clay's ordinariness. Clay wondered why Forrest Langley couldn't have lived with that. Why had he had to thrust it back down their throats? Well, maybe these were better men than Forrest Langley, Clay thought. Maybe they could accept the inevitable with more grace. At least he would soon find out.

The lawyer that Duncan Hatch had found for Cloudman preferred an insanity plea because he feared otherwise the case would require the building of a new gallows. Cloudman, afraid only that he would never see his daughters, refused to go to Pleasant Street.

"Besides," Clay added, "he wasn't crazy. He was angry, furious, and that doesn't count."

"Something has to explain why he boiled the kid," Duncan Hatch said. "Otherwise there's little chance of a reduced charge."

"Well, he was guilty," Clay said. There seemed to be a desire, almost a need, to get Jonas Cloudman off, as if he were in fact innocent.

"That's just the point," Davis Scales said. He smiled, but Clay recognized the professional smile of the undertaker and the smooth way he peeled ash from his cigarette. Clay knew the point concerned the three men sitting before him, but though he was good at the small talk that preceded a sale, he had difficulty if the business itself wasn't finally discussed directly.

"The point isn't guilt or innocence," Zack said. With both elbows on the table and looking over his cigar just past Clay's face, the big man seemed suddenly philosophical. "The point is results. What's going to happen to a man who goes down to Newfound for trial? Are those people going to say here's a man who was angry and grieving because his daughter was made pregnant by a boy he considered a bum and a lout? Or are they going to call him a murderous maniac who tortures teen-agers, somebody who ought to be executed for the good of society?" Zack looked straight at Clay. "It's how someone else, people not even from Enoch, are going to interpret it. Do you see?"

"Besides which," Duncan Hatch said, "it's not even certain Jonas would let them mention that Linda's pregnant."

"Pride can't be allowed to interfere with truth," Clay told them. He was barely sipping his Scotch; the soda was losing the struggle to calm the rebellious acids in his stomach. "If Jonas Cloudman doesn't want that brought out in open court, he's got to realize there's a price to be paid for keeping secrets."

"And if you want things to stay cozy for you and your Marjorie Langley," Zack said, "you ought to stop prying into other people's silences." There it was, all out. Clay felt as though he had stepped from a slowly drifting boat onto the firm shore. What awaited him was uncertain, but he at least was on dry land.

"You know, Clay," Davis Scales said, "there are more than a few people in Enoch who think hers was the hand on the knife."

"Or helped another thrust it in," added Duncan Hatch.

Davis Scales snubbed out the Lucky and went on. "Now, the grieving widow, the woman crazed with grief, wildly accusing the whole town, turns up with a boyfriend."

"So the question is," Duncan said, "how long will it be before she'll sell off the place to disappear with the man and her husband's money?"

Zack said, "She was a crafty woman, Clay. To have lived with him all those years she'd've had to have been crafty. It's just that none of us thought of her that way." Zack peered over his cigar, which was aimed like an extended finger at Clay. "Now, maybe you know things we don't."

In the silence Clay looked down at his glass and counted the breaking bubbles. "New Year's morning," he began, "four men came out of my cousin's barn. Three of them are sitting at this table. The fourth one they dragged across the field like a dead calf and dumped him into the river."

Duncan said, "What do you expect us to do?"

What he expected them to do, and no less, was to go to the police; whether it was Henry Dodge didn't matter. It could be they would want to get a lawyer and go to the attorney general's office in Concord, because that would be where they would find the man in charge. And do what? they wanted to know. Zack relighted his cigar, which had gone out earlier while Clay was leading into business. Duncan Hatch went quietly to the bar and prepared a fresh round of drinks. As he was telling them they would have to confess, it occured to Clay not to drink from the full Scotch and soda Duncan set in front of him, but he found himself sipping from it after all. Dryness from the cool bubbles refreshed his mouth.

The truth, he told them, would clear up the cloud under which the town lived. Outside of Enoch people talked about it as a place of evil and sin, and in the town itself people were afraid. They asked him if he was afraid. No, he told them, he wasn't afraid. That wasn't the idea, because if he had been afraid he could have gone to the police way back when he had first realized that he held the answer to the secret that was the source of fear. Then why didn't he just go to the police now? they asked. Then he wouldn't be dependent on them.

"Because you're my friends," Clay said. His eyes traveled over the three faces across from him. It seemed to him that they were the tribunal and he the accused.

"A man doesn't send his friends to prison," said Duncan Hatch. "A man sticks by his friends."

"Langley was his relation," Davis Scales said. "Blood's thicker than water. Could be that family is more important than friends to Clay." Once again the undertaker smiled professionally and slowly twisted his signet ring.

"Some family," Zack said. He set his cigar on the table like a loaded gun.

Clay said he didn't know what would happen to them in court. They were all businessmen, respected men, and if they confessed, went and admitted their wrong, he didn't think it would go too hard on them. What, with the whole town looking for a scapegoat? they asked. We'd be taking it for practically every individual in town. We'd be there right along with Jonas Cloudman, a gang of cutthroats facing a noose.

"You didn't cut his throat," Clay told them. "You went there because like everyone else in Enoch you were upset by the beating Forrest had given Billy Harmes. None of you liked

Forrest or had ever liked Forrest, but this went beyond like or dislike. And Billy Harmes was special to people in town. If he hadn't been, he or the men he works with would have gone there and fixed it so that Forrest Langley would never raise his hand against another human being again."

As Clay talked they said nothing. Only the sounds of glasses being raised and the metal clicks of Davis Scales's lighter responded to Clay's words. They hadn't gone up there to kill a man, he told them. No weapon had been found because, he was positive, there was no weapon. Probably they had had a few after Duncan had closed the lounge from the party. Clay looked across the table, but Duncan spun the pack of Luckies around like a roulette wheel. From it he pulled a cigarette and spun it again. He ended up facing Clay, who shook his head. He didn't want a Lucky Strike; he didn't want a cigarette.

He said that they'd likely just gone up to teach Forrest a lesson. It had been late; maybe they'd talked about it most of the night. If someone else did it, they'd be caught. You wouldn't want that. And no one man would go up against my cousin. Maybe at first you didn't even think about hurting him. Only talking to him to try to make an impression on him.

"Maybe you'd had a few too many that night, and it got the better of you, eh, Zack?" Clay tried to nudge the big man, but he moved out of the way so that Clay's elbow struck empty air.

"I don't recall drinking much New Year's," said Zack. "And I wasn't drunk. I haven't been drunk since my brother's wedding twenty years ago."

"I remember New Year's very well," said Duncan Hatch. "You guys helped me close up, and we all went home. I walked back to the trailer, and you two drove off with your wives." There wasn't a trace of a smile on Duncan's face. Other than that he looked like a reflection of the undertaker.

"If you had a wife over in the trailer," Clay answered, "she could alibi for you, too. Too bad you didn't think about that."

"Don't be overly clever, Clay," Davis Scales told him. "You're not a lawyer."

"Besides," said Zack. "Duncan couldn't go up against your cousin, not all by himself."

Clay spoke a little faster now. The presence on his stomach seemed to ease. Or else his viscera had gone numb. "Waiting for him in the barn," Clay said, "you decide to give him a dose of his own medicine, an eye for an eye. After all, it's in the Bible, and the three of you are more Bible men than Henry Dodge. It isn't really a police matter, you figure, more of a town affair, and there you are with a selectman right there with you." Staring at them does no good, Clay decided when Duncan Hatch didn't return his look. He went on, still speaking rapidly.

"So as he comes in, you grab him. Zack whips some rope around him and you slap him around. He's nasty to you. I know my cousin. He could be as nasty a man as ever walked. You hit him. Somebody, maybe Davis, remembers what he did to Billy with the milk lid, so you hit him harder. Then he's dead."

Waiting for one of them to pick up the story, he took a large swallow from his drink. Some of the fizzing liquid went down the wrong way and made him choke and cough. His three friends across the table remained silent.

"It could have happened this way," he went on. In the back of his throat a raw tickle annoyed his speech. "You didn't hit him at all. When he came in, you gave him a talking-to, a rough talking-to. I know my cousin. Such a thing would set him in a rage, a rage fit to burst his brain. Now, there he is dead on the floor. Davis checks that he's dead. Stroke, coronary, whatever. You panic. Fear of being falsely accused of what practically everybody in town's been talking about settles on you like a blanket of snow." Clay tried a smile on them, a small smile, but it did no good. They stayed stonefaced. "You put the rope around him to make it look like murder and drop him off the bridge." Finished, he drank, slowly this time, from his Scotch. It soothed his throat.

Zack picked up his cigar. "Clay," he said, "do we look like men who would panic?"

Indeed they didn't, none of them. Each was a man who when his mind was made up to do a thing, did that thing. Come hell or high water, the phrase lingered in Clay's mind. Zack lighted his cigar.

Davis Scales pulled a cigarette from the pack of Luckies. "Do you honestly believe," he asked Clay, "that someone would put a rope around a dead man to make it look like murder?"

Before Clay had a chance to answer, Duncan Hatch asked him another question. "If you saw this back on New Year's, why are you coming to us now?"

"Because," said Zack, "the cops would ask him the same question. Or they just wouldn't believe him." Like a tall genie Zack blew out a smoke ring that circled and tumbled on itself.

How many times had Clay asked himself that question? Why didn't he know immediately what had happened? Why hadn't he told the police? But now he had told Marjorie Langley, and it was imperative that the three men go to face the truth. Because if they didn't, Marjorie would see that their deaths were certain.

"You've got to go to the police," Clay told them.

"We put Henry Dodge in office," Davis Scales reminded him.

"I wasn't in the barn to see what you did," Clay explained. "Maybe you did worse than what I imagine. I'm just sure it was the three of you."

"Everybody else in town has kept quiet about it," Zack said. "It wouldn't be just us you're talking on."

Clay pushed his empty glass to the center of the table, next to the pack of Luckies. "No," he said, "but it's your three names I gave to Marjorie Langley."

Halfway to his mouth Zack's cigar stopped. Holding position there, it released a tall stream of blue smoke. The big man looked over the smoke with eyes that told Clay nothing except that he was not in control of the situation. "You just have to go overboard in everything you do," Zack said. He lowered his head a minute, then puffed on the cigar. He seemed to be musing on his next move. "You could have left well enough alone." Zack didn't even look at Clay. He just followed the smoke he exhaled across the table.

"Everybody else in town did," said Davis Scales.

"Practically everybody," Duncan Hatch added, "except you and her and that goddamn minister."

Clay said, "I suppose Henry Dodge made some inquiries." It was sarcastic, but he didn't want to offer them sarcasm. He wanted to offer them talk. Talk was his strength, he thought, always had been, because no matter how long he lived, he was not going to be bigger than Zack. "Jonas Cloudman worked up on her farm every day until he was arrested. He wasn't on your side."

Zack grinned around the cigar held in his mouth. "There aren't 'sides.' There's just a mean son of a bitch that died and some fools trying to make something out of it when no one else wants to make anything out of it."

"They just want to forget it," said Davis Scales.

"At least we can help Jonas," Duncan Hatch said. "At least I have been."

"But we're not talking about sides here, huh?" Clay said. He stood up. He saw the three of them still sitting on the opposite side of the round table. "I'm telling you because we're friends."

Davis Scales said, "Friendship's a two-way street."

"You remember," Zack said, "the streets you use are the streets of Enoch. When you're thinking of friendship, think of that."

Clay had seen his chance and had left. Without asking if they were threatening him or asking them if they would go to the police. Without asking anything, he had taken the stairs two at a time, his hand pulling himself on the narrow banister. In the darkened dining room the tables were covered with ghosts.

Clay couldn't remember if he had said good night. Still his stomach quivered with this strange new feeling. He would go to Marjorie, though not tonight with this rampaging stomach. He would go to her because he didn't want her to do anything else. He left the three men who sat in the Down the Hatch, three friends, three murderers. At least they could have told him if he had guessed right about how the death had happened, because all the other possibilities were frightening. In his fright was anger because Marjorie had been right about what happened after, even if she didn't know what had happened before. Clay would have bet his life she was wrong, but she wasn't. Then he understood the name of the awful turbulence in the pit of his stomach.

25 / *Looking for Help*

Linda Cloudman was home. She and her sister had already milked the cows, the two of them lifting each forty-quart jug into the cooler, and had gone through the house, cleaning and picking up. They had done all that, and Linda had said they would buy groceries after lunch, when Billy Harmes pulled up in the yard. The girls stayed in the kitchen and waited while he walked through the dogs to knock on the door of the ell.

I should have called, he thought, but he had driven straight from the dairy. It had seemed silly to stop at Hatch's to put a nickel into a telephone, then drive on down here anyway. Besides, he wasn't exactly sure what he would have said. Standing in the kitchen with two girls sitting at the table, he still wasn't sure what to say.

"I'm sorry," he said. Linda Cloudman looked up at him while her mouth seemed to fatten. Her sister stared at the glass of milk in front of her on the table. Billy was glad he'd come.

"I'm here to offer any help I can," he said. "I know with your father away—"

"Jonas is in jail," said Linda. She swirled the remains of the coffee in her cup. "You sit down, Billy, and I'll get you some coffee."

He sat, and while she was getting the coffee from the stove, he told her what he could do to help. His own sister, a heavy girl, moved with chunky motions, as did his mother, and he was fascinated with the smooth way Linda handled the cup and spoon and coffeepot. He had trouble imagining this girl and her younger sister hoisting the hundred-and-twenty-pound milk jugs into a cooler. Gently as he could, he insisted that he would take no money for whatever he did.

"I don't think money's going to be much of a problem," said Linda. The spoon in her hand dangled in the coffee before her. Slowly her fingers twisted it, and the coffee swirled. Even her idleness seemed attractive to Billy. "Jonas always fixed everything," she said. Then she looked at Billy, her eyes raised to his. "We'd need to keep the pickup running. And sometimes things go wrong with the plumbing, you know, the toilet." Her sister giggled. Her hand went to her mouth, and she turned her head. Linda grinned at Billy—about the sister, he understood, not the toilet.

"What about milking?" he asked. "And haying?"

"When my mother was alive, she did all that," Linda explained, as though it were no more than addition or subtraction.

Billy sipped some coffee. It tasted bitter, and he imagined that was how Jonas Cloudman preferred it. Linda had probably learned from watching him make it, just as she must have learned to tend the cows from him, every night going to thin stalls with a bucket and a three-legged stool. Only with Jonas it was more likely an upturned milkcase he'd picked up somewhere. But Billy was certain the farmer had not instructed his daughter, had not had her out in the barn before supper (certainly not before breakfast) to tell her how to handle the cows. She had learned on her own.

"When your time comes near—" Billy began.

"That's a ways off," Linda said.

But he wouldn't let it go at that. He pointed to her sister. "She's not going to lift any milk jug," he said. Sonny was dead, and her father was in jail, not likely to get out. Lucky if they just kept him there and didn't hang him.

"I'm not ashamed, you know," she said. She knew he was thinking of her at the center of things.

"With your sorrows, I didn't imagine you were," he said. He sipped some more of the coffee. He could show her how to make it smoother. She probably hadn't tasted much else than the bitter coffee her father preferred. Billy guessed she drank it only because that was all she had known. He guessed the same thing about Sonny Rutherford, though he didn't say so. He did mention the coffee.

"Linda wasn't allowed to make coffee for Dad," said her sister. She came over from the sink to talk to Billy. "She had to make it like his, or he could have told the difference."

The milk money from three hundredweight a day wouldn't go very far even with one grown man not eating there. Billy wondered where the money to make up the wages Jonas Cloudman earned on the Langley place would come from. And someone would have to pay for a lawyer. Billy understood there was no question of bail. Jonas Cloudman was accused of murder. In the fall there would be cause for other money, money that Billy didn't much like thinking about, much less mentioning. But he did.

"How are you going to afford the hospital?"

It turned out that many people were giving her money. Both Duncan Hatch and Marjorie Langley, through their separate loyalties to Jonas, were providing money for the girls to live on. The money Forrest Langley had sent Billy after beating him was still in the bank. Billy promised Linda her father could have whatever he needed of it for a lawyer. The two hundred and fifty dollars for the hospital would be paid by Sonny Rutherford's father.

Billy didn't want to know any more about it. At the dairy he had told the men that Sonny was in love, but what Linda had felt, he would have to invent. Creativity was not his strength. He rather accepted what had happened as an accident. Linda, drowned, run over, tied up in the emotions and lust of a wild boy like Sonny, got pregnant as someone else might lose an arm or an eye. In the back of Billy's mind, though, lay the thought that once in the cars or woods or whatever, she saw a way out of the trap of her love and obligation to her father. He just let that thought lie.

"Quite a feather in your cap," Marjorie told Henry Dodge. "Solve my husband's murder, and you'll have quite a reputation." He had asked where Peter was. Not knowing Peter's name, he had stumbled in his speech, finally saying "your boy." Marjorie knew the words he had held back, words that would not embarrass him. Dodge said he wasn't interested in a reputation. No promotion was possible for him. Unlike some men, ambitious men, he was happy in the office that he held, in the town that he lived in.

"Do you know anything about baseball, Mrs. Langley?" he asked. As he explained, he didn't look at her. His profile to her, as if someone had told him it was his best side, he looked out his office window to the paved area where she had parked her car next to his. A symmetrical pattern of raindrops had formed on the wide hood of his car. On hers was simply dark metal, rounded in multiple curves. Clay had told her she should put wax on the car. In the front seat stood a bottle of Scotch, which she had driven to Newfound to buy. Standing in the state liquor store, she had scanned the brands and their code numbers, then written down the number and passed the slip to the clerk as if she were in a library. She hoped it was the right brand. Never in her life had she bought a bottle of liquor.

"So you understand, Mrs. Langley, there is only going to be one pitcher in this game." He had looked at her directly to say this. From a drawer in his desk he took a pack of gum. His mouth slightly open, he chewed with the gross motions of a child. Marjorie half expected him to swallow the gum, then wonder where it had gone. On the desk lay the discarded wrapper, white with a green arrow.

"What if you had the names of the men?" she asked.

"What makes you think I don't?" he said.

It became clear to her that he knew what she was there for. Pleased with herself that he had underestimated her, she now knew she had underestimated him. And the three behind him. He went on about Jonas Cloudman, how busy he had been with Jonas Cloudman. The paperwork for expenses was enough to make a man cry. The D.A. from Concord was on the telephone about twice a day, Dodge complained, usually at mealtime.

"And that's a simple case," he said. Somehow he had propped his feet against the desk and tilted his chair back in a position of precarious arrogance. "Like Grimsley. Simple. Now, I didn't call you in to make it complicated. Just simple, Mrs. Langley."

The gum wrapper from the desk now in his hand, he leaned his chair back farther. He crumpled the paper and threw it toward the wastebasket by the file cabinet. It missed, but he remained in his chair as Marjorie left.

26 / *The White Speckled Boulder*

Billy Harmes took Linda Cloudman bowling with the men from the dairy. He took her and her sister to church, where they heard the Reverend Treadwell preach. The men from the dairy had been polite. Too polite, Billy had thought. He was happy that they had not used the language and teasing they usually did, but their very quietness had made things seem unnatural. For Billy it was important that taking Linda Cloudman bowling be no different from dating any other girl in Enoch. He had heard the men speculating about Marjorie Langley and Clay Freeman, and he did not want to be put in the same category, the area of the unnatural, the unaccepted, the wrong. He didn't like them putting Marjorie Langley in that category either, but he didn't see anything he could do about that.

Escorting Linda to church had been easy. She had readily agreed, and when he had got to the farm, both she and her sister were dressed and ready to go. Billy accepted their offer of coffee because if he hadn't, they would have arrived before everyone else, including the Reverend Treadwell. What he hadn't expected came after the service. In the church, for the first time in his life, Billy sat in the pew on the left-hand side toward the rear, a pew that Jonas Cloudman had occupied for twenty years. More accurately Jonas or his daughters, for after his wife's death he had attended less often, driving the girls to the service and returning for them at the end. Still, he had gone often enough for Billy to feel he was sitting in Jonas Cloudman's pew. His own parents, as usual, sat on the right-hand side about halfway down. Only his sister grinned at him as the family moved down the aisle. In the back of the church Billy saw Clay Freeman. He was glad Marjorie Langley wasn't there too.

The sermon on God's grace had struck Billy as an unusual one. The minister for a change hadn't talked about the social and economic problems of the world, nor had he preached on the trials and sins of their own community. Instead he spoke on the difficulty of human life. He called his sermon "The Wound" and said the only balm was God's grace. The usual sermons on social problems had interested Billy, who believed that Christianity demanded charity, which meant work. The words of this sermon, however, didn't include charity or work. Throughout the service a button that hung from stretched thread on his sports jacket annoyed Billy.

"Why does God love us?" the minister asked. "It's a gift, a gift on the occasion of our birth into the grace and love of the living God."

Faced with dismissal, Treadwell looked for divine love. Life on earth was too hard for him. Billy was fortunate, he knew, because he could act. He could drain the oil and lube Jonas Cloudman's truck. And he had told Mrs. Langley that since she was paying Jonas Cloudman's wages, he would come over for any repairs or heavy work that needed to be done. Since she was selling to the dairy in Newfound that had a bulk tanker, there was no need of fooling with milk. But she had thanked him for his offer. She had said it would save her waiting for repair people to drive up from Newfound. There was no other man in Enoch she'd allow on the place except Clay Freeman or the minister, and she wouldn't allow either of them to so much as fix a clothespin. When she had told him that, Billy had laughed, and it had made it easier not to say anything about her condemnation of Enoch. The Reverend Treadwell did not look as though he had laughed in a while, and Billy wondered what had condemned him. He looked worse than Jonas Cloudman.

In any case Billy didn't think of love as a gift or rain or whatever. It was acts. But if the men who had killed Langley thought they were doing something for Billy, they were dreadfully mistaken.

As Billy and Linda left the church the minister, standing at the door, put his hands on their shoulders. He said he was so happy they had come. Together, he said, he had meant. He seemed to be trying to give them something, a word or gift that he couldn't find. Behind them people began to pile up, and some of them went around the three of them and down the church steps. Even Linda's sister passed them to wait on the grass in front of the church. Finally Billy offered his hand to the minister, who looked at it for just a moment before he took it. Before they got to Linda's sister, Billy whispered to Linda.

"That man's in trouble," he said.

"I wish I'd known that before." She looked back at the minister. "He convinced me to tell Jonas I was pregnant."

After a Sunday dinner of roast chicken, Linda's sister rode her bicycle to a friend's house. Billy was glad of the chicken and mashed potatoes and peas because it was what his mother usually cooked at home. Linda apologized for the meal.

"It's all Jonas ever asked for," she explained. She had set coffee on the table. Billy missed some pie or ice cream, but he supposed her father didn't demand that. He resolved to bring ice cream the next time he came, maybe some of the ice cream he had made and packed himself.

Stretched out behind the house was an ancient chicken coop that had seen neither feather nor egg for years. As they walked past it a breeze carried the smell of manure, no longer ammoniac nor even dead, but just warm, dry. Along the bottom of the boards a black line had formed where the earth had rotted the wood to its own color. Billy could replace those boards easily, he thought, if Linda wanted to raise chickens, but he didn't ask her. She was talking, lifting her face to his, then pointing away at something, and he preferred to listen to her talk. They were beyond the chicken coop. The odor carried only a little way.

Linda was pointing to a sedan in the tall grass. The car had rusted so uniformly that from a distance it looked as though someone had painted red primer on it. At first Billy wondered if Jonas Cloudman had been in the process of fixing it; then, before he was much closer to the car, he looked back at the chicken coop and the half-painted house and laughed at his own thoughts.

Linda touched his forearm. "What are you laughing at?" She was smiling.

"Nothing," he said. It was so automatic to say that, but her hand was still on his arm. Her fingers were soft, warm. "I was just thinking that it'd be funny if your father was rebuilding that car." He smiled too. "My father's always trying to rebuild something when he ought to start off from scratch."

"Jonas never tried rebuilding," Linda said. "Just keeping things up took all that he had."

Billy couldn't tell what she felt about that. He said, "Whose car is it, anyway? Where did it come from?"

"I don't know," she said. "It just ended up here." She released his arm, and they walked on past the car. The car was from the thirties, the end of the thirties, Billy knew, a square-boxed, bull-nosed Chevrolet, and he wondered if the rubber on the tires had rotted into the ground.

Linda broke from him and darted off the path into the tall grasses. He could hear her giggling. He called to her, and the giggling stopped. By the side of the path bent grass showed where she had cut through. Again he called her name.

"Come on, Linda," he said.

"Was one of the seven dwarfs called Practical?" she yelled back.

Stopping at the edge of the path, he folded his arms and knitted his brows. Sleepy, Sneezy, Dopey, he couldn't remember. "I don't think so," he said. When she laughed this time, he found himself laughing. Still laughing, he ran off into the grass until he came to a boulder of white granite like a giant speckled egg in the sun.

"I'm going to find you," he announced. Then, giggling, he sneaked around the rock. "I'm surrounding you," he said. The crushed grass smelled green.

On the other side of the rock she pulled him down. "Surround me," she said. "Mr. Practical, surround me."

The sun warmed his bare forearms as they encircled Linda between her breasts and her swelling belly. Her back to him, she nestled against his chest, her hair just under his face. She smelled of soap and the green grass, a sweet smell that made him feel awkward about the tobacco odor on his fingers. His face was newly shaved and shiny, a bright cheek above her tanned skin. Even with the breeze he was warm in his white shirt and dark gabardine trousers, but he didn't move. He sat and waited.

"When I was a little girl," Linda told him, "my mother used to bring us out here to play." She didn't look at Billy while she talked, though her eyes kept moving over the rocky field that was slowly growing back to forest. "She'd bring Jane out here, and we'd spread a blanket and picnic. When Jane fell asleep, my mother and I'd play hide-and-go-seek." She looked up, not so much at Billy as at the sky. Billy glanced up too, noticing nothing but a small white cloud. "You know she would never let me hide. Only she could hide, and I always had to be the one to go seek. Why do you think she did that?"

Billy thought Linda might cry. He pressed his chest to her. "Probably she wanted to keep an eye on your sister," he said. "And maybe she was afraid you'd hide so that she couldn't find you."

"I always found her," said Linda, moving back against Billy. She rested her hands on his forearms. "Did you know my mother?"

He told Linda he could remember her in church. Only there, sitting next to Jonas Cloudman, could he visualize her. He had wondered why such a pretty woman had married such a fierce-looking man. At eight or nine he had even thought she was beautiful in her hat with the lacy fringe of veil that seemed to mix with her hair. And Jonas Cloudman, not a homely or ugly man, had looked every bit as fierce as he did now. Even when he held the hymnal, one thick-fingered hand strong enough to keep it in front of him and his wife, his singing mouth still seemed ready to chew on a man. Over Linda's shoulder Billy stared at his own fingers, swollen and cracked by the alkaline detergent of the dairy.

"She was a pretty woman," Billy said. He wanted to add something, but he couldn't. "A very pretty woman."

"Once, when I was very little, we went down to the river for a picnic. I don't think my sister had been born, anyway I don't remember her with us. She had all these things wrapped up in a big towel that she carried, and I kept worrying that something would fall out, the Thermos or something." There were other things she hadn't liked about that picnic, Linda told him. The shore had been mucky, and yellow jackets, attracted by the sweet jelly in their sandwiches, had buzzed around them. And when she had tried to sleep, she had dreamed something came out of the water at her. "That's about the first dream I remember," she said. "Funny because I don't have nightmares at all now, not even after finding the body with Sonny."

Billy glanced down at her. Her small mouth was slightly open, and she was looking out where she used to picnic with her mother. "Real things aren't half as scary as dreams," he said.

"Finding Mr. Langley was plenty scary," said Linda. Her folded hands rested on top of her stomach.

"Not finding him would have been even worse," Billy said. "I just wish it hadn't happened in the first place." She was crying. Before he even looked down at her face, he knew there were tears, and then her body began to shake. He held her and hoped she wouldn't convulse because he was afraid that might hurt her or the baby. No shame or guilt entered his mind. He decided that she couldn't hate both of them, she couldn't even hate one of them, and so she would have to cry. He offered himself as someone to hold her while she cried.

Love offers itself to be of service, he thought, remembering the minister's sermon, and when it is performed automatically, as his was done, it shows itself to be genuine, sincere. He wouldn't have to force himself to find things to do around here to be of help. They practically jumped out at him.

"He's my father, Billy," Linda said, "and he just couldn't stand it." She sobbed and twisted so she could look directly at him. "But sometimes now I can't stand it either, and with Sonny gone." She turned away and looked down at her belly. The rhythm of her sobs slowed, and she remained motionless, head down as though she were sick.

"It's like some things shouldn't happen at all," Billy said. Linda turned her whole body to him. While he talked, she pulled blades of grass and laid them crossways on his trouser leg. "But

when they do, there's not much you can do about them after."
Awkwardness in presenting his thoughts usually slowed Billy or
kept him quiet, but when he paused, Linda said nothing. She
began to arrange the grass on his leg into changing shapes, first
a star, then a rectangle. "I didn't want anything to happen to
Mr. Langley, nothing like what they did. I suppose they thought
they were doing the right thing, something to get back at him
for me. It was a cinch I wasn't going to do anything to him."

"Everybody thinks they're doing the right thing," said
Linda. "Even when they know they're not." She held a spear
of grass suspended over the arrangement. "They heard Mr.
Treadwell talk about it."

"And now we all have to live with it," Billy said. "And
trying to make it right again will just make it worse."

Linda picked up the pile of grass and rained it on her own
lap. "Are you thinking of Marjorie Langley?"

"Some."

"Just remember, Billy, what they did, they did." A single
blade of grass stuck to the heel of her hand. She peeled it off
and dangling it in the sunlight, smiled at it. "What you do has
got nothing to do with it, had nothing to do with it. There's no
need for you to get mixed up with any of them."

He took her hand, gently, aware of the roughness of his
own. "It's not your fault," he said. Her eyes were downcast,
and he saw that what made the sorrow so hard for her was the
blame that had blended into it. "The baby," he said, "the baby
will be all right."

She looked at him with clear eyes. He could see neither
mourning nor guilt. "It's not the baby," she said. "It's me."
She grabbed him to her. Her fingers dug into his flesh. "It's
me."

For the first time Billy doubted what help could do in the
service of love. And he realized too how much blame he had
made himself responsible for, realized that Linda had seen it,
and had tried to help him absolve himself. But holding her,

there was more than blame and pity, and though he was frightened of it, he put his face to hers and kissed her lips.

They sat quietly for a while in the warm grass. A pair of Baltimore orioles flew past them to the high branches of an oak. In the leaves hidden from their view hung a nest. Billy and Linda watched the birds flying from the tree to the ground and back. After a while they got up and walked past the old car and chicken coop to the house. They smiled at each other, but they did not kiss again until Billy left. This time it was Linda who bent to his face while he sat behind the wheel of his car.

"I've had a wonderful time," she said. Her face was very warm.

27 / *Lovers' Talk*

In bed Clay would hold Marjorie with his arms around her back, a shield of warmth. Slow and gentle he was, as though hiding something. But out of bed he was a bumbler. A fumbler. He had waited to tell her about the killers and waited to tell them, and now nothing had happened.

The red cotton skirt she took from the closet fit closely around her waist. She had matched it with a white sleeveless blouse, which showed off her arms and neck. At her age she was proud not to have added weight to her upper arms. She was flattered to think the woman in the mirror on the bedroom door was still attractive.

In the kitchen she took out the ice cube trays, the dull metal sticking slightly to her flesh. In the refrigerator next to the milk stood the fifth of Scotch, a surprise for Clay. He was her man of habit, habitual disarray, her fumbler.

When Clay came in, he sat down and gently rested his chin in his hands. "They didn't do Henry Dodge any favors when they made him chief," Marjorie said. "Did he tell you that silly business about being a pitcher?"

"Henry's young enough to be entitled to a large scoop of foolishness."

"He knows who they are." She was certain Dodge knew who killed Forrest. She couldn't understand why he thought he could be in charge, since those three so obviously controlled him. What she did understand, enough to make her angry, was that Henry Dodge would be of absolutely no help to her. "With what's gone on in Enoch, I'd think he'd have to do something."

"Some people in town," Clay said, "think he ought to investigate Ned Grimsley's accident."

"Yes, he threatened me with that too."

"I'm not sure he does know," Clay said. He drummed his fingers on the table. "They probably didn't see any need to be specific with him, and no one else is talking."

"They have too much contempt for him to bother telling him," she said. His silence again. She tried to see him virtuous in it. After all, what had her noises accomplished? Virtuous or not, it made no sense to ask him to go to Dodge. How many others in town knew but were afraid to say anything? Probably most of them thought Henry Dodge was aware of everything, his investigation a pretense. That's what he meant by being a pitcher, knowing where everybody stood, making sure no one moved. What could her fumbler do against that? "That was a warning from them," Marjorie asked, "that business about Grimsley?"

"They aren't powerless," he said.

"I think I balanced the scales with Jonas," she said. While Henry Dodge, two of his specials, and a state trooper had squatted behind their cars and trained their rifles on Jonas's half-painted house, Marjorie had crossed the open, dog-littered yard, gone into the kitchen, and brought Jonas out. "Gunless," as

Henry Dodge kept saying, until the state trooper reminded him the word was "unarmed."

Clay smiled. "I think he fancied himself one of those television heroes, half crew-cut, square-jawed big-city detective, half powerful highway patrolman. But when it was all over, the drone was left with nothing to do but deliver Jonas to the county jail and the jurisdiction of the attorney general's office." Nodding his head, he let his smile grow into chuckle. "And at that the poor bastard had to worry about the gas and the mileage on the cruiser because the selectman might ask him why he didn't let the trooper take him down there and save the town of Enoch car expenses, to say nothing of the salary for the special who went along for the ride."

From the glass came a crack as the ice cubes warmed. She poured the Scotch nearly to the top. As she set the glass in front of Clay, she allowed her left hand to rest on his shoulder. She let it linger there a moment before she sat down. She felt young, a youth full of energy and frustrations such as had not actually existed in her adolescence. Had she lived through it, she reflected, she might know better what to do now.

"So," Clay said when she sat down. A word of all things, "so"; of question and answer and consequence. Marjorie nodded her head. Her hand wanted to reach across the table and grab his, to warm all the "so"'s from his head, from their conversation.

"They're going to fire Timothy, aren't they?" she said.

"He's out of place here," he said. In his look was nothing of the salesman, nothing that flattered or cajoled, prodded or eased the way. The bright wonder of his eyes showed him so much better than the other men of Enoch.

"Everyone good is out of place here." Jonas Cloudman, without anything out of place or inexplicable, had succeeded in his crude business. But, Marjorie decided, he had been wrong.

"There's no soda in this!" Clay coughed. In his watery eyes was a look of accusation. "Soda!" he shouted. "You have to put soda in it!'' He raised the glass for a cautious sip. ''Good, though.''

''I'm glad,'' she said.

''Where's Peter?''

''Playing.'' She pointed to the garage. ''He plays on his own. It gives me time.''

''I suppose with the cows—''

''You know what I think of cows, Clay?'' She had both hands on the table as if to keep it from flying away. ''I hate them. And just as soon as I finish my business here, I'm selling out kit and kaboodle. To hell with them.'' She stopped and looked at him. His hair was neatly cut. He was the only handsome man she had met who didn't know it.

''So,'' he said. That ''so'' that could be anything was now perhaps a plea.

''I won't be going far, Clay,'' she said. ''Maybe Newfound. A place big enough for us.'' ''Us'' had a soft, undefined sound. It frightened her. She noticed Clay too looked frightened; a scream held mute, legs locked by a panic to flee. ''Your candy will get warm in the car. Didn't you say some of it melted last time?'' She went to him, her sad fumbler. She pressed her cheek to the back of his neck and squeezed his shoulders.

''Did you tell Gladys about us?'' He didn't look at her. Between his thumb and forefinger he ground dust.

She started to pull away from him, then pressed against the smooth skin of his neck. ''Does she know?''

Clay sipped from his Scotch. He shook his head, unsure if his wife did know. ''His wife,'' Marjorie thought, not ''Gladys'' but ''his wife,'' as if Gladys had somehow disappeared. Marjorie could wish them all disappeared, all but Clay. ''Are you through with me?'' she asked.

Clay reached his arm around her waist, his hand resting gently on her hip. ''I'm worried.''

''You know I wouldn't tell her,'' Marjorie said. ''Don't even imagine I would think of telling her. Did you think I had?''

"She just worries sometimes," he answered. "How could she know?"

Marjorie wouldn't ask him why he had doubted her. She could feel the fear in him. She knew how hurtful it was for him to have these ugly truths chewing on him, sharp bitey things about his town, his friends, and now himself. There was little she could do for him except leave him, and she wouldn't do that. She let him hold her in his grief.

28 / *Love and Love*

Billy Harmes loved smells. All through high school the boys had teased him about the number of onions he could eat, the amount of pepper he shook on his food, the skunks and trees and other cardboard figures that hung from the radio knobs of his car. They laughed and said that when he got done fixing a hamburger it looked more like one of those pizza pies you could buy in Newfound. Never, though, did the girls tease him about his fondness for aftershave. More than any other boy they would date or talk to, he noticed their perfumes and colognes, and as an artist could do with colors, he would detail to them the subtle variations in their fragrances. He was wearing Aqua Velva when he took Linda to the company picnic.

Liquor for the Land Dairy picnic arrived in the private cars of the employees and stayed in them all during the day. No keg, no table of fifths, not even a case of beer appeared in the open. Instead the men were forced to go to their cars and prepare drinks in their own backseats. What they emerged with, as long as it was in a paper cup provided by the company, was their business, but the purity of hot dogs, hamburger, pies and Land's

Dairy ice cream was not to be sullied by liquor. After last year, when Jelly had added ginger ale to the final shots that lay in the bottom of his Canadian Club and then walked around fifth in hand, Mr. Land had threatened to end the picnics, which had meant free food, time off, and a small celebration at the company's expense. There were not many celebrations, and the men did not intend to botch what they had.

On the grass beside the dam the open-doored snub-nosed cars looked like a flock of ducks with clipped wings, unable to fly. Billy in the backseat of his Chevrolet mixed rum Cokes, or rather mixed one for Linda Cloudman and poured one for himself. With his flower print shirt he bore a resemblance to a tropical bartender, not a native but a slick, black-haired transplanted American, a soldier of fortune going incognito. But his country accent and the thick hide of his hands betrayed him, so that close up he was not even an imitation of a tropical adventurer.

"I love the colors," he told Linda, "and the fruit-juice smells and music. My aunt brought back a record of the music they made with steel drums and gourds and all." Linda had worn no perfume. It disappointed him. The time she had gone to the bowling alley she had smelled of Evening in Paris, a gentle scent sold in the five-and-ten in Newfound. His mother worked there, and both she and Billy's sister wore it. It was, he thought, a contradictory scent, because the color of the bottle was so blue. Stronger and richer than the fragrance. The shape and color of the bottle were similar to his container of Aqua Velva, yet the perfume smelled nothing like his aftershave.

After the food and drink, after the softball game, after everyone else had left, he danced with her in the slow evening light. In a while she ran down to the beach, and he was glad he felt sober enough to go into the water with her. The turned-up cuffs of his pants turned dark in the warm water. From the shore came long shadows stretching out over the river, the dark lines of trees. Turning her back to him, she unbuttoned her blouse. High up on the wall of the dam he could see the cement changed to pink by the setting sun. As she pressed against him she raised his shirt so that her breasts touched his skin. Her belly was large.

When they got off their blanket, the woods were dark. Naked, they returned to the water and waded in as far as their waists. His hand rested just below the small of her back on the small rise of her cheek. The flesh of her breast was warm against his side. The two of them stared across the quiet river. He wondered what she was thinking. What he was thinking was that he had been terribly wrong about love just being giving and sacrifice.

29 / *Legion*

Clay was tired. All the way down from the mountains he had been rubbing his eyes and pinching his cheek. It wasn't his fault. Hadn't the car stalled out right in the parking lot of the Old Barn Gift Shoppe, the distributor wetted by a puddle that shouldn't have been there? Now, he supposed, the rubber Zack put on is probably worn out, and they'd tell him to get a new car. When he'd bought this one, he'd planned on its lasting four years, even though four years was a lot of miles in his business, once around the clock. With his car they'd have to spin the odometer forward, he thought, to make it come out right before they resold it. It wasn't time yet. He'd hold on to it another year, no matter what they said.

Gladys would say he should have called. She didn't give a damn about the car. That was her trouble; she didn't give a damn about any of these things or try at least to see how he did. In the middle of trying to make a sale to that woman who ran the Old Barn, he'd had to fool around with the distributor, getting his hands covered with grease. Was he supposed to fool around with telephones when the very appearance of his hands could kill a sale? And these people didn't keep things to themselves. If some sugar went bad at one place, he'd hear about it all down the line at every one of his outlets.

A lack of faith seemed inherent in women, part of their constant attention to day-to-day matters that gave them no larger view of life, no vision. Clay had a vision. An idea, he called it, because vision seemed too grand and dream too unrealistic. As his business grew, eventually he could hire somebody to make the sugar while he was on the road distributing it. From there it would be a short step to having a crew, raising a building, and Enoch would have its first factory. By the time he was sixty, he told himself, he'd have a fleet of salesmen on the road, just as when he worked for the spice company, only he'd be the one sitting behind the big oak desk planning how to increase his territory.

It was a practical idea, he had told Gladys. Hadn't that outfit in Vermont started pretty much the same way? During the thirties the guy had taken payment in kind because ready cash was as scarce as Catholics up there. Clay knew the story well, how maple syrup had become the early spring crop to buy seeds and how the guy had packaged and shipped those little maple leaves and Indians and state maps made from the golden sugar all over the Northeast. At the factory now were tours, tours Clay had taken more than once to study the operation and plan, as he said, for Enoch's first factory—Clay Freeman and Son, Maple Sugar Candy. With his little cakes, an exclusive trademark, Clay was sure he could make a success of it. Gladys had asked him, Do you want to sit behind a big oak desk? Maybe he didn't, maybe she was right and he couldn't sit still longer than it took to eat dinner. But that was the trouble with women, they didn't have a vision, a dream, a plan.

It would put Enoch on the map, his factory. Forrest had made a success of his dairy herd, but that was just money. And it was just for himself. Now the only thing famous about Enoch was a rotten murder or accident or something that made the woman who ran the gift shop shake her head and the kid who'd helped him with the distributor snicker. Things ought to be better than that, if you had a plan.

An hour later, when he reached home, Gladys was gone. On the coffee table in the living room lay two sheets of her yellow stationery. She had listed in longhand those things she wanted shipped to an address in Duluth, Minnesota, which Clay recognized as her sister's. Through the rest of the house he searched to see what she had taken besides two suitcases and his son. In the kitchen he found the note, also written on the yellow stationery, propped against the bottle of Scotch he kept beside the cookie jar. Before reading the note he chunked ice into a glass and dumped in two shots of Scotch and filled it with soda. As he took a swallow he wondered why she had taped the note shut.

Clay—

I have long known about you and Marjorie but now others know too. I cannot live here with that, nor can you expect me to. You wanted to get involved in all that despite what I wanted. Despite what I warned you about. Of course, I have every right to be angry and I am angry. Don't think it will blow over. I have examined my own behavior and can find nothing to blame myself for. I see no need to stay and talk, particularly since it's now eight o'clock and you're not even home. I hope if you stay here, you'll be careful. You still have a responsibility to me and Dan.

—Gladys.

It sat there like a stain on the table while he finished his drink. He looked at it, the names plainly stated at beginning and end, as if that were all. Reading the message again, he argued with it. There was no "long" for her to know about him and Marjorie. Nor had he *expected* her to be humiliated or embarrassed. He searched the note, but those words weren't there. *No* word for what she felt was there. Angry. All right, she was angry. He'd been angry, many times, angrier than she could get. He didn't use it as an excuse to just run off.

After mixing another drink, he spoke aloud. "Well, she's got goddamn plenty to blame herself for now." Gladys had listed all the things she'd wanted sent and carefully written the Duluth address, but she'd left no place to call. It took him fifteen minutes to find his sister-in-law's telephone number. Information, he remembered, could have given him the number. To hell with information. "I want to talk to Gladys."

But, of course, she wasn't in Duluth. She was in Boston, staying in some hotel, whose name his sister-in-law either didn't know or wouldn't tell. The train, leaving the next morning, wouldn't get to Minnesota for a couple of days. His sister-in-law, calm through his cursing, stopped talking. Not until the operator came on did he realize she had hung up on him.

Fresh ice cubes stuck together in his glass. He told himself not to bull ahead. Wait awhile. He made himself walk into the living room and sit down. When had he last been alone in the house? He couldn't remember, maybe never. Night after night on the road he had been alone in hotel rooms, but that was nearly twenty years ago. Now Gladys and the boy were alone in a hotel room.

Louise Langley called. Because she so seldom did, he guessed it was about Gladys. After talking to Louise, he drove straight to Marjorie's without bothering to call.

Dressed in her housecoat, she opened the door. She was unharmed. "She's left me," he said, and while Marjorie made him a drink, he told her about the note.

"Are you going after her?" asked Marjorie.

He shook his head. "I want to leave here," he said, "with you."

Louise had driven Gladys to the train station in Newfound. As she had told him that, Clay realized Gladys would not come back. In her note she had written, "Others know too." Then she had gone and involved others, asked his cousin to drive her to the depot. Her and the boy and the two suitcases. They were gone. Maybe he could get out with Marjorie.

Marjorie led him into the living room. Beside him on the

couch, she lay her head on his shoulder. "A while ago," she told him, "I prayed that somehow you could come with me. Now it seems too soon."

"She had hardly mentioned anything—a little suspicion. Now she's gone."

Marjorie's fingers rubbed along his neck to his cheek. "She must have given you hints, something you missed?"

"I missed the hints because I'd already lost her." He tried to think of his house and sugar kitchen for sale. It would not be a temporary move. There was plenty of liquid left in his glass. The couch felt comfortable. Across the tops of his shoulders formed knots of pain from the long drive.

"Maybe I'm being selfish," Marjorie said, "but I want you to come to me for me, not to take Gladys's place."

"I want you to go with me because I'm afraid of losing you."

"You won't lose me," she said, "unless you want to. You can come here anytime. Maybe by the time I leave, you'll have settled in your mind—"

"I have settled in my mind." He sat up and put the glass on the coffee table. The several things he wanted to say clogged in his throat. "It's not my fault, damn it."

"Of course it's not." She kneaded the aching muscles at the back of his neck.

"Louise said it was my fault."

"The hypocrite!"

"No," he said, "no. Not because of you. Because of them."

Slowly he told her what Louise had said. Gladys hadn't left in anger but fear. They hadn't threatened her or the boy. They had just called to say maybe she ought to know about Clay and a certain widow.

"They?" Marjorie asked.

"One of the three. She wouldn't tell Louise which one."

Threats weren't necessary because if they dared to call, Gladys could imagine what worse they dared to do. He talked about where he and Marjorie might go. Newfound probably wasn't far enough. He had figured out that he could run the sugar business from most anywhere in the state. Louise had said to forget about Forrest because no matter what, he wasn't coming back. And Gladys wasn't coming back either. He hated to lose the sugar bush they had tapped on Marjorie's farm, the best source of syrup east of Vermont. Of course, he had even considered moving to Vermont.

"They are disgusting," Marjorie interrupted. "You aren't to blame. They are." Her hands encircled his face. "And you aren't afraid. You don't want to leave. You want me to leave."

"Louise said as soon as possible," he admitted. He was sure she understood why he had avoided telling her all this at first. He was sure he had been right. Now she reacted as he had feared she would.

"No." She sat apart from him, her hands in her lap. "They've done enough. They're not going to do this too. Not to you."

He was comfortable on her couch. The note, his fear, had combined to make him artificially awake. At last the long day and the liquor brought fatigue. As she explained why she wouldn't leave, he realized he didn't have to go home. So he didn't.

30 / *Billy Harmes*

August 1956

Billy Harmes had never been to the county jail before. Many times on the way to Concord he had ridden past it, following the road that threaded between it and the brick building that was the county home. For the aged, he thought. All of those old folks looking across the road at the prisoners, young men mostly, guys in for brawling or child desertion and a few accused felons waiting trial. And Jonas Cloudman, murderer. Below the jail was the barn full of cows that provided milk for both the home and the jail. Linda said it saddened her for her father to be a hundred yards away from the largest dairy operation other than Langley's he'd ever seen.

The hand of the jailer was just above Jonas Cloudman's shoulder as they came into the room. Other than that Billy couldn't see any vestige of the terrible fierceness of the man whom few men in Enoch had ever touched, even so much as to shake hands. It occurred to Billy that killing Sonny Rutherford had not required Jonas to grab or strike. All he had to do was turn on the steam, then seal up the tanker. Billy and Linda took the place of the girl and her brother-in-law at the wire divider.

"Something wrong with the truck?" Jonas Cloudman asked. His eyes switched briefly to Billy, then back to Linda. The rest of his face showed neither motion nor feeling. Though he had had to clean the corrosion off the battery terminals the day before just to start the pickup, Billy said nothing.

"I wanted Billy here today," Linda told her father. "We want to ask you something, Jonas."

His eyes went through Billy to the back wall where Billy had sat. "Never was often anybody'd ask me something," he said. His eyes remained on the wall. Though he brought his hands up, fingers pointing at Billy and Linda, palms open as if he held something invisible, weightless, and absolutely precious. "This year Langley started in on me, then Henry Dodge, and now you two." The drop of his fingers on the wood of the divider made a thump, as though he actually had had something in his hands. His eyes came back to his daughter. "Are you going to get rid of it?"

"He knows," she told him. Neither of them looked at Billy. He felt a long ways from the people who had sat there before him, but it still wasn't a good feeling. In fact he felt like a thief caught before he'd grabbed the treasure.

"Of course he knows," Jonas Cloudman said. "Everybody knows."

Billy said, "I want to marry Linda. I mean we're here to ask your permission for a wedding."

Jonas Cloudman rubbed his wrists. He raised his eyes to Billy, and a narrow smile creased his face. "Hell of a place to give away a bride, ain't it?" He shook his head, seemingly knocking off the smile. Billy felt better with the self-mocking smile gone. "Don't you want her to get rid of it?"

"Jonas," Linda said, "we've talked about it."

"I want to hear it from him," Jonas Cloudman said.

"She's right, Mr. Cloudman," Billy told him. He didn't say any more because the only thing he could think of to say led nowhere. Much as he hated being in this position, he knew that without the baby he wouldn't be here at all.

"Do you know how little I like being in here?" the man asked. His cocked eye wrinkled his forehead.

"No," Billy answered, "but I have an idea." Cloudman's wrinkles looked sharp enough to cut through the wire separating them. For the first time Billy felt terribly afraid.

"Even so, I'm not sorry. I'm not sorry a bit."

"Jonas, do we have your permission?" Linda said. Her hand went to smooth the hair at the back of her head. Billy glanced at Jonas Cloudman, expecting him to make some similar gesture, but the man simply folded his arms.

"Not yet," he said.

Billy told him they hadn't planned to be married until fall. He didn't say after the trial, though he thought Jonas Cloudman must have guessed. Then he realized the man was still holding his permission. Inside his suit Billy was hot. Sweat ran down his leg, tickling the hair.

"Daddy," Linda said.

"I can't shake hands or even have a drink with you," Jonas Cloudman said.

"Your word's always been good," Billy said.

"Yes," the man said, nodding his head, "yes." Billy

wasn't sure if that showed agreement about his word or the engagement, but he didn't want to ask.

In the car on the way to Enoch, Billy said it didn't seem right to see Jonas Cloudman in those pale blue clothes. "Your father never favored light colors that I know of. Always, even working in the barn or under the tractor, he'd be in something dark. He don't look right this way, and they won't even let him work."

Linda began to swear. "Goddamn son of a bitch," she said.

Attacking him, the words hammered his fingers from the wheel, swerving the car to the center of the Sunday-empty road. His mouth was open to speak, but when he looked at her, she was staring ahead. Even the jarring of the car and its swing back into the lane didn't move her. Shocked, then startled by the car's veering, Billy closed his mouth as if to contain his careening heart from jumping.

"That goddamn son of a bitch," she said again.

Billy wanted a cigarette, but the motions of getting out his lighter and snapping it open seemed somehow indecorous; coughing during prayer or sneezing in the middle of the benediction would have felt the same. On went her cursing, careering now into those forbidden areas of sexual reference Billy had never heard any girl use. Then she ended.

"Cunt-headed bitch fucker."

Before he spoke, Billy lighted a cigarette and tapped it gently on the ashtray he pulled from the bottom of the dash. He was engaged to marry a girl whose rage had shocked the sense out of him. Pulling the car to the side of the road, he reached across the seat and held her. Like a statue, not cold stone, but stiff, warm wood, she sat in his embrace, staring at the vacant highway. Out of the side window he watched the tall grass heavy with cylindrical heads wave on the raised bank of the railroad track. For some reason he was reminded of a television show, something his sister watched after supper. He wished he could ask Linda, even though she didn't have a set. He didn't know what to say because he didn't even know whom she had been swearing at. He didn't want to ask.

When she began talking, she faced him. Her body, pulling slightly from his grasp, became softer. She said she hated her father. He had killed the boy she loved and had said he had no regrets. After all the years she had been with Jonas, going to school, keeping house, looking out for her sister, she thought she deserved more. To be allowed to make a mistake was not such a big thing. Besides, it wasn't a mistake.

"You wanted to be pregnant?" Billy asked. He let his arm surround her shoulders as casually as a shawl. They could have been on a first date or just friends.

"Going with Sonny wasn't a mistake," Linda said. She took the cigarette from between his fingers and sucked in smoke. "He wanted to kill my baby just as he killed Sonny. That's what he wanted, another death. And he's not even thinking they're going to kill him."

She handed back his cigarette. Though he'd never seen her smoke before, he decided not to mention it. Renewed talk about Sonny gave him time to be quiet and just let his hand slip over her shoulder. At the dam, love had been nothing of charity or kindness or doing for others. A passionate selfishness had taken over him, and he had enjoyed it. Because Linda too had enjoyed it, he called it love. Enjoy, he thought, was too weak a word, like the mixture of milk and water on the cement floor of the dairy when he had to hose away the spills.

Recognizing that sort of love didn't make him happy; it made him think of Sonny. Now he couldn't hate Sonny, couldn't even blame him, though since the evening on the floor of the forest, he wanted to destroy Sonny. Once he understood the feeling he had for Linda, at least once it came to the surface and stood still long enough for him to recognize it, he experienced a thousand things all antithetical to what he had thought about love. Chief among them was the wish that Sonny Rutherford could be erased from the earth. But he couldn't. He was already dead. Instead of a winner, a champion, even a lover, Billy saw himself as a vulture.

"Jonas turned so quickly," Linda was saying.

"He loved you too much," Billy said. After it was out, he hoped she knew he meant her father.

Quickly, she cursed him again, calling him "Jonas" between the obscenities. And just as quickly, she leaned back into Billy's shoulder and cried. The wet trickle of tears that ran beside his own nose surprised Billy. It was all surprise, ambush; the invaders wore masks. No trains used the tracks on Sundays. Only the thick heads of wild grass moved beside the car.

"The Lone Ranger," Billy said. A smile broke through his tears, tasting salty on his lips.

Neither cursing nor crying, Linda turned to him. "What?" she asked. In the darting of her eyes he knew she saw his tears.

"Those weeds," he said, "reminded me of a television program, and I couldn't remember it. It's the Lone Ranger. They show a field of wheat or oats or something before the ads."

Smiling, she dug her elbow into his ribs. "Well, it's nothing to cry about."

31 / *The Unpleasantness After the Wedding*

Clay didn't like to talk about it. What's to be gained? he asked in that polite and reasonable way men used to hide the fear they couldn't admit. So she talked about the wedding instead.

Treadwell, as his last official act as minister of the Enoch church, had married Linda Cloudman and Billy Harmes. They had driven Timothy out and Gladys out, though she didn't mention it because she knew he didn't want to talk about "them."

"I wish you had been there," she said. In the living room they drank their after-dinner coffee. She liked to have him sitting on the couch beside her rather than across the kitchen table. "Peter had on his new suit with the pink shirt the clerk in Newfound told me went so well with the pearl-gray. It has a button-down collar."

Clay laughed. "I hope he didn't draw attention from the bride."

"You know," she said, "even with all the layers of white, she showed. Not that I blame her for wearing white."

"I hope no one blames her." He looked sideways at Marjorie.

"No, they wouldn't do that." She caught herself. Linda in the church had all her faults revealed while others sat smugly in their pews. "Duncan Hatch gave her away."

"He was a friend of Jonas's."

"I know," she said. "I was surprised Zack was there. I thought Catholics couldn't attend."

"He does what he wants in that regard."

There was a brazen quality about the service station owner, she had decided at the wedding. A disregard for things that drove her to anger and Clay to his fear or timidity or caution or whatever it was. Zack had destroyed the two men she loved.

"A funny thing happened when Davis Scales and his wife came in." She put her hand on his wrist as if to reassure him she wasn't going to bring up anything unpleasant. "When they got to the front of the church, she went to sit on the right, he on the left."

"I suppose the contingent from the dairy filled up Billy's side."

"They ended up sitting behind Hatch," she told him. "The Scaleses. You know, I never realized how big Zack is until he brought me a drink at the reception."

"He talked to you?" Clay set his cup in his saucer.

She didn't mean to frighten him. "Hatch opened bottles of pink champagne. Zack was bringing them to people." Zack, smiling, his close-cropped hair brushed neatly away from his face, had walked across the room like an ambassador. He had chatted to her about what a fine reception it was and how happy Linda seemed despite the unpleasantness with her father. A vision of him formed in her mind, like the hazy smoke from his cigar.

"Good to see the town turn out for an affair like that," Clay said. He put his arm around her. "Good of you to pay for their honeymoon."

"Jonas was good to me," she explained. She didn't want to go on with it. She sat there, her hand running scales across his shoulders. But she knew she'd always be driven back to it. "I had an accident yesterday."

"Why didn't you tell me?"

"We weren't hurt." She really had. On the way home from Newfound, her wheel had slipped into the sand of a soft shoulder. White, Peter had screamed, white, as though the guardrails were ripping through the car like teeth.

"You crowd the ditch too much," he told her. "Did you bang up the car?" He set down his coffee cup, glad to discuss some safe details.

"I don't think so, except there's a smell of gas."

He went out with her to inspect the car, then back inside for Forrest's toolbox. She watched carefully while he raised the hood. He told her he didn't smell anything.

"Zack's going to look at it tomorrow noon," she said. "You told me it was time for an oil change and lubrication. It's only when I'm driving."

Clay followed a tubelike pipe from the center of the engine. Finding a fitting, he took a wrench from the box, adjusted the jaws with his thumbs, and turned the fitting. From the motor came the sharp, clean smell of gasoline.

"That's it," she said, laughing.

"Turned it the wrong way." He tightened that fitting and

the other farther back on the gas line while she watched. "That should take care of it."

"If it leaked much, would the motor still run?" she asked him.

"It won't leak now," he said, her fumbler, so helpful.

She wanted to tell him her purpose, but he was too vulnerable, vulnerable in the way men didn't recognize they were. She remembered right after Forrest's death, she had wanted to shock Clay, bring him around. No more. She couldn't hurt. She listened to him talk about Gladys and his son.

"I don't miss her—you know." She knew. In no conversation had he discussed sex with Gladys. Marjorie wondered how much love there had been. With her he was a gently passionate lover. She didn't think how he might be elsewhere. She recognized his claim for an excuse to talk about Gladys. "It's that there's no one there."

She knew that, too, had known it from the time she had woke the second time to a cold bed. "Forrest," she said. While she fixed Clay a Scotch and soda, she heated the last of the coffee. On the tray she placed a cigar.

"It's an awful thing to say," Clay said, "but I don't miss the boy so much. I suppose I was gone half the time, and she was always taking care of him. I know she'll take care of him."

Pulling the cellophane from the cigar, she put it to her mouth with the paper ring still on it, the way she had seen Zack do at the station.

"What the hell!" Clay said.

With each puff the flame of the match jumped. At first it had been difficult to draw in air enough to light the cigar without choking on the smoke she sucked into her mouth. Practice had accustomed her to the taste, which she had learned almost to like.

"You take up smoking?" Clay asked. He obviously saw that she could light one without a cough.

"Only cigars," she told him. "Cigarettes always smell dead and stale. I was glad neither you nor Forrest smoked them. But a cigar has a flavor. It tastes better than it smells." She knew he didn't approve. When the cigar went out in the ashtray, she didn't relight it.

"I suppose he'll grow up out there," Clay said. He began to cry. She wanted to take him upstairs where he would put his arms around her and press her body to his. In a short time she had learned the rhythms of his body. His sorrow, though, came at moments she couldn't predict. She ran her fingers between his.

"You were right, you know," he said. "I don't want to leave Enoch."

"I knew that. I knew why you said we had to go."

"My business is here."

She noticed he didn't say friends. Or family. The only family he saw now was Louise. "I said I'd stay as long as you want."

"But you do want to go," he said. "You would have gone except for your pride." He was in control of himself again. His hands, at first lightly tickling her ribs, found her breasts. Soon he would be in control of her. Before he was, she spoke.

"That's not so. I need to stay for a while."

But in bed all thoughts of staying or going left her. His lips on her lips, her neck, her ears, drew out every feeling but one. On her bare skin his hands were soft. Slowly she ran her fingers down his back. Then something changed. Pain bit her breast. His body on her was rigid, his movements frantic. Dread ripped through the fine texture of his love. Marjorie was horrified. But as he slept beside her, his hands on her flesh, her horror changed.

Clay was surprised that she didn't wake when he got out of bed and dressed in the dark room. Or maybe she had and had lain there, eyes open, wondering if he would come back. In any case he didn't speak to her as he padded out of the room. Downstairs he picked up his shoes before driving home.

It was cool, a morning lowering of temperature that changed

the humid air to fog in front of his house. Another morning, not much longer now, a morning with clear air would bring a killing frost. Now the same fog that protected the tender plants hid Clay as he paced on the low wall outside his house. In the pain that had driven him wild the night before, he had hurt Marjorie. She must think he still loved Gladys. He didn't. The miserable feeling inside was apprehension. Nerves, he told himself. With a steady, cardiac rhythm Clay's bare feet beat against the flat cement top of the wall.

From a distance even the wall itself, which ran across the front lawn and up one side of the driveway, was little more than a dark shape in white mist. Closer, the large rounded stones took form. Back and forth strode Clay, as though he were a sentry. On his face was no sign of a smile, grin, or any awareness of how he appeared. It was important to stop thinking of appearances. He thought of Marjorie.

If they lived somewhere else, without his house to remind him, without the cows she hated, he wouldn't have fits of wildness. She wouldn't turn hurtful. Maybe one day Peter would be on his own. It wasn't impossible, seeing the progress he'd already made. And Marjorie would go with Clay to help make deliveries. A fine-looking woman like her, who knew how to dress so well, would be an asset to his business. Of course, he'd do the driving.

For only a moment did he laugh. There were two things that he loved, Marjorie and his business. They could buy a sugar bush in Vermont and work together, travel together. Both of them had things to forget, and with each other they would forget. It didn't even matter if they went to Vermont, just that the syrup was better there.

In the morning she would be up with him and busy. Forrest had never let her help him. Gladys had never wanted to help Clay. The two of them, Clay and Marjorie, would make the candy kitchen hum. Until one day he'd have his factory. Then he could think of retiring, because Marjorie was a woman he could imagine himself being retired with. Just being with her and traveling the whole country, all the places he'd never seen. It was what he wanted, a fresh start that would stay fresh.

A half hour elapsed before the mist began to rise. It was quite possible to see Clay pace the right-angled wall. No one did. His parade, a valley away from the village, went unnoticed. At the meeting of the two walls he turned, awkwardly, unmilitarily, and went off in a different direction. With the passing of the fog, he entered his house.

It still seemed empty. For over a month Clay had tried to get used to the absence of clothes in the closets, toys on the floor. No room he entered was ever occupied. Although he knew Gladys would not be back, he had not tried to change the order in which she kept the house. Nothing was different except there was less. What's the use? he asked himself. He wondered if he could ever leave.

From the corner of the kitchen counter he took his route book. He had to go to Newfound today to fill jars in half a dozen places. One outlet, requiring a good-sized order, had called yesterday. He had enough sugar on hand for today. Tomorrow he would need to cook up some more. Despite all his troubles he had at least kept up with the orders. A man who didn't tend to business might just as well cash it all in.

He wasn't much on making his own breakfast. Not that he had ever troubled Gladys about it. If she were sick or still in bed, he just dropped over to Hatch's. In the past month not once had he been to Hatch's. It would be convenient, maybe even smart, but he wasn't going. Marjorie would have gotten breakfast for him. After packing his beach wagon, he drove to Newfound, where he ate in a grill. No one there spoke to him.

By noon he'd finished his deliveries. Hunger gave him an excuse to stop at Louise's apartment. She was surprised to see him, and he was barely inside the room when she asked him what was wrong.

As he told her about crying in front of Marjorie, he looked around the apartment. Years ago, when he and Gladys had first been married, they had rented a place. Bigger than Louise's place, though. He couldn't quite remember how it had been laid out. He could live in an apartment again. All he really needed was a place to make his candy.

In front of him sat an untasted sandwich. He told Louise that Marjorie's staying in Enoch worried him and pleased him at the same time. Gladys had just packed and left. For him, moving was not easy. Louise said that Gladys was driven out, just as Marjorie was driven to stay. But she risks too much for that, Clay told Louise.

On the way home Clay pulled into the overlook for the dam. The water, low now, barely moved. On the opposite bank a few maples showed a premature red. Below him had lodged Forrest's body after its journey downstream. The sumac, always early, burned scarlet. Soon the white birches too would turn, their yellow muting the land. But he could leave. He would have to leave, and Marjorie would go with him.

Back on the road he felt cheerful. It was a plan to sell. Once he had told Marjorie that he would say the three names, she would agree to leave. Of course, there would be no reason for him to stay. He would speak the three names anywhere—to Dodge, to the town, to the whole world. She would be at Zack's having her car fixed. All right, he would start there. Tell them both. He would prove to her and to Zack simultaneously his power. She had waited long enough and risked enough.

Selling the house and land would give him enough money to expand his candy kitchen. It might actually be possible to develop the business so that it did more than support him. And Marjorie would help him. He knew she would. He felt magically happy.

At the station he smelled gasoline. Marjorie was not in the office, though her car was parked over the lube pit. Then he smelled fire. Before he saw Zack, the smell of seared flesh overcame the gasoline fumes. On the cement floor of the lube pit lay the big man, even his eyebrows burned off.

A sound, starting from the hollow of Clay's chest, roared

from his mouth. It echoed in the garage as though it would pierce the metal of her car and crack its glass.

"NO. NO. NO."

The anguish of the words echoed in his head, but he stopped his mouth, the necessity of silence on him like a cold hand. From above he could see no movement in the lube pit. The clothes, the familiar uniform with the red winged horse, seemed scarcely burned.

He called Marjorie's name. He remembered tightening the fuel line for her while she watched, learning from him. Now he had to go into the pit: Around on the other side of her car he descended the ladder. In Zack's outstretched hand was a droplight, its bulb blown out by the blast. The outer layer of skin was burned away. Feeling for a pulse, Clay winced as his fingers touched the wet flesh. With the shirt open, Zack's chest revealed whole skin, though underneath beat no heart. The cigar with a band of ash near the narrow end lay a little ways off. Clay hesitated only a moment before nudging it closer to the dead man's hand. Once more he called Marjorie's name, though by now he was certain she had gone home.

Gone home, leaving this mess behind her, leaving her cigar as the only part of the mess he could clean up. So he edged it again closer to the seared flesh that had been Zack. Now he would take her the "no" that would save her.

Marjorie was in the bathroom with the door closed. She vomited and vomited, stopping only when she heard Peter's cries on the other side of the door. Her legs, tired from the quick walk home, were weak. Downstairs she drank water to rinse out the foul taste in her mouth. Then she began to peel potatoes. The slam of the screen door startled Marjorie so that she nicked her finger with the peeler. Half stripped, the potato in her hand thudded into the sink.

"Goddamn it all to hell," Clay said. "Goddamn it, Marjorie."

She stepped to embrace him. He backed away, leaving empty space between them. From her finger came a slow ooze of blood. "I was making potato salad," she said, "for us."

"He's dead."

Of course he would know. Outside there was no sun, only gray sky and humid, windless air. They would be gone soon, gone from Enoch. "Clay," she began, but he cut her off.

"He's dead."

He wouldn't listen to her, and he had to listen. She wanted to grab him and shake him. Instead, finger to mouth, she sucked the slow blood. Why did she always have to tell him everything? With her hand she wiped the tears from one cheek. Under her eye streaked a thin line of blood. "He killed Forrest," she said. "He was the one." She wiped her other cheek, smearing more blood on her face.

Staring at her face, he looked as if he were seeing something grotesque. "Go fix your cut!" he yelled.

In the bathroom she stopped crying. After flushing the toilet to rid the smell of vomit, she bandaged her finger. She returned to see him pacing the floor, his heels smacking on the linoleum while between the palms of his hands he crushed some invisible substance.

"You of all people," he told her.

She ran at him, her face gleaming like metal. "Me! Me! Good God, what about them?" She gripped his forearms, her fingers digging through the layers of cloth to force him to feel her.

"Don't you see what you've done to me?" He brought his arms up sharply, thrusting her hands away. "I gave you their names."

"If you had spoken his name where you should—" She put her arms around him, her face in his neck. "Don't shout," she said. "Please, no more shouting." She had expected Peter to come in from outside. She had expected many things, but not Clay looking at her as if he held some bitter candy in his mouth. And she about to accuse him.

"I don't want to talk like this," he said.

In the wooden chair by the table he sat. The rung on the right side was worn from Forrest's foot resting on it evening after evening. For a moment she watched Clay, then went to fix him a drink. Before she had gone to Zack's, she had tried to fix one herself.

"You know why I went there?" he asked.

She wouldn't tell him why she had gone. She wouldn't make him see the necessity of her going, of freeing them both. Still, she listened to him explain how he had planned to tell everybody, starting with her and Zack. She didn't even point out to him that he had already told both her and Zack. As she started to cry she thought if Peter came in the room, she'd stop crying. She wanted to stop crying.

"What's going to happen?" she asked him.

"He looked like a charred bit of sugar boiled over on the stove," Clay said. Raising the glass to his lips, he opened his eyes to her. "They'd kill you if they found out." Then he told her about moving the cigar. "You set it all up, even the fuel line."

Outside the house she had felt cold. Her fingers, shaking with the cold, had been barely able to twist the wrench on the fitting. She had thought of her murdered husband, her conscience-stricken lover, and told herself not to tremble. She knew all the laws and bounds and principles her fury had pushed her past. She had tried to concentrate only on the details.

"How can they do it?" she asked Clay. "How can these people maintain their perfectly sane balance every day?"

"For the first time in a month I felt completely happy," Clay said. "We could just end it."

"I have ended it," she said. She wouldn't let him go.

"No," he said, "you've just reduced it all. Law, justice, whatever—it's just life now."

Her face softened until she knew he could see her sorrow. "They did that," she said, "when they murdered Forrest."

"Well, it's time to stop it."

Stepping out of the car, she had worried about falling into the lube pit. She had almost forgotten her handbag on the car seat. In the office she had taken a cigar and lighted it. Like some crushed insect the cellophane from the cigar crinkled as it tried to reshape itself in the concentric circles of the metal ashtray. Only a small ring of ash had formed on the cigar when the smell of gasoline seemed strong enough. She had stepped to the door and tossed her cigar into the pit.

"There was a terrible crack of light," she said. That's all she would tell Clay, not how she had made herself look at Zack, not which of the several reasons for killing Zack had been the final one. "Clay, you wouldn't tell them about the cigar?"

He said he hated to think about it. What could help? he asked. Henry Dodge was useless. On and on he explained, the words frantic facts to avoid the truth.

"Stop it, Clay! Stop it! Stop counting all the crumbs."

Some of his drink slopped onto the table. Lowering her voice, she talked to him about going away. They could move to Minnesota if he liked, be near his son. With the sale of her place, there'd be money enough. Her hands on his shoulders, she could feel his desire. But in his face she read refusal.

"Come away with me," she said. "Don't you trust me?"

He watched her face. She knew that years of shuffling feet and discussing the weather had taught him to recognize the quick exhalation of breath, a kind of courage to start, that preceded and signaled a moment of honest talk. She knew he had heard that breath from her, that it had whispered trust to him.

"You do," she said. "You know you do. Come away with me. All this will be over."

He smiled at her, but he sat unanswering. Gradually he looked down. Across his brow grew a line. His eyes went cold. He stared at the spilled drink as if it were all the carelessness in the world.

"You have to go," he said.

And she knew he wouldn't, so she took the burden from him. "Yes," she said.

Near the top of the kettle bubbled syrup turning to candy. The steam from the candy covered the window. Clay sipped the coffee he had made first thing. It had gone cold. He thought if a man were to live long enough, his skin would wear away, flake off without being replaced. He would become a walking sore, a wound from whom truth would be no different from salt. The syrup grained and raised quarter-sized bubbles.

Clay had a bucketful of tasks this morning, enough for a month of mornings. But the fall foliage, which meant tourists who would buy his candy, wouldn't wait a month. He had to stock the gift shops. And he had to visit a lawyer, because whatever it took, he was going to see his son this winter. After he had poured the last batch of sugar into the molds, he would set off for the dairy to see Billy Harmes. Marjorie wanted Billy and Linda to run her farm, run it until they could afford to buy it. She had had it all written up for them. Clay, already practicing the pitch he'd present to Billy, wanted him to produce syrup for the candy business.

He'd have his factory yet. Standing outside while the liquid hardened to the leaves and cakes, he knew he'd have to wear a coat. Still he stayed, leaning against the edge of the candy kitchen and looking across the valley to Enoch. Someone would buy Zack's station. Stations like that were always folding and reopening. Davis Scales, he'd heard, was moving to Manchester because his wife had decided it was time she lived in a city. So that left Duncan, but Clay didn't see Duncan, not even so much as to stop in the restaurant for a cup of coffee. Before he left, Clay slipped on his coat because the cold was beginning to bother him.